MY (NOT SO) SLUTTY PROFESSOR

D. K. SUTTON

1

MADDIE

PROFESSOR EMERSON GESTURED EMPHATICALLY, stopping only to tuck a stray blond hair behind his ear as he explained the significant impact of blight on the American chestnut tree. A guy in the front row asked a question about the offending fungi, but I didn't hear the answer. I was too focused on Professor Em's long fingers as he flattened his Beam Me up Scotty tie against his well-defined chest.

I am going to fail this class.

That thought haunted me day and night. And by fail I meant get a B. Same thing. I had one semester left at Southern Missouri State University before graduating with a Bachelor's in Wildlife and Conservation Management. I'd already been accepted into their graduate program and had even taken a few accelerated classes. On track to graduate summa cum laude, my life was planned out, all the way down to moving to Denali, Alaska after graduate school. I couldn't fuck this up.

I'd never gotten a B in my life. In high school I got close, but it was gym class. Did that really count? I was good at sports, so that wasn't the problem. Gym class was difficult because as a freshman in high school, I realized girls were not my thing, and boys were my everything. Even skinny freshman boys with big blue eyes and awkward smiles. My problem got worse when Couch Hale decided we needed to do squats—

Speaking of squats... *Holy hell.* My wandering mind screeched to a halt, then jolted back to my Forest Ecology professor. Was he trying to give me a heart attack? He was bent over picking something up off the floor, and I couldn't take my eyes off him. Those thigh muscles resisted the confines of his black pants admirably. Was it ironic that the very thing that almost got me a B in gym was getting me a B or worse in this class? Eye candy. Guys. Way-too-hot professors. It wasn't fair.

I'd had cute professors before. So why was I struggling in this class? I mean, Prof. Em was hot as fuck, but I needed to get past this. I just had to focus, but I couldn't. On anything. Except his ass as he wrote on the whiteboard. His longish blond hair as he ran his hand through it only to have it fall back in his eyes. His classically beautiful face with a chiseled chin, a wide smile, and those gorgeous cheekbones. He had intelligent blue eyes that somehow seemed innocent. I didn't stand a chance.

But I was determined to do well despite my yummy professor. Any difficult professors I'd had before and even ones I wanted to jump, had never distracted me enough to affect my grades. I would just study harder. Last semester, my Ornithology instructor wore shorts to class that showed off his muscled legs. My bestie Rae and I both drooled over him. As long as I had a textbook and shared notes with my gal-pal, I could make it through any class and get my A.

Professor Emerson's class was different. I couldn't focus on the material in class or out of it. When he talked about the deforestation of the rainforest, he made it sound sexy as hell. I couldn't hear Latin anymore without getting hard.

When I tried to study the material on my own, all I could think about was his sexy voice and those gorgeous lips, and then I'd be gone. Thirty minutes and a hundred tissues later, you'd think I'd be fine, but no. I guess that was the curse of being twenty-two.

My thirst to understand everything, especially when it came to nature, helped me maintain my perfect grade point average. But focusing on Forest Ecology meant focusing on Prof. Em. I thought about asking him to wear a baggy sweatshirt instead of that formfitting button-down shirt that made me want to slip each button off slowly, exposing his muscled chest and stomach. Sure, I could have looked at my paper and just listened to him if he hadn't had that sexy voice. He could literally read off the composition of dirt, and I'd be as hard as a rock, just like I was fifteen minutes into today's lecture.

"Mr. Evans," that sexy voice said, "could you tell us where the chestnut blight originated from and why it is so detrimental?"

I might have whimpered in appreciation at the way he said my name. Rae nudged me, then nodded towards the front of the class. I glanced up into bright blue eyes. Oh wait, that wasn't in my head? He really *was* asking me that question. *Shit.*

He raised his eyebrow at me, not giving an inch. *I wish you would give me an inch or two or three or nine.* Thoughts like that were not helpful when he was waiting for my answer.

"Yes sir," I said. "Could you repeat the question?"

My sister Jen was a successful lawyer, and I'd learned a few stalling techniques from her.

He asked again, but it didn't help. My mind couldn't process the words coming out of his gorgeous mouth. He crossed his arms with a frown. His hair was messy like he'd just gotten out of bed or had no idea how to control it. I wanted to run my hands through it, but that had nothing to do with a tree-killing fungus.

Everyone stared at me as I struggled to find an answer that would satisfy him while every part of my brain decided to go on strike. I knew their demands: give us the sexy professor and we'll work again. I would have loved to give my brain and my cock what they wanted, but it was literally out of my hands.

I mumbled something about it being bad for the bark, and I could tell even before his aggravated sigh that it wasn't the answer he wanted.

"Anyone else care to enlighten Mr. Evans?"

About a thousand hands went up. Showoffs.

This never happened to me. I was always prepared. If I arrived ten minutes early, I felt like I was late. When I was in third grade, I grounded myself from recess because I misspelled the word 'climb' on a spelling test. I never again forgot how to spell that word. I could even use it in a sentence. 'I want to climb my forestry professor.'

But grade school was easier. I didn't have #ProfEmHottie to distract me. And yes, he had his own hashtag, although I sincerely doubted he knew about it. Or Twitter.

Normally, I'd be more upset that I'd missed a question in class, but the look of admonishment Prof Em gave me made up for it. I stowed that piece of info in my spank bank for later when he would punish me in my fantasies for not paying attention in his class.

Fuck. I was a goner. I might not even make a B. And a C in a major class actually *was* failing. I was so screwed.

Speaking of screwed, I'd tried that. I'd had sex with different guys to get him out of my system, thinking that would help calm my libido. It did not. It left me feeling unsatisfied. Like eating imitation cheese. Jen had a severe milk and dairy allergy, so we had to have the fake stuff growing up, and trust me, the real thing was always better.

And I had rules. About dating, not cheese. Less was better. Never go on a fourth date. Most guys didn't make past two.

"That's all for today. Remember, unless it's raining, we'll be at the Woodlands for lab on Wednesday. Please come prepared."

I chanced a glance at the front of the classroom, and as I suspected, Prof. Em was staring right at me. He turned away for a second to answer a student's question, and I gulped in a breath of air. As his gaze returned to me, he cleared his throat. Even that had a sexy sound to it. How was that possible?

"Mr. Evans? Can I have a word with you?"

"You are in so much trouble," Rae said, shaking her finger at me and trying not to laugh. My bestie had bright pink hair cut in a pixie style. Edgy. And that described her perfectly.

I shrugged as I put my stuff away, but inside, I was a mess. How was I going to get through a face-to-face talk without embarrassing myself?

As she walked by, she patted me on the shoulder. "It's not your fault, Maddie. Seventy-five percent of the class is in love with him. All the girls and half the boys. Lucky you. Here I was trying to impress him by knowing the answers. Who knew slacking off in class would do it?"

"What am I going to do Rae? I need to get over this obsession."

"Too bad you can't date him," she said with a chuckle. "You'd be bored by midterms."

My mouth dropped open as my brain decided to reengage.

"Sorry. That was harsh—"

I gave her a hug and kissed her cheek. She stared at me like I'd gone crazy.

"Thank you. You've given me a brilliant idea."

"I did?"

"Mr. Evans. I don't have all day."

We both turned to stare at our instructor. He glared at us.

"Oh fuck, that's hot," Rae said, biting her lip.

"Coming." I waved my hand at him for emphasis, but when I tried to turn, I couldn't. Rae had grabbed my bookbag.

"Wait...What are you going to do?" she asked, glancing at our irate professor and back at me.

"Don't worry," I said, brushing her and her concerns away with a wink. "I have a plan."

As I made my way to the front and my pissed-off professor, I held my bookbag in front of me to hide my inconvenient reaction to him. I thought of the many students in this class—approximately thirty—and multiplied that by two. Sixty or so disgusting feet currently heading for the exit. And in a few months, when it became warm again, most of them would be wearing sandals. I shuddered at the thought. Success. Hard-on deflated.

That lasted until I reached the front of the classroom and faced Professor Em. I'd never been this close to him, and I realized lusting from afar was a lot easier than admiring him up close. His hair appeared softer, his eyes bluer, and I could smell a woodsy, musky scent that made my dick forget about feet entirely. Hello Professor Gorgeous.

His skin looked perfect, and my fingers itched to touch him. I opened my mouth to speak, but nothing came out.

Get a hold of yourself, Maddox. Focus on the plan. This had to work. I smiled my most charming smile. The one that got me free ice cream from the servers of the Tasty Treats downtown. "You wanted to see me, Professor?"

His cheeks pinkened slightly as he combed his hand through his hair.

Was he angry, embarrassed, or turned on?

Didn't matter. I could work with any of those.

Operation Seduce Professor Emerson was a go.

2

REID

I SHUFFLED the papers on my desk and threw them in my bag just to have something to do with my hands. Nervous energy surged through me. His eyes watched as I gathered my stuff and myself together.

What was going on? I was an assistant professor. I didn't get nervous around students anymore. When I first started teaching, I was a mess. The freshman classes would laugh and make me jittery, causing me to drop things. My hands seemed to have a mind of their own, deciding that holding onto things while talking was too difficult a task. The senior classes were different, but no less embarrassing. They watched me in shocked silence. I was a grad student at the time, going for my doctorate... and only eighteen. But to be fair, I looked more like twelve.

That was a few years back and a different school altogether. I had no reason to be nervous now.

"Professor?"

I jumped slightly, bumping my hand on the desk and knocking my pens to the floor. I ignored them. They could just sit there for all I cared. My gaze flew up to his face. He had a strong jaw and dark hair that was perfectly styled. He reminded me of every popular kid I'd ever been tortured by. Charming, cocky, and way too full of himself.

His dark eyes focused on the whiteboard behind me. I'd already erased the evidence of our class, so I wasn't sure what he was staring at. I almost turned around to look. Most likely he was irritated at being called out. I sucked at reading social cues. Give me plants and animals over people any day.

"Mr. Evans. Look at me."

"Yes, sir."

It had been an automatic request to regain control, and I immediately regretted it. His eyes reminded me of the night sky. They had a depth to them. An abyss I could easily fall into. I steadied myself by holding onto the desk. My body shook from the inside out, and it reminded me of the tingling feeling when my foot would fall asleep and then regain feeling. An eruption of some type seemed imminent. Unfortunately, or maybe fortunately, what spilled out was a string of words that together made no sense.

"I...you...missed." I clamped my mouth shut, forcing my words to assemble themselves in the correct order.

"Sir?"

"Mr. Evans," I started again. "If you would stop calling me sir, that..." Might help. "It just isn't necessary." I'd never been averse to being called that, but now it seemed to be doing something strange to my mind, making it difficult to think. I resorted to an old trick I'd learned when I became nervous. Make him do the talking.

"Do you know why I asked you to stay after class?"

His eyes cast down, studying my desk. "Yes, sir."

"Don't call me sir."

"Sorry...Professor?" A small smile appeared on his face as he glanced up at me through his lashes.

I tried to ignore the bubbles popping through my body. *Focus, Reid.* "Professor is fine. Or Dr. Emerson."

"Got it. Professor Em."

I cleared my throat, determined to get back on track and to somehow stop my words from jumping out before I was ready. "At the beginning of the semester, you were doing quite well. Now, your attention has been slipping, and so have your grades. You should have easily answered the question I asked in class today."

"Yes," he said, and then he pressed his lips together.

"But you couldn't answer it."

"No."

"This is where you do the talking," I said, resisting the urge to strangle him or at least put my hands on him to regain his attention. "Explain yourself."

His face darkened, but I couldn't tell if he was angry or embarrassed. Would anyone else in my situation know? Or was it just my lack of understanding when it came to human interactions? My mom thought I was on the autism spectrum at first. It made sense. I was highly intelligent. A genius, in fact. But I was never good at connecting with people. It probably had more to do with growing up too fast and being so focused on learning and not so focused on people. I graduated high school at fourteen. Once I got behind when it came to socialization, it was difficult to catch up. There was always a gap between me and everyone else. And it didn't matter if the gap was because of age, intellect, or maturity. The results were the same.

I decided the direct approach was best.

"What's this about?" I gestured toward his face.

His skin got darker, if possible, and his eyes widened. "What?"

Crap. I'd done it again. Pointing out someone's embarrassment probably wasn't something normal people did, but I really wanted to know. And how else was I going to find out?

He glanced down at the backpack clutched in front of him. "I usually know the answers. I don't like not knowing."

I nodded. That, at least, made sense.

"I don't understand," he continued, raising his eyes to meet mine in what felt like a challenge. "I'm getting a B. I'm passing. Are you asking every student getting a B to stay after class to talk to them?"

"Of course not. That would be thirty-seven-point-five percent of the class. But those students have been getting a B all semester and are fine with it. Are you fine with a B, Mr. Evans?"

"No," he said, his voice sounding rough. "I've never gotten a B in my life."

"Me neither." I don't know why I said that. Maybe to show him I understood.

I waited for him to continue. He shrugged. What did that even mean? "You're more than capable of getting an A. Are you having difficulty in your other classes?"

He shook his head.

"Then what's going on?"

Even I could tell he was struggling to answer that question. He tilted his head and started to say something and changed his mind.

"Take your time. I can wait all day, Mr. Evans."

He smiled, and his face seemed to light up, causing another chain reaction of bubbles in my stomach.

"That's not true, Professor Em," he said. "You have another class in less than thirty minutes."

I narrowed my eyes at him. "How do you know that?"

"Social media." His cheeks tinged pink. Was it hot in here? Maybe that was causing his reaction.

I glanced at my watch, verifying that I did, indeed, need to leave soon.

"I'm distracted."

When he didn't offer more, I made an educated guess. "I've noticed that sometimes seniors close to graduating get tired of studying. They drink more alcohol. Party more."

He scowled at me. Okay, that one I got. He wasn't happy with my suggestion.

"I don't party," he said. I couldn't look away. His eyes held me in place. "I might have a drink now and then, but I'm not in college to have a good time. I'm focused. Except in this class."

"Why this class?" I asked softly.

"I'm distracted by...someone."

The pieces fell into place. I'd seen that before as well. And I'd noticed he talked to Miss Watson quite often. Was she why he was distracted? She was attractive, I supposed, in a spirited rebel kind of way. Although I was glad to finally know what was bothering him, a sense of disappointment came over me. What was that about? "You can move seats if the person next to you—"

"It's not Rae," he mumbled. "Someone else."

I crossed my arms, trying not to say what I was thinking, but I finally gave in. "Maybe you should get to know them. Sometimes the excitement is more than the thing itself." I knew this from many things. Dating was not one of them. But it made sense? Right?

He laughed, his eyes bright as he looked at me. I felt like maybe I'd surprised him. And for some reason, that made me happy.

"I'm sorry," I said, tucking a stray hair behind my ear. "Your dating life is none of my business."

"No worries. It's good advice. I'd actually been thinking the same thing." He traced the edge of my desk with his finger before turning that smile on me again. The one that turned my brain to mush. "Maybe I should give it a shot."

I smiled in return, but I didn't feel happy about the advice I'd given him. And I wasn't sure why. "If you need me to help you with anything..."

He raised his eyebrow.

"Not, of course, with that. I'm sure you can get dates on your own." I clamped my mouth shut, trying to get control of the words falling out. What the hell was I going on about? "I mean, with the material. I can help you with the material. In the class."

"Why would you help me when I've admitted to slacking off?"

"I know what it feels like to get distracted by...life." I shrugged, trying to erase some of the intensity of my words. "The need to prove yourself. And I think you want that A more than anything. And together I think we can make that happen."

"Thank you, Professor Em." His voice was full of gratitude. Or awe. Or...something?

"I have to go. Drop by my office at ten tomorrow, and we'll see what we can work out."

"See you tomorrow." He left with a grin and a wave.

As I finished packing up my things. I snuck a glance at him. He held his backpack in front of him like a shield, and it seemed to affect the way he walked. I felt good in my decision to help him, but something didn't seem quite right. Did I do something wrong? I replayed our conversation in my head. Something nagged at me. The clues were there. The tightness of his face, the way his eyebrows shot up, and even the grin at the end. But there wasn't enough evidence to decipher it. Or, more likely, there was enough information, but I wasn't knowledgeable enough to understand it. For a moment, I thought of asking Gal, my best friend and fellow professor. She'd helped me before in deciphering social cues I just didn't get. She also laughed at me, but it was always in such a fond, nonjudgmental way that I couldn't take offense.

But this time, for some reason, I hesitated. I wasn't sure I wanted to share this with Gal. Yet. That should have been my first clue that I was out of my depth.

3

MADDIE

I slogged through the last class of the day. Environmental Soils Science lab. My favorite. Sarcasm was my friend. My brain was firing. Just in the wrong directions. The conversation with Professor Em bounced through my head like a pinball machine. Up close, he looked sweet and innocent. Sexy and kissable. My plan of seducing him didn't make it past that first smile. I felt like I was thirteen again and standing in front of my Social Studies teacher, embarrassed by his praise but willing to beg for more. Okay, maybe not at thirteen, but I was not beyond begging now. And then when he suggested I date the person distracting me? Did he realize it was him? How could he not when I'd poured on the charm and batted my lashes at him? That usually got me whatever I wanted.

Not that I used my power like that. Okay, sometimes, I did. But would you tell an intelligent person not to use their brain? Or an athlete not to use their talents? I just happened to have it all: brains, talent, and charm.

I'd had to adapt early to my surroundings. A runaway dad, a devastated mom, a sister in college. Someone had to pick up the pieces and put things back together. That had been my job. Make everyone happy. And I was good at it. So, if I sometimes got an extra scoop of ice cream or out of a speeding ticket or got laid, no one was hurt by it.

All those thoughts distracted me. It was the only explanation for why I added the hydrochloric acid to my control sample.

Did we have to start the entire experiment over again? Yes. But no one got hurt. My ego took a small hit, but that might have been for the better. I never messed up in lab.

I sighed, putting my head in hands. This was bad. Very, very bad. My problem was seeping into my other classes. If it wasn't so late in the semester, I'd just drop Professor Em's class. As much as I hated the idea of giving up and not seeing that cute little ass three times a week, my grades were more important. My future career was more important. I couldn't always convince my brain of that, but it was true.

And now the stakes had ramped up. Things had the potential to get better or much, *much* worse. I had a date with my professor.

Okay, not a date. It was just a get-together where he told me what he wanted from me, and I told him what I wanted from him. It reminded me of a lot of dates I'd been on.

I shook my head, trying to clear my thoughts, as I scribbled notes on what we'd found during the first part of the experiment. We were working in sets of four. The others glared at me as we completed the steps again and waited the required fifteen minutes after adding the last ingredient. The rest of the class had left. We were the last group to finish, and it was because of my screw-up. I hated that. We only had one more part to add, and then we'd be ready for the professor to check it.

I couldn't wait to get out of this class and be done for the day. A nervous pinging had started in my body, and I needed it to stop. Maybe I could go for a bike ride or take a bubble bath or just scream into a dark room. I had options.

When it came time, I measured out the hydrochloric acid and started to add it. A hand on my arm stopped my progress. My lab partner José stared at me. But not with his usual flirty adoration. He had hit on me many times over the last few months, but I never slept with him. He was my lab partner. I tried not to mix school and sex. I'd learned early that it never worked. Why couldn't my Prof. Em-obsessed brain get that message?

"Maddie, stop." His eyes narrowed as he glanced from me to the specimen jars to the other two students scowling at me.

I'd never seen that look on their faces before. At least not as it related to me.

"You're about to fuck this up. Again. Is this a cry for attention or a death wish?"

"What? No." I checked the label of the jar I was about to add it to. The control sample. Again. I set the dropper into the beaker and stepped away, glancing over at him helplessly. Was I losing my mind?

"I got this," he said as he carefully added the acid to the correct sample.

"I'm sorry, José." The words felt foreign to me. Not because I didn't apologize but because I usually didn't allow myself to make mistakes. Not like this.

He smiled at me. "It's no problem, Mads," he said. "You've carried my ass through this class many times. It's my turn to have your back."

I appreciated the words and his friendship, even though messing up grated on my nerves and made me feel *less*. I had to get through this and back on track as soon as possible.

"Is he hot?" he asked, his voice low. He stared at the mixture, watching for any reactions, but I thought he might also be avoiding my gaze.

"Who?"

"The guy you're thinking about." He finished scribbling some notes and glanced my way, a small smile on his face. "Is that why you never give me a chance?"

My standard response got stuck in my throat. It wouldn't come out, no matter how hard I tried. Turns out José wasn't expecting an answer. We seemed back to normal by the time the teacher checked our work. Finally, after grumbling about incompetence from my least favorite professor, we were cleared to leave. I couldn't wait to get to the sanctuary of my bedroom and process this new development.

I stepped into my apartment, dismayed to find a party going on.

Great. Just what I needed. It was a study party, and although that gave it legitimacy, it didn't make it any less annoying. It was still loud and crowded with people eating pizza and drinking alcohol. My roommate Atticus waved at me as I put my stuff away and headed for the fridge. I just needed to get something to take to my room. I wasn't in the mood for company. He poked me from behind.

"What's this?"

"It's a Diet Coke," I said, lifting the soda I had in my hand.

"No, I mean the sour look on your face. What's that about?"

"I didn't expect to walk into a big party."

He crossed his arms and raised an eyebrow at me. "Seriously?"

"What?"

"It's on the calendar."

I glanced at the giant calendar hanging on the kitchen wall. It took up most of the unused space and included our school schedules and his work schedule. But most importantly, in big letters on today's date, the words 'Study Party' were written in purple pen. It had been there for weeks. I knew this was coming up. I'd just forgotten.

"Whatever."

"What's with you? You've been acting weird for weeks."

"Weeks?"

"Well, it's been going on longer than that, but I didn't care back then. Now you're bothering me. Now I care."

I chuckled. Atticus never sugarcoated anything. "It's nothing. I'm taking care of it."

"Thank God. That's all I want to hear. Going to your room?" He loved giving me a hard time. I scheduled my studying. I scheduled everything. Hence the giant calendar.

"Yeah."

"We have pizza if you change your mind."

Pizza and calculus. Two things that went well together.

I nibbled on swiped pizza, sipped my Diet Coke, and tried to unravel my brain. My nervous energy was gone, leaving in its place a ball of worry. My third-grade teacher had a rubber band ball. I'd thought it was cool at the time. She'd let me put the bands back on when they came off. I felt like that rubber band ball was making its home in my stomach. As it started to unravel, the bands wrapped around my ribs and squeezed me tight. I couldn't catch my breath. It was almost a relief when my phone buzzed.

"Rae?"

"How did it go with Professor Yum?"

"Fine."

"Why are you holding out on me?"

"I don't tell you everything, Rae."

"We have a bond, Maddie. Born out of surviving Professor Emerson's Forest Ecology class together. You owe me something."

"You make it sound like we're in combat together or hell."

"Maybe not hell, but I do feel like I'm burning up all the time. The hotness quotient is out the roof," she said. "Maybe you guys are star-crossed lovers, just needing a chance."

"I think you've missed your calling. You should sign up for creative writing. Rosen Hall is just across the quad."

She ignored that. "And Prof. Em is so clueless. He has no idea everybody's lusting over him."

"Or why students are always asking him for help." I pushed away the ball of guilt squeezing my chest. That wasn't what I was doing. Not really. I needed his help.

"And he helps everyone. He's such a Boy Scout. This is his thing."

I sat up, suddenly paying more attention. "Are you speaking from experience?"

"I may have needed a little help...in the beginning."

"And you didn't tell me?"

"I don't tell you everything, Maddie."

Touché. "You tell me yours and I'll tell you mine."

"Kinky. But I'm not doing it over the phone."

"Kinky," I replied with a smirk. "The Coffee House?"

"It's a date."

I was out the door and walking across campus within minutes. Atticus rolled his eyes and waved me out. I ignored him. I'd get my two-point-five hours of studying in. Later tonight.

As I got closer to our favorite coffee place, the aroma called to me. I loved the smell of coffee, but I couldn't stand the taste of it. It was the story of my life *and* my dating life. I loved the thought of guys, but when I got to know them, it was like tasting coffee all over again. Some were like a cappuccino—*eh*. Others were like straight black coffee. *Oh hell no.*

I stopped. Right in the doorway, forcing people to go around me. It suddenly made sense. I felt lighter than I had moments ago. And not because I'd stripped off my jacket. I'd been on the right track all along.

I loved the thought of the thing more than the actual thing.

This was the solution to my Professor Emerson situation. Just like coffee. He smelled good. He looked tasty. Of course, he probably really, *really* tasted good. My dick perked up at that. Traitor. I wasn't going to taste my professor. That wasn't the point. I didn't need to have sex with my professor to get him out of my system. Spending time with him would do the trick. Like a book and its cover. Sure, it looked good, but once you got inside...

Okay, I needed another analogy because thinking of being inside my professor with that sweet little ass was not helping my situation. At all. Maybe I needed to wait until I got back to my apartment to work through this so I could take care of any issues that popped up. In private.

Rae waved me over, and I sank down in the chair with a sigh of relief. She'd already ordered me a Chai tea latte. I loved this girl.

She gave me a moment. Probably realizing I needed it. I didn't have my bookbag to hide behind. I was halfway done with my tea when she raised an eyebrow. I guessed I was going first.

I told her about our meeting, skipping over my body's reaction to everything he said and the near meltdown I'd had in soils lab.

"Damn," she said. "When I asked for help, all he did was explain everything. Clearly. So I could understand it. No dating advice. No offers of...what exactly was he offering?"

"I don't know. And to be honest, I'm not sure he knows."

"Kinky."

After out little study break, I headed back to my apartment and studied for my test in Environmental Soil Science class. Spoiler alert. The class was mostly about septic tanks and sewage. Important stuff to know. But still. Ew. Just like the teacher. Prof. Mt. Surly. That wasn't his actual name. More like his Twitter hashtag.

No one could blame me for treating myself one last time to thoughts of Professor Em. His wide mouth and pretty lips. His tight ass and muscled chest. And those innocent blue eyes that begged for knowledge. I moaned into my pillow as I thought of all the things I could teach my nerdy professor.

Tomorrow, I'd focus on getting to know my professor better. Then once the shine had worn off, once I'd tasted the coffee, everything would be back to normal. I ignored that little voice in my head. The one reminding me Professor Emerson might not be coffee. What if he was Chai tea instead?

4

REID

SOMETHING WAS WRONG, and I had no idea what it was. Clearly, Mr. Evans needed my help. I examined that fact and could find no fault with it. His grades had been slipping. He had been distracted, he said. He needed help getting caught up. All those things were logical. We were meeting today at ten to discuss what could be done. Perfectly understandable.

And yet something had me unnerved. This clawing feeling in my stomach as if a hole had opened up, and if I wasn't careful, I'd fall right through. It made no logical sense. And yet I couldn't dismiss it. I'd learned early on that in some ways my body understood more than I did. I grew up fast. After high school at fourteen, I'd gotten my bachelor's degree at sixteen and completed graduate school and had my doctorate by the time I'd turned nineteen.

I could recite the social and biological responses to puberty with no problems. I had a near-perfect memory and had read countless books trying to understand what I was going through. But without the actual experiences to go with it, it had been like someone explaining how amazing butter pecan ice cream tasted. You could memorize the details, but that didn't mean you understood it.

Not unless you experienced it.

I was always younger than everyone else. Intellectually, I was smarter than those around me, including my teachers. But socially, I was awkward, always trying to catch up. The truth was I gave up trying. I had assumed there would be plenty of time when I finished school and started my career to figure that stuff out. Now that I was there, I had no idea where to start. It reminded me of driving. I'd never needed to know how to drive in high school because I wasn't old enough. Then when I got to college, it was easy enough to get along without it. Now everyone assumed that I already knew how. I was a professor at a university, so of course, I knew how to drive. Of course, I'd been in relationships. But I didn't, and I hadn't.

Substitute everything else in my life except academia and you'd have gotten the same answer. The things I really struggled with were the things I couldn't learn to do on my own. Others just didn't seem important until they were suddenly very important. Why did I need a Twitter account again?

I hated that feeling of inadequacy. I'd struggled with it my whole life. And it perfectly summed up how I felt going into my meeting with Mr. Evans.

Even though I didn't understand my uneasiness, I couldn't dismiss it. There was a reason; I just didn't know what it was. Mr. Evans was attractive. But many of my students were. That had never been an issue. And it wasn't an issue now.

He needed my help. He wanted to do better. I wasn't completely naïve. Students lied and had their own agendas. I rubbed at my chest. I knew that better than anyone. But I didn't get that feeling from him.

I still felt off balance as I ate my breakfast of egg whites and wheat toast. Shaking it off, I prepared for the day. It would do no good to dwell on it. After my meeting with Mr. Evans, I was sure to understand.

My first class was Intro to Forestry, and I could teach it in my sleep, And obviously in their sleep as well. A few snores reached me and pushed me right over the edge. I had a cowbell from my brother's farm that I had used the first week or so of classes. Time to remind them of how much I hated it when people wasted my time.

Everyone jumped, even those paying attention. I heard some strong language from the back. I ignored them.

"Now that we're all awake, let's turn to chapter six and review the basics of site assessment and the tools we'll be using."

My nervous energy lasted throughout the morning. I ran up the stairs of Hudson Hall instead of taking the elevator to my office, hoping to dispel most of the energy before my student appointments. I enjoyed the exercise. Walking was my usual mode of transportation, unless I was riding my Vespa. I'd gotten some strange looks at first, but now, no one cared. It was better for the planet anyway. Those thoughts preoccupied my mind, which was the excuse I gave myself for running into and bouncing off of Professor Oliver.

"What the hell, Emerson," he said, glaring at me, like I'd done him bodily harm.

"I'm so sorry, Professor." I glanced around, but he hadn't dropped anything or spilled anything or had anything happen that would warrant the hostility he was sending my way. Not that he needed a reason to be unpleasant. That was how he looked at me all the time.

I stammered as I walked around him, cursing myself for being so awkward. To be fair, I felt awkward ninety-nine-point-nine percent of the time. The only time I didn't feel awkward was when I was in the classroom teaching.

Someone grabbed my arm, pulled me into my office, and shut the door before breaking down with a loud cackle. I recognized that crazy laugh.

"Gal? What are you doing?"

"Isn't it obvious?" she said between laughs. "I'm saving you from St. Oliver. The look on his face." She shook her head, jet black curls falling around her face.

"It's not that funny."

"Are you kidding me? You bounced off him. Literally bounced off him. But by the time I got my phone out to record it, the whole thing was over. Could you go out and do it again? For me?"

"No. I make it a habit not to redo embarrassing mistakes."

"Oh, Reid," she said. "Redoing mistakes just for the hell of it is the reason we're human and not computers."

I shook my head and slumped into the chair behind my desk. I didn't have the energy to contradict her because all my nervous energy was centered in my stomach and shooting through my muscles. I flexed my hands, trying to dispel it through my fingertips. It was no use.

"Something's going on with you."

"Nope. Nothing."

"Liar."

"Gal..." Her name was actually Galdina. Which I adored and she hated. But no one dared make fun of her name or treat her like a "gal." My best friend was fierce. Like Wonder Woman. She hated being called that, too.

"Talk." Her gaze never wavered.

"I have students coming in. I don't have time for whatever this is."

She glanced at the Zelda clock on my wall. It was nine forty-five. Most of my students came in late for their appointments but if his attendance in class was anything to go by, Mr. Evans would probably be early.

"You're right." She pulled the other chair around so we were face to face.

"I am?"

"We don't have time to play the you-avoid-me-and-I-worm-it-out-of-you game. Just fess up now. Save us both some time."

"You haven't actually asked me anything."

"Oh, my bad," she said. "Reid, my sweet little nerd. Why are you all jacked up?"

I huffed out a breath. "I don't know."

She opened her mouth and closed it again, squinting at me with her X-ray vision or whatever superpower she had that always seemed to be just as effective against me. "You don't know, do you?"

"I said I didn't."

"Guess."

"You know I don't like to speculate. It's messy and ineffective."

"But Reid," she said with an exasperated tone. "We're short on time, so it'll have to do."

I crossed my arms, mostly to hide the slight shaking of my hands. Maybe it could contain some of that energy. "I have a student coming in. He needs my help."

"And?" She waved her hands around, making it seem bigger than it was.

"And...I'm nervous about it."

She slammed a hand on the desk, and I couldn't help the squeak I let out. "Dammit, Gal! Stop that. I'm nervous enough already without you scaring the crap out of me."

"But you're never nervous with students. Not anymore. What's going on?"

"I can see it would do me no good to remind you that I don't know. Even though I don't. He's in my Forest Ecology class. He's normally an A student, and he's getting a B. This is for his major, so he needs to stay on top of it. I offered to help him." It was something I'd done a thousand times before.

"Is he cute?"

"That's not relevant."

"No. It shouldn't be relevant. But in this case, I suspect it is."

I gave her my most serious look. "He is attractive. But I don't sleep with my students."

She cackled again. I'd always thought she overdid her laugh just to bring a smile to my face. This time, I resisted the urge. "I don't."

"I'm sorry. I shouldn't laugh. But your honesty and lack of filter crack me up. No one would suspect you of sleeping with your students."

I slouched in my chair and swallowed the ball of shame stuck in my throat.

"Reid..." she said, putting her hand on the arm of my chair. "I forgot. I'm sorry." She moved closer like she wanted to hug me. She knew I didn't like people touching me. I appreciated her restraint.

"It's fine." It wasn't, but I didn't want to dwell on the past. I looked up at her. "I don't sleep with my students."

"Sweetie. Give yourself a break. You're in the prime of your sexual life. It is okay to be attracted to a hot guy. Do you think that's what this is?"

"I don't know. A lot of my students ask for extra help…"

She snorted at this, but I decided to ignore it. I'd never turn a student away. This was my passion. Teaching. Giving students what they needed to grow. Not dismissing them because they didn't get it. Not dismissing them because they were too smart.

I avoided her perceptive gaze. "And a lot of them are attractive in some way. But this feels different." I sighed. "Sometimes I wish I could be as smart as you."

She laughed again, but this one sounded more self-deprecating. "You're a genius, Reid. You don't want to be as smart as me."

"But you get people. You understand them. I'm clueless. Animals make sense. Plants make sense. Nature makes sense. People are messy and confusing and infuriating."

"And that's what I love about you," Gal said, kissing the top of my head before I could tell her not to.

A knock at the door had me shooting looks at the clock. Just as I suspected, Mr. Evans was early. Gal's eyes widened, and she bit her lip with an excited smile. Dammit. I'd hoped she'd be gone before he showed up. But maybe I could use this somehow.

"Should I get that for you?" she asked, sounding gleeful.

"Yes," I said. "But just a second." I straightened up my desk and took a deep breath before pushing it out again to clear my mind. "Okay. Let him in. Maybe later you can give me your thoughts."

She smiled warmly and winked before answering the door.

Maddox Evans filled the entryway with his presence. He wasn't physically a big guy, but he somehow filled the space he was in completely. I shook off those fanciful thoughts. They were unlike me and completely unnecessary. He glanced at Gal and then the door and then looked down the hallway as if he'd somehow gotten the wrong room.

"Hi," Maddie said. "I have an appointment with Professor Em."

Gal backed up so he could see me, and a smile lit up his face. I reacted to it before I could stop myself. There was something open and inviting about him. He was confident in a way that I wasn't. Was that why my stomach was in knots?

I stood up, even though my legs were shaking. "Come in, Mr. Evans," I said, motioning to the chair that was supposed to be in front of my desk. Of course, it wasn't. It was where Gal left it, sitting close to mine. My face heated up as I moved it to a more appropriate spot.

But he didn't seem to notice. "Call me Maddie. And you're Professor Ramon, aren't you? I've heard amazing things about your organic chemistry class."

"Really." She smiled. "Aren't you adorable. Well, I'll leave you two to it. Professor Emerson, we'll finish discussing that thing we were discussing later. I'll just go check on Professor Oliver and make sure he's not still bouncing around."

Before I could stop her, she shut the door.

I had been prepared. But Gal threw me for a loop. Because now all I could focus on was the fact that she had closed the door. I never met with my students behind closed doors. The reason I had to leave my last school in Maryville was never far from my mind. So, I kept the door open. Always.

But now if I walked across the room and opened the door, it would look suspicious, like I was afraid to be alone with him. Which wasn't true. At all.

"Professor? Are you okay?"

"Yes, of course."

"Before we start, I wanted to tell you that this isn't like me. I don't do this kind of thing. I work hard. I get good grades."

I nodded my agreement. He'd never gotten anything below an A. At least, not at this school. I'd checked.

"So? Can you help me?"

"That's why I'm here," I said. "I'm at your service. Whatever you need."

"Really? I wasn't sure you'd be willing. I mean..."

That was the moment the hole opened up and swallowed me. Not actually, of course. But it felt like it. Like I was falling. Was this the reason I felt nervous all morning? And yet I still didn't understand. What was he saying exactly? He seemed to think we were on the same page. But I wasn't sure we were even using the same book. My body seemed to understand, but since it wasn't communicating with my brain, it wasn't helpful. If I needed answers, I had to get them myself. "Excuse me?"

His mouth opened and then closed. "I heard you were helpful," he said, trying again. "When students needed help."

"Mr. Evans—"

"Maddie."

"Maddie," I finally agreed. It felt like I was giving in already, and that wasn't a good way to start. I wanted to tell him I didn't understand what he wanted from me, but that wasn't what came out of my mouth. "I don't sleep with my students."

Gal would have cackled at the look on his face. His eyes were impossibly wide, and his mouth was hanging open. He closed it with a click.

Oh, no. I had everything wrong. Completely. And I'd just humiliated myself. My face burned in shame. What was wrong with me? "I mean..." But what did I mean? I had nothing more to say. What a disaster.

His eyebrows scrunched together, and he looked...annoyed? That would be my guess. But I hated guessing. "I've worked hard for every A I've gotten. I certainly don't need to sleep my way into graduate school." His cheeks were tinged a dark pink. Anger or embarrassment? Maybe a bit of both? And it was hot in here with the door closed.

"I wasn't suggesting.... Anything. I'm sorry. Sometimes I don't have a filter." There was more I should say, but I wasn't sure what that would be.

"No. It's my fault." Maddie picked up the small rake from the Zen Garden on my desk. Gal had bought it for me mostly as a joke. He smoothed out all the swirls in the sand and avoided looking at me. I'd tried to use it before, but it had never worked for me. He sighed as he leaned closer to make his confession. And I knew somehow that this was going to be a confession.

"You're the reason I'm failing."

My pulse jumped. Was he suggesting this was my fault? "I disagree with ninety-nine percent of that sentence," I said. "First, you're not failing. You're getting a B. Second, *you* are the reason your grades are falling. You have to take responsibility for getting the grade you want."

He rolled his eyes and smiled. It was a shy smile, but I didn't believe it for a second. This man didn't have a shy bone in his whole body. Then I had to shut down those thoughts of his bones and his body. I shook my head to clear it. His smile grew.

"You're right, Professor Em. It is my fault. I told you I was distracted by someone in class. What I didn't mention is that person is you."

His eyes met mine, and a shock went through me. For just a second, I could see something in his eyes, and it was unlike anything I'd seen before. Which didn't make sense. I'd been hit on from guys before. I was told I was attractive. I'd seen what I thought was desire in others' eyes before I quickly looked away. This wasn't that, exactly. This was something that shot through me and jumpstarted every nerve ending in my body. It was like adding electrical current to every cell I had. The reaction multiplied over and over, causing something major...

The uneasiness I didn't understand became clearer. It wasn't that I was afraid my student would want to have sex with me. It was that, for the first time in my life—no matter what my last college thought —I might be interested right back.

5

MADDIE

SOMETIMES YOU GOT LABELED things in life that were totally unfair and unearned. I'd been called impulsive, reckless, and way too charming for my own good. That was mostly by my dad. I liked to consider myself bold. Ready to go after what I wanted. Because fuck if anyone else was going to get it for you. Those labels implied I didn't think things through. Untrue. I did the mental calculations in my head, and once I had my answer, I went for it. Why torture yourself for hours beforehand? Today, I totally earned those labels. Well, maybe not the last one. Professor Em did not look charmed at all. He looked shellshocked.

"Mr. Evans—"

"Wait." I couldn't let him throw me out of this class or, worse yet, report me to the dean. Not that I'd done anything wrong. I hadn't said what I wanted, which was more along the lines of, *Let me fuck you, just once, on your desk, and I think I'd be good for the rest of the semester.*

Thankfully, I swallowed those words... and all thoughts of swallowing him. Fuck. It was being *this* close to him that messed me up.

His eyes darted around like they weren't sure where to settle. "I... am I still waiting? Or...not?"

"Sorry," I said, taking a shaky breath. "I shouldn't have said that. I mean, we've already agreed you don't sleep with your students. And I don't sleep with my professors. But I made it even *more* awkward. The thing is, Professor, being attracted to you is a problem. And I don't know how to deal with it."

"But it's your problem. Not mine."

Wow. That felt like a slap and not the good kind. "You're right." I started to stand up, perfectly aware that this time, I didn't have my bookbag to hide behind.

"Wait..." He ran his hand though his messy hair, and I followed every movement. "I'm not good at saying things," he admitted. "I meant, you came here today for help. I'm not sure how I can help you."

I eased back into the chair, grateful not to be flashing him with my interest any longer. "I thought maybe you could review some of the material with me. Help catch me up."

He tilted his head and chewed on his bottom lip. The man oozed sex and didn't even know it. He had a chiseled face that still gave off a youthful vibe like he hadn't quite matured yet and an innocence that I wanted to dirty up. I shook those thoughts away.

"It seems...counterproductive," he said. "If I'm the reason for your difficulty, then my assisting you is destined to fail."

"Not necessarily. Have you heard of exposure therapy?"

"Of course, but I don't make you anxious."

"I could challenge that opinion, but it would get us off track. I've never been in a serious relationship."

"Excuse me?" He squinted at me like I was one of the geodes on his bookshelf, and he wanted to see if I was real or not. "I don't follow."

I tried again. "I've dated lots of guys. But none more than a week."

"Because of your anxiety?"

I couldn't help but laugh. "No. I don't have anxiety."

"Then why are you going through exposure therapy?"

"No. I mean..." I shook my head and then slammed it into the top of his desk over and over, avoiding the Zen Garden. Okay, so I didn't slam it, but I tapped it. Kind of hard.

"I'm sorry. I don't always get things. I mean, chemistry, I understand. Nature, rocks, soil, bugs, animals, I understand. People. Not so much."

I hated the frustration in his voice. It was my fault. I just needed to spit it out. But once out there, I wouldn't be able take it back. I raised my head and looked at him. "I love guys. When I'm attracted to a guy, I can't wait to f—date them. Only after one or two dates, I get tired of them. Bored. Not interested."

"We can't date, Mr. Evans."

I rolled my eyes. "I—" But the cute half smile on his face told me he was kidding. Professor Emerson had a sense of humor? Of course he must. His ties were geeky, and whimsical, and nerdy as shit. Today, he had on a thin tie with pink and black glasses all over it. And tight gray pants that should have been outlawed. Or stripped off him as soon as possible.

"You think being around me, amazing person that I am, will cause you to lose interest?"

"Yes. I mean no."

"Which is it?"

"I feel like I'm insulting you."

He smiled. "Not at all. Sexual interest is a biological response. A lack of interest could be a deep-seated fear of commitment on your part. Nothing to do with me."

The way he looked at me—his eyes clear and innocent and damn, I wanted to grab him, kiss him senseless, and work him totally out of my system. Now. On his desk.

Something in my look must have scared him because he leaned back, blinked a few times, and crossed his arms protectively. "Let's say I help you get caught up and where you need to be in my class. What do I get out of it?"

My mouth dropped open. "I'm sorry, what?"

"I think you heard me."

"You're my teacher. This is your job."

"You think it's my job to waste my time going over information I already taught you because you can't stop staring at my ass during my lecture?"

I coughed. Almost choking on my tongue, which seemed to be tied up in my mouth. Oh, holy hell. "No?"

He raised an eyebrow at that.

"What do you want?" *Please say a blowjob. Please say a blowjob. Right here. Right now.*

"I want you to teach me about social media. The tweeting and stuff. I mean I can read about it, but there's these unwritten rules and things I don't get. And the whole being social thing."

"Didn't you have friends in high school?"

"I was twelve."

I couldn't have heard him right, but I checked my ears, and they seemed to be fine. And he had a serious look on his face. Waiting for me to laugh at him. No way.

"I can help you with that. But why not ask your friend, Gal? I mean Professor Gal."

"I can't. I don't want to explain it. Just...will you help me?"

"Absolutely."

He beamed, and it lit up his entire face. And my entire body. God, he was gorgeous.

I stood up. I needed to get out before I propositioned him. Or proposed to him.

"So, how..." He couldn't look at me. "I mean, should I try to be ..."

"Sexy?"

His face turned beet red. As red as the geode crystal on the shelf behind him.

"Although I'd love to see you try to be sexier than you are..." I looked him over, drinking my fill, because it seemed, at least for the moment, that I could. He shifted uneasily under my gaze. I wanted to check and see if he was getting as hard as I was, but I thought that would have been too much. "Just be you, Prof Em."

I headed for the door. "Same time, tomorrow?" I asked, turning as I reached my goal.

He nodded, his lips open slightly. Damn, I'd be dreaming about them tonight. I wasn't sure if I wanted this to work so I could focus or not. As adamant as he was, Prof. Em couldn't hide the fact that he liked me *and* my attention.

6

REID

"Wʜᴀᴛ ʜᴀᴘᴘᴇɴᴇᴅ?" Gal asked, following me into my office the next morning. "You barely answered any of my texts last night."

"How is that different from any other night?"

"Answer the question, Reid."

I dropped my leather bag and sat in my chair, looking anywhere but at her face. "I honestly don't know."

"Hold up. Rewind." She twirled her finger in the air. "You don't know something? You?"

"As we've established, there are many things I don't know."

"Reid Emerson," she said with a fierce glare. "Tell me what happened, before I strangle you with your Doctor Who tie." She advanced on me, and I scooted my chair back as far as I could. I wasn't scared of her, but she could be fierce when she wanted.

"Did he pounce on you? Proposition you? Or did you guys just eye-fuck?"

I stared at her, ignoring her dramatic eye-rolling and hand waving. "No pouncing. Or propositioning. And definitely no eye— what is that anyway? It sounds disgusting."

"Seriously? Where have you been for the last twenty years? It means staring at each other like you want to fuck."

"No." I turned toward my desk. I didn't really have time to go over everything. Not that Gal could be dissuaded when she wanted something. "Seriously. What is wrong with you?"

"He's cute."

"He is my student."

"Whatever. Quit stalling and tell me what happened."

What had happened? It was a blur now, like I'd been blasted by a Dalek. Maybe I *should* stop watching Doctor Who late at night. "I'm not sure," I admitted. "Everything happened so fast."

"Everything what?" She grabbed my chair to turn me around.

"Stop that." I shooed her away. "We just established some boundaries. I told him I didn't have sex with my students."

She laughed, slapping a hand to her mouth, her eyes wide and mocking or maybe just amused. "Did he offer?"

"Well, not exactly."

"Oh my God."

"He did seem offended."

"You think?" She sat in the other chair staring at me. "What did he say?"

I thought back. I wanted to get this right because sometimes I didn't. "Just that he worked hard for his grades, and he didn't sleep with his professors to get them."

Gal burst out in laughter. Cackling, actually. It was gleeful. Practically hysterical. She was bent over, holding on to her stomach. I watched the door. Professor Oliver would be over here complaining soon if she didn't quiet down. He loved to complain.

"Gal!"

"Sorry," she said, trying to catch her breath. "It's just you were so determined to be good, and...and... you actually propositioned *him*."

I waited for her laughter to quiet down. It took a while. I wasn't offended by her mirth. She didn't have a mean bone in her body. I was just embarrassed. "I didn't proposition him."

"Sweetie, you brought it up."

"It wasn't like that. The things he was saying... he implied..." I covered my face with my hands. "What have I done?"

She reached across the desk and touched my arm. "It'll be okay."

"How?"

"I don't know." Her eyes sparkled, and she bit her lip.

"I'm glad I could amuse you."

"Sorry. Tell me what he said."

"I don't remember."

"You have a photographic memory or close enough. You remember everything."

"Usually, yes. That's true. But for some reason, my head was swarmy." I glanced at her quickly, and her eyes went wide.

"Is that a scientific term?"

"Of course. Haven't you heard of it?"

"Wow. Now you're even making jokes. This guy has gotten to you, hasn't he?"

"No," I said. "We set boundaries."

"No sleeping with each other." She even managed to say that without laughing.

I ignored the big smile on her face.

"So how did you leave it?"

I didn't want to tell her. It was embarrassing. I tapped my fingers on my desk, trying to figure a way out. I reached for my Zen garden and remembered the way he'd handled the little rake, sliding through the sand, and I just couldn't.

"Reid? I see we're doing this the hard way. Are you meeting with him again or not?"

"Yes."

"And?"

"I'm helping him catch up," I said. I wasn't going to mention the exposure theory. It was ridiculous, but it made him feel better. And she would enjoy it too much.

"And?" she prompted again.

"And what?"

"You're twisting your tie. When you do that, it means you're lying or holding out on me."

"It does not." I shook my head, but I let go of my tie, trying to smooth it out. I might as well tell her. "He's helping me as well."

"Oh, really? Are you struggling in Forest Ecology? I didn't realize."

I huffed. "No. He's helping me with... social media."

She didn't say anything, which prompted me to look up. Her mouth was open, her eyes wide.

"What?" I didn't mean it to come out so gruff.

"I'm surprised. Not that you don't need help with navigating anything with social in the name, because hello, you do. But I have been trying to help you with that for forever, and suddenly, Baby Doll here comes along, and you just melt."

"That is not what happened. And helping him is helping me."

"You're helping him because it's your job. Why is he helping you?"

I shrugged my shoulders. "I think it just makes him feel better about taking up my time. I mean, it's his fault for getting behind, even though he blames me."

"Wait, back up. He blames you?" She tipped my chin up so I had to look at her.

Why did I say that? My face was on fire, but she held onto my face so I couldn't look away.

"Why does he blame you, Reid?"

"He says I distract him. Because he finds me attractive."

"That smooth mofo. I'm not sure how to feel about this. Did he use the term attractive? I bet he didn't. What exactly did he say? You can tell me."

I rolled my eyes. It wasn't something I usually did, but it was called for in this instance. "He said I was hot."

That set her off again. She laughed and banged her hand on my desk.

A knock at the door startled us both. Was it Maddie? Mr. Evans, I corrected myself. Why would he be back? I was both excited and appalled by the idea. Gal winked at me and ran for the door, but it wasn't the gorgeous senior standing there. It was an irritated Prof. Oliver.

"What do you want?"

Prof. Oliver ignored Gal, but he always did. Like she was invisible. Inconsequential.

"Would you please hold down the racket? Some people have work to do." He stepped into the room while he complained. Gal stood slightly behind him, mocking him. I tried not to laugh. She'd helped me get through the last couple years which weren't always easy. Professor Oliver didn't like me, for some reason. I wasn't particularly fond of him either, but I didn't wish him ill. I knew he'd complained to the dean about me. But the dean was a kind old gentleman, the grandfatherly type. He'd taken me under his wing as soon as I got there. Was that the reason Prof. Oliver was so angry? He probably thought I was the dean's favorite. Which was ridiculous. Were we in high school again? Were we teenagers? I mean, I was a teenager when I got here, but that was beside the point.

"I'm sorry," I said finding my voice. "Prof. Ramon told me a funny joke. Hilarious, actually. We'll keep it down."

He glared at me for another second and wrapped his arms around his huge belly before turning and looking at Gal as if he'd not seen her there. He stormed out of the room the same way he'd entered, by slamming the door.

Unsurprisingly, Gal cracked up again. But she held her hand over her mouth to keep from being so loud.

"Don't you have work to do?"

She ignored me. "I'm Prof. Oliver," she said, waddling around the room. "I suck the fun out of everything.

"Seriously, I've got to prepare for today."

"Is that when you see lover boy again?"

"His name is Maddie." And I immediately wished I could take back the words.

"You're on a first-name basis with Maddie. I like it. Maddie and Reid."

"Stop it. Get out."

"Okay, I'm going, but I expect a full report."

"Absolutely not."

"A half report? Quarter? Highlights? A catalog of any physical contact?"

I didn't say any words. I just pointed towards the door. She skipped all the way out to the hallway.

THAT NIGHT I treated myself to Chinese food from the place around the corner. I normally didn't eat takeout. I tried to eat healthy, but I'd struggled lately with sticking to any of my plans. Like the plan to not get involved with my students. Not that I was involved with him, but this was more involved than usual. And I thought about him way too much.

What had I been thinking? Spending almost every day with him one-on-one? I mean, I could control myself. That wasn't a problem. But it would make things awkward. When it came to school, academia, I had a lot more knowledge than him, even though he was no slouch in that department. But when it came to other things, other personal things, like relationships, intimacy, social cues, I was like a freshman again. I had no idea what I was doing. It reminded me of those awkward days when I first started college. I'd struggled. Not with my studies. Never that. But I'd tried way too hard to interact with the other students and got ridiculed or used in the process. I'd wanted to learn all that human interaction stuff. But I was awkward. And I looked twelve.

You couldn't learn the nuances of social interaction in books. And I realized early that staring at people to try to understand resulted in a shove or a punch in the face.

And yet, all through dinner, cleaning up, grading essays, and trying to fall asleep, it didn't hit me. The most difficult part of this whole thing didn't register until the next day when I was making my way through the halls and avoiding the bustle of students. While also trying to ignore the glares from Prof. Oliver and the winks from Gal. That's when it hit me. The hardest part of this whole situation was that I still had to see and interact with Maddie in class. While it was embarrassing being one on one with him and feeling awkward, it was going to be even worse seeing him in the classroom, in front of all my students.

But I'd had to face difficult things all my life. Growing up too quickly and not knowing if people were laughing with me or at me. Spoiler alert: it was always at me.

I could do this. I was the professor. He was the student.

I arrived early to class, wrote some things on the board, and waited for time to start. I forced myself not to watch the door to see when he came in. I didn't need to know. His grades, his classes, his ability to pay attention and not focus on my butt were all his problems. The timer went off on my watch, indicating it was time for class to start. I scanned the rows of students, hopefully giving off the impression that I had everything under control. I had become rather good at faking it, so I thought I did a good job.

I started with a discussion on fungi and how they were introduced from Canada. Several students, the usual, answered questions or engaged in the discussions, and I started to relax.

Then Maddie ruined it all.

He raised his hand.

I couldn't ignore him. Could I? I bit back a sigh. "Yes, Maddie?"

The room went silent. All eyes ricocheted from me to Maddie and back to me again. His mouth had dropped open, and he snapped it shut.

It wasn't like professors didn't call their students by their first name. They did all the time. I just never had. I had needed that protection of those labels—boundaries, mostly. It was because of the age difference or actual lack of age difference. I was the same age or younger than many of my students.

But showing weakness was not something I was prepared to do. "Do you have a question, Maddox, or not?"

I intentionally used his name instead of his nickname to try and put in a little distance without giving in.

He caught on rather quickly. "Yes, Professor," he said. "Can you explain more about the mycorrhizae and how it relates to roots? I'm not sure I understand."

"Can anyone help Mr. Evans out?"

Miss Watson raised her hand, and it seemed to dance in the air. I could almost hear her chanting, "Pick me. Pick me."

I didn't want to pick her, but it was spiteful. I had no reason to be jealous of her or the fact she spent so much time with Maddie, so despite what I wanted, I called on her.

"The term mycorrhizae refers to the association or the structure, not the fungus or the plant. And there are two main types: endo and ecto." She smiled playfully at him.

Why didn't he ask her for help? Was it really so he could work through whatever distraction issues he had? Or was I being naïve? Or set up.

There were plenty of people who didn't like me, Professor Oliver being one of them. He'd take any opportunity he could to get me in trouble. And if he found out about Maryville... Those thoughts twisted my stomach into a knot. I felt sick. I needed to cancel the whole thing. Tell Maddie to get a tutor. That would have been the appropriate response, not whatever the hell I did.

As I finished class and then the next one, I became more determined to tell Maddie I couldn't help him. We were set to meet at two this afternoon. So not only did I have to make it through my classes first, I also had to make it through lunch. Lunch with Gal.

"I thought you'd be more excited," she said, "Why are you picking at your lettuce?"

"Is that what this is?" I pushed the wilted leaves away from me.

"Okay, what's up?"

"I'm going to tell Maddie I can't help him."

"That didn't take long."

"I called him Maddie in class."

Maybe I should've waited until she wasn't taking a drink of her soda. I moved back as she sprayed liquid everywhere.

She cleaned herself up, tilting her head at me. "But that's one rule you never break."

"Exactly."

"Reid, sometimes rules were made to be broken."

"I reject your hypothesis. Rules are designed to keep order."

"This is not a bad thing." She took another bite and then waved her fork at me. "You've got a wall up that keeps people out."

"It's for protection."

"I get it. When you were fourteen, you needed protection. Now, not so much. It's time to start letting people in."

"I let you in." I picked at my salad, trying to find something edible and avoiding her look.

"That's because I'm amazing. I got your back, boo."

I rubbed my eyes. "Don't call me that. Why are you pushing this?"

"Because you need more than me. You need a guy, not a Gal."

"Funny. Even if I did need a guy, it wouldn't be a student."

"I agree. But—here's the thing, Reid. I've been telling you this since I met you, three years ago. And never in that time did you show interest in anyone, student or otherwise. Whatever it is about Maddie, he has your attention."

"But I can't..." The humiliation of being used. Of having to leave. Start all over again. I couldn't go through that again.

"Then maybe our mission should be to find you a guy."

"You should focus on you."

"I don't want a guy."

"We can find you a girl. You like girls."

"Correction, Professor Emerson. I like women. And I don't need help finding any."

"Are you seeing someone?"

"Nope. Not changing the subject. We are focused on you and your man drama."

I smiled at her. She always had a way of making me feel better. "I need to find someone. I get that. If only so I'm not the sole virgin at this school."

"No worries there." She nodded over to a freshman struggling with the strap of his backpack wrapped around the legs of the chair. He knocked it over with a crash, and I cringed a little. Poor kid.

"You don't know he's a virgin," I said.

She raised a brow at me.

"Right now, I just want to make it through this semester without doing something stupid."

She leaned in closer. "Like sleeping with a student?"

I leaned in even closer. "Like losing my job. I have enough people out there who think I shouldn't be here. That I'm not mature enough. I certainly don't want to give them actual reasons to think that."

She reached over and squeezed my hand. "I know," she said. "I get it. I'm here for you whatever you need. I won't even harass you if you keep helping Maddie the cutie pie."

"Really?"

She scrunched up her face thinking about it. "I can't really make that promise, but I'm here for you no matter what. Now eat your wilted salad before it slides off your plate."

Once I got back to my office, I prepared for my meeting with Maddie. I felt better after my conversation with Gal. Not sure why since she didn't reassure me at all. Maybe it was her unconditional friendship. I could do this. I made a list of the things I wanted to say so I wouldn't forget. It didn't matter.

My resolve to not help Maddie crumbled five minutes after he stepped into my office.

7

MADDIE

Rae jumped in front of me as I tried to leave the classroom after Professor Emerson's class.

"Hey."

I tried not to barrel into her as the students around me practically stampeded to get out. I grabbed her shoulders to keep my balance and held on until the rush had passed.

"Sorry," I said. "I didn't mean to..." I wasn't sure what to say, so I just waved my hands around.

"Manhandle me?" She had one pierced brow raised and a smile on her pink, sparkly lips. "No problem. Totally worth it."

I studied her face trying to figure out what she meant. Nope. Still didn't get it. "What?"

She slipped her arm through mine. "I need coffee. What about you? Ready for tea?"

"Always."

She led me out, glancing back right before we slipped out the door.

I started to turn my head to see what she was looking at.

"Don't look," she whispered. "Keep walking."

We settled into our normal table at the Coffee House, each of us with our drinks. Rae had a dark roast coffee, and I had my Chai tea. I waited until I was able to take a drink without scalding my tongue. "What's up?"

She shrugged. But a smile played around her lips, and excitement shone in her eyes. "How did your meeting with the professor go?"

"Fine."

She sipped her coffee and set it down before raising both brows at me. "Liar."

"It was fine."

"He called you Maddie in class."

"Whatever. He said he'd help me."

"I bet."

"What is that supposed to mean? Prof. Em is a good guy."

"Whoa." She raised up her hands. "Down, boy. I'm not attacking your precious professor. But I think it's interesting how possessive you both are of each other."

"That's not a thing."

"Really? Because when you were holding me—"

"You mean keeping myself from falling?"

"I don't think that's how he saw it. He was glaring at me. And as much as I'm enjoying this, if I start getting a bad grade because your professor is jealous of us...Well, it won't be pretty."

"You're imagining it." But I couldn't help that little bit of hope. What was I hoping for? That he cared about me? That he was attracted to me? None of those things would actually be good. I only had to convince my body of that. And my brain. And my heart.

After a few minutes of silence, Rae tilted her head. "When is this all happening?"

"Later today."

"Where at?"

"Seriously, Rae. This is not *Downton Abbey*, okay?"

"No, it's more like *The Graduate*."

"I know that movie. My mom loves Dustin Hoffman. It doesn't fit at all. Professor Emerson and I are about the same age. And he's not taking advantage of me."

"Ha. You're Mrs. Robinson in this scenario. Our sweet little professor is the innocent graduate."

"Don't you have classes to study for? Or more interesting things to do?"

"Nope. My life is boring. I'd rather talk about you and our hot professor."

"I'm done. Next topic."

"How's your mom and stepdad?"

"Good. I talked to them a couple of weeks ago."

"And how's your dad?"

"Next topic."

"Talk to me, Mads."

"I think this is a bad idea."

She glanced around the room and down at her coffee. "This? Or your meetings with Prof. Em?"

I closed my eyes, trying to make sense of the thoughts fighting for attention in my head.

"Maddie?"

"I thought being around him would desensitize me."

"Was this the theory behind your three-date plan?"

Why did I share that with her? "I get bored with things easily. I start on a series and get tired of it after a few episodes."

"Are you comparing Prof. Em to something you binge on Netflix?"

I ignored her, staring instead at the cute barista cheerfully serving coffee to exhausted students. No one should be that happy. But I wasn't seeing him. I was seeing the excitement of the first day in class when Professor Em was happily telling us that classifying trees was exciting and fun.

"Are you actually going for the full three days?"

"What?" I glanced back at her. What were we talking about?

"You've met once, day one. Today will be day two. Are you giving him three days to bore you?"

"That's not... not exactly what I meant. I just think being around him will take some of the shine off. Some of the excitement. And maybe I can focus."

"How's that working for you so far?"

"I still want to jump him, if that's what you're asking."

"Were you able to concentrate more today?"

I sat up straighter in my chair and stared at her. "A little. Isn't that weird? I mean, I still stared at his ass, but I didn't want him to think I was slacking and just staring at his ass, so I tried to focus more…"

"So, it is working?"

I smiled. "In a weird way, I think it is."

"Just don't sleep with him."

"I wouldn't. Not really. And I told him that…"

She grabbed my arm. Thankfully, I'd put my tea down. "You told him you wouldn't sleep with him? I mean, you actually talked about having sex with him?"

"He…" Nope. I could not go there. "Listen. It wasn't like that, Not really. Just let it go, okay?"

"Fine. But we will be discussing this at some point."

"Yeah, yeah."

I TRIED to contain my excitement when I settled in the chair across from Professor Em's desk. No scaring the hot professor. He didn't look at me, but that wasn't unusual. The grim line around his mouth *was* unusual. I didn't like it at all.

"Class was so awesome today," I said, causing his gaze to shift to me for the first time since I'd entered his office.

He stared at me like I was crazy.

"How was that awesome?"

"You called on me—"

"I called you Maddie."

"That was pretty freaking great. Did you see everyone's faces?"

He frowned even more. If that was possible. "It was a mistake."

"But that's not what I was talking about. You called on me, and I knew what you were talking about."

"You didn't know any of the answers."

"But I asked a question." I held out my hands for emphasis. His expression didn't change.

"You asked the question because you didn't know the answers."

"Right," I said. "But—wait for it—I knew what question to ask. And that's a step in the right direction."

"If you say so."

"I hope you're not bailing on me already. Seriously, I need you." I reached out and touched his hand on the desk. As soon as our hands made contact, he snatched his away.

"We have rules."

I studied his flushed and growly face. Usually, Prof. Em was all sunshine and sweetness. Did I bring out the worst in him? "I don't remember touching not being allowed."

"I'm your professor."

"Sorry. I'm a touchy-feely kind of guy. I just like to touch and feel people." I winked at him.

He shifted in his seat and cleared his throat. Then he pushed back the lock of hair that had flopped into his face. "No touching," he said. "We have boundaries for a reason, Mr. Evans."

"Okay, I get it. But fuck, don't go back to calling me Mr. Evans, again."

"Language."

"English. Is that what you want to know?"

His lip twitched, and I took it as a good sign. "Vulgar English. Barely English."

"Good thing you didn't know my English teacher. She knew some words."

"Can we focus on trees? What part are you struggling on?"

"The chapter on tree growth and fungi keeps getting mixed up in my head. Maybe if you explain it in your sexy professor voice, that might help."

He shook his head and seemed to be asking someone for patience. Did he believe in God? Or was he talking to himself?

But something in me wanted to impress him. Make him proud. I ignored the similarity to my childhood and my need to make my mom's life easier by being the perfect child. This was nothing like that. I was by far not the perfect student. But I wanted to be. And I wanted to be that for him. Instead, I told him which part still wasn't clicking with me and asked if he could explain it. When I didn't get an answer, I glanced up.

He was biting his lip and staring off. I called his name again. Nothing. He was going to tear his lips up if he kept chewing on them. I gave in and watched him for a second. His lips were red and slightly swollen, and I wanted to taste them. That way lay madness. I shook my head and called his name once more, slapping my hand on his desk to get his attention.

He jumped, his eyes going wide. "What?"

"I asked you a question a couple of times. Are you okay?"

"Yes. Absolutely. What was it you wanted to know?"

"I asked about the two main types of mycrosia..."

He started to answer, but I help up my hand.

"That's what I asked, but what I really want to know is—have you ever kissed a guy?"

8

REID

THIS IDEA immediately went from the worst idea of all time to apocalyptic levels of not good. I couldn't respond. Intelligible words escaped me. All the blood in my body centered in one place. Had he really asked me that? We'd just talked about rules. Maybe I needed to be clearer. Not only with him but with myself. When he'd told me exactly which part of the lesson he'd been struggling with, I had realized in that moment that I got it. I understood what he was going through. Everything about him distracted me. There was a clean scent about him—citrusy. But it wasn't just that. I couldn't focus.

And now it was even worse.

"Prof. Em?"

"Yes?" I squeaked out.

"I'm sorry. I shouldn't have asked you that." He stood up, and for a moment, I thought he was leaving. And while that would have been best, I wanted to yell at him not to go.

Instead, he stretched his arms to the sky and took off his sweater. Watching all his muscles work so hard to look so good made my mouth go dry. He had a T-shirt on underneath that pulled up as he removed his sweater. His tight abdominal muscles taunted me.

I was never going to survive this.

"Sorry," he said, with a smile. "I was hot."

I waved my hand, indicating it was okay. But my gesture did not convey the absolute need in my body for him to continue shedding his clothes. At one point in my life, I'd wondered if I was someone who wasn't attracted to people in real life. I'd hardly found anyone I wanted to have sex with. Maybe the terrifying thought of trying it overruled any lust in my body. But that was not true with Maddie. Not at all.

Boundaries, Reid.

He carefully folded his sweater and tucked it into his backpack. Then he returned to his seat and faced me. "So, have you?"

"Have I what?"

"Kissed a guy."

"We... I..." I took a deep breath, expanding my diaphragm to get my blood and oxygen flowing elsewhere. "Mr. Evans—"

"Please call me Maddie."

"We have rules. Boundaries. There are some things we cannot talk about."

"Like if you've ever kissed someone? Or felt the touch of another man? Or experienced the burn as someone —"

"Mr. Evans." I stood up, trying to fight the blush spreading across my face. To keep the want out of my voice and the images out of my head. I didn't have to look down to see that I had an erection and that standing up was a bad idea. I sat down quickly. "I'm not sure this is a good idea. I think you should leave."

"I'll be good. I promise. I really am sorry. It's just so easy to get a reaction out of you."

"It's a normal biological response."

He held up his hand. "Not the reaction I'm talking about. You get flustered. It's cute. But I stepped over the line."

I battled with my conscience. This wouldn't end well, but I wanted to help him. And I was enjoying my reactions to him. Something I hadn't experienced with anyone before. Could I give that up?

"Fine," I said. "But you're on notice."

"Duly noted." He turned to look over the contents of my room as if he'd never noticed them before. Was he really interested or was it a way to distance himself? No matter the reason, I appreciated the chance to get myself together.

"You're a plant and tree guy, but you have all these cool rocks."

"Is that a question or an observation?" I asked, trying not to admire the way he bit his bottom lip when he was concentrating on something. "I have PhDs in wildlife biology and geology. But rocks are more of a hobby."

"You have a hobby? That makes you seem like everyone else."

I bristled at his comment. I'd been different all my life. I didn't mind that. The world was unique. There were over seven hundred and fifty species of butterflies in the United States alone. And if you were paying attention, you could appreciate the variances in each. But things like friendships and intimacy often eluded me because of those differences.

"That's not what I meant, Professor." He leaned closer, his eyes catching mine. "You're wicked smart and too good for all of us. Especially me."

His words warmed my heart, taking the frost off his earlier comments. Had he read my expression? My body language? He seemed to be good at that.

"Can I see them?" He motioned to the shelves behind me. "The jade and the amethyst geodes?"

"You're into rocks?" His words surprised me. Although, considering his major, they shouldn't have. I placed the two rocks side by side in my hand and held them out to him.

"I became obsessed when I took my first geology class."

I expected him to take them, but instead he lightly rubbed his thumb over them, caressing the crystals and dipping into the cavities. His fingers lightly touched the back of my hand. He wasn't crossing any boundaries or doing anything wrong, and yet my body didn't get that message. Every touch sent tendrils of excitement through me. I wanted to tell him to take them, but to do that, I had to admit what he was doing to me. Admitting my attraction—already blaringly obvious, I was sure—made me vulnerable. Would I be able to stop myself from begging him for more? I handed the rocks to him so he could explore at his leisure.

I thought it would make things easier, but it didn't. Seeing the geodes in his strong hands did something to me. Was I jealous of my rocks? He gave them his full attention, rubbing and stroking the edges, even bringing them up to rub against his jaw. Could I make it through the rest of the hour without embarrassing myself?

"Did you get the amethyst from the northeast part of the state?"

"Yes. When I was in Maryville, I had a chance to rock hunt in Kahoka." I was amazed he recognized where it was from. "I found the jade in Kachemak Bay in Alaska."

His eyes shone with excitement. "That's my dream. Working in Alaska or someplace like that. The unspoiled beauty of nature." His fingertips skimmed across my palm as he handed them back. He bit his lip, glancing up at me. He knew exactly what he was doing.

How could I be mad when he smiled at me that way? In a way that no one ever had before. I'd had guys try to pick me up, but I'd felt more like prey. Maddie made me feel alive.

But it didn't matter. None of it mattered. Because even if he wasn't my student, he was one of those guys. Popular. Charming. Everyone loved them. They knew exactly what to say and do to get people to fall all over them. But it wasn't real. It was an act. I'd learned that first-hand. Not only in high school, when it was fun to mess with the four-teen-year-old senior, but it reminded me of Maryville. A student needing help. He was sweet and cute and a liar.

So, while I could see the attraction of Maddox Evans, I couldn't let myself believe any of it. I desperately wanted to feel that intimacy with someone. My short-term goal was to shed the virgin label, but I had no interest in just sleeping around. It was scary enough letting one person get close to me. Doing it over and over with different strangers sounded torturous. My long-term goal was to find that one person I could be myself with. A partner.

But I wasn't sure I'd ever find that. I was okay with being on my own. I'd survived until now without it.

The rest of the session went smoothly. I focused on what needed to be done and not Maddie's broad shoulders or flirty smile. His earlier admission that he would get bored easily had stayed with me. Would we have any more of these sessions?

After he left, my office seemed empty. I felt a moment of panic. What about after? When Maddie didn't need me anymore? Once he moved on from my class, my life would feel as empty as this room. I'd never been one for Shakespeare and romance. Or fanciful stuff. I was a scientist. But I had gotten a glimpse of what poets were lamenting about. What drove country songs and rock ballads. Tales of love and love lost.

This was crazy. I barely knew him. And yet he'd already had an impact on my life. While scientifically I didn't quite believe in things like love at first sight or having an instant connection with someone, I understood the ripple effect. Drop the stone in the water and the ripples changed everything until another semblance of calm took over. That was exactly what happened. My world was calm—Gal would say too calm. Maddie had sent ripples through it. More noticeable because of the lack of waves normally in my life.

That had to be it. In fact, maybe Gal was right. Not about Maddie but about needing to date again or really at all. If I let some small ripples in, then they wouldn't be so earthshattering when the big ones happened.

I couldn't dwell on this. I had an afternoon class to prepare for. I avoided Gal for the most part, only saying *hi* and *everything went fine* when she asked. I didn't want to get into details about my gorgeous but off-limits student.

I dragged myself home to my empty apartment that never seemed this empty before. I cooked chicken and broccoli and saved the leftover chicken to have in my salad tomorrow for lunch. I needed to stick to my routine and keep doing things the way I've always done them. It was the only way to stay focused on my goals: teach for another five years, get my research published and move up from Assistant Professor to Associate Professor. Once I had tenure, I could breathe.

Nothing was going to pull me off course. Not a meddling best friend, bumbling archenemy—at least in his own mind—or a sexy student with strong hands and a hot body that could definitely teach me a thing or two. I loved teaching, but I loved learning even more. But thoughts like those—of what Maddie could teach me—were dangerous. I needed to do everything I could to keep things between us professional.

I did allow myself a moment of self-indulgence. I relaxed in a lavender bubble bath and let thoughts of Maddie wash over me as I surrendered to my body's needs.

"Want me to strip for you, Prof. Em?" my imaginary Maddie asked. "Do you like watching me?" He stretched his hands over his head to take his shirt off, exposing all that lovely muscle.

"Yes, please."

He stripped his pants off. His ass was round and perfect. I wanted to touch him. He stepped into the tub and slid his body over mine. I imagined what it would feel like skin to skin. I'd never touched another man like that, but it didn't stop me from creating that moment in my mind, stroking myself to thoughts of Maddie, and whispering his name as I came.

It was a natural biological response that was demonstrated in nature and throughout humanity, but that didn't stop the shame I felt at using Maddie's image to get off. I had convinced myself it would be better to get it out of my system, but I may have made it worse. How could I face him tomorrow knowing I'd jerked off to thoughts of him? My office was small and private. Being that close to him, I was in real danger of begging him to take me.

I needed a new plan. And I needed it fast.

9

MADDIE

T HE FIRST TEXT came in during a quiz in my Plant Taxonomy class. I heard the ping, but I didn't look at it. Using your phone during the quiz was considered cheating. But I did wonder at it for a second. My roommate rarely texted me. Rae was the most likely culprit, but I could see her head down as she focused on the test. I had tons of so-called friends, but not that many had my number. It almost certainly was my parents. Why would they be texting me during the day?

Those thoughts came and went, but I didn't have time to worry about it. This test was kicking my ass, and that was unusual. Plant Taxonomy was easy for me. It was mostly classifying plants. But even one plus one equals two was difficult when my mind would rather focus on the way a blush could easily heat up Prof. Em's skin. The way his hair fell forward and his shy, almost innocent, smile. The outrage on his face while he tried to hide his body's reaction. I shouldn't have pushed him so hard. It wasn't fair to Prof. Em. He was helping me, and if I pushed him too far, he would stop.

"Five minutes, class," Prof. Aubrey said. She raised an eyebrow at my guilty look. Damn it. She was one of my favorite instructors.

I drove all thoughts of my forestry professor out of my head. I had an A in this class, and I wasn't going to mess that up.

I rushed to finish, getting done right before the buzzer. Yes, she had a buzzer.

As I made my way out of the room, someone grabbed my arm and pulled me forward.

"I wish she had the buzzer right up her ass," Rae said. "I hate this class so much. I'm sure you aced it."

"Maybe not," I said. "I had a hard time concentrating. But I think I did okay."

"I'm sure you did more than okay. Otherwise, you'd be freaking out."

"True."

"Distracted by our yummy professor?"

"She's cute and all, but she's a little too.... What's the word? Oh, yeah, female for me."

She hit me on the arm, and it hurt. I had found out early on that Rae packed a fairly good punch. I couldn't help but laugh. Despite struggling on the test, I was in a good mood. Later, I'd be meeting with Prof. Em. It would be our third meeting, and that thought brought me up short. I stopped, causing students to run into us and then bitch about it.

"Okay, first, you know I meant Prof. Em. And second, why did you stop? I'm getting trampled by starving students fleeing the torture known as chemistry."

I shook my head, not wanting to get into it then and there, and started walking again.

"Don't worry. I'll get the whole story by the end of lunch."

And of course, she was right.

"But he's still willing to work with you?"

I shrugged and took another bite of my burger. We'd gone to the little diner right off campus. It served the best burgers and fries in town. And by fries, of course I meant sweet potato fries. Dusted with sugar.

"I don't know how you do it, Maddie. You smile, and everyone falls all over themselves."

"That's not true."

She put down her fork and stared at me. "What about the girl behind us when we were paying for lunch?"

"She tripped on her shoelaces."

"She was wearing boots."

"Really? I didn't notice."

"And yet you noticed the scarf she was wearing. Enough to compliment her on it."

"It was a beautiful shade of blue-green." And very close to the color of Prof. Em's eyes. But I did not tell her that. "What's your point again?"

"My point, Mads, is that only you can proposition your professor and get away with it."

I smiled at the memory, and she scowled. "I'm sorry. He's just so adorable when he gets embarrassed. I mean, I feel bad. I hope he doesn't change his mind about meeting with me."

"Did you check? Maybe he sent you an email."

I started to tell her he wouldn't cancel when I remembered the text notifications I'd gotten earlier. I closed my mouth and pulled my phone out of my back pocket.

"Maddie?"

"I have a text," I said. "From an unknown number."

"Kinky. Tell me more."

I waved her off. "I should probably wait until after we eat."

"No way. Check it now."

"Bossy." But she was right. Putting it off would just worsen the churning in my stomach. It probably wasn't even from him. Then I'd have been fretting for no reason. It could be a notification telling me my dentist appointment was next week. Not that I had a dentist appointment next week, but you never knew.

I couldn't look. I glanced around the diner instead. The place was packed with students and faculty. A mixture of different people. A girl wearing Grumpy Cat pajamas stood in line behind a man dressed in expensive-looking pants, a baby-blue button-down shirt, and a slim gray tie. Sometimes, Rae and I came here just to people watch.

"Maddox Josephine Evans."

"It's Joseph." But I relented, opened my phone, and put in the passcode. I had four missed messages. That was odd. I read them in order. The first one said, *Maddie, this is Reid.*

My heart sped up. The second one made me laugh out loud.

"I swear, Maddie, if you don't share with me right now..."

She let the threat hang there. She didn't need to elaborate. She was good for it. I leaned in closer so we wouldn't be overheard and told her about the messages, reading the first one off to her. Her eyes grew big. And then I read the second one. *Please ignore my first message because I don't know how to delete it.*

Rae giggled. "He's so freaking adorable."

The third one said, as if he hadn't sent the first two, *Mr. Evans, this is your Prof. Emerson. Instead of meeting in my office, I'd like to meet in the student center.*

"Huh. I guess *your* professor doesn't want to be alone with you. Smart."

I felt disappointed but also relieved. I wouldn't be tempted to do or suggest things I shouldn't do or suggest.

"Wait—I thought you said there were four messages."

I smiled, thinking of Prof. Em writing the last message. "The first messages were minutes apart. But the last message was from almost an hour ago. He must've freaked out when I didn't respond right away."

"What does it say?" she asked.

"I just realized I might have the wrong number," I read. "I got this from your student file. If this is not Maddox Evans, please disregard and delete all the previous messages. Immediately."

We both laughed. I felt like I was fourteen again with my first real crush. Okay so my first crush was at twelve.

"You should text him back before he hunts you down. What are you're going to say?"

"Not sure." I typed out, *Gotcha, I'll be there* and quickly deleted it. *Can't wait. Looking forward to it.* Nope. Too needy.

"Give it to me. I'll do it."

Oh hell no. *This is Maddie*, I typed out. *Thanks for letting me know. I look forward to it.* I hit send before I could change my mind. Maybe I did look too eager, but I wanted to be honest with him. At least as much as I could.

"Well?"

I handed her my phone because I didn't want to say the words out loud, but that turned out to be a mistake. She started typing, and I grabbed for the phone. She scooted back out of my reach as she finished whatever she was doing.

"Rae? What the hell?"

"Don't worry. I am not texting him. See?"

She handed the phone back. The anonymous number now had a name.

"Prof. Em Hottie?"

She rolled her eyes. "Would you prefer Dr. Stud Muffin? Prof. McSlutty? I can do this all day."

I glanced around making sure no one was listening. No one was. No one cared what we were talking about. "He is not slutty."

"Didn't he bring up having sex first?"

"He brought up *not* having sex first."

"It's adorable how protective you are, Maddie. Especially since this is your third meeting with him. Isn't that when you're through?"

"It's more of a guideline than a rule."

"Guideline. I see. Quick question. How many squares are on this table—just the black ones?" She stared at me like she knew me so well. And maybe she did.

"Look, it doesn't really matter anyway —"

"How many?"

"Geesh. 24."

She raised her brow in triumph.

"Smug doesn't look good on you."

"Everything looks good on me, sweetie. Give me your phone. I'll change it back." She held out her hand, but I could see the mischievous glint in her eyes.

"No way are you touching my phone." Another text came in, distracting me.

PROF. EM HOTTIE: *Thank you for letting me know. I was a bit worried I had the wrong number. I look forward to seeing you as well.*

The number of words he managed to put in one message, with perfect punctuation, was endearing.

"You're smiling."

"I'm not." But as much as I fought it, I couldn't help the grin on my face. None of the guys I'd ever dated had made me this happy just by texting. I had a feeling this wasn't going to end well for me.

THE STUDENT CENTER wasn't just for students. The upper floors contained conference rooms, a study room, and a small auditorium. The main floor almost resembled a food court in a mall with a coffee place, a grill, a healthy salad place, and one place even had sushi. Tables were everywhere from long tables set up for groups of people to small tables set for two. An area near the wall with tall windows had comfortable chairs that might have been more at home in a living room than a college student center.

The campus store was located on the main floor. The bookstore was downstairs, leaving the main part to sell everything SMSU related. The school colors of purple and gold spread throughout the aisles of the store, covering everything from clothing and cups to the banners displayed at sports games, proudly proclaiming SMSU Badgers. It was obnoxious in a school spirit kind of way.

I used to go to the student center regularly. It had a fun vibe to it. But once senior year hit, I didn't care about anything but focusing on my studies and graduating.

Atticus occasionally dragged me to poetry night where an open mic enticed would-be poets to express themselves. Atticus loved poetry and everything romantic. Not that I'd ever seen him with anyone. But he had a romantic soul. His poems always seemed to jolt me into realizing how stale my love life had become and made me wish for more.

Rae and I came for sushi occasionally, but I had to admit, except for snacking on poetry night, it had been a while since I'd eaten there. Most of my classes were in Hudson Hall, which was in the Natural Science building. I was too busy or lazy to trek across campus unless I had a reason. I definitely had a reason now.

This late in the afternoon, the center was crowded with students and staff. I still had no problem picking out Prof. Emerson. And not just because he was the hottest guy in the room, even though he was. Tables were packed with students laughing and having fun. Some were off the main area studying in their own little groups. Everyone seemed relaxed or at least comfortable.

Prof. Em looked like he didn't belong. Scratch that. He looked like he *did* belong but didn't believe he belonged. He wore a rainbow striped tie, and he'd chucked the blazer he usually wore. He looked hot in a semi-casual way with the sleeves of his white button-up barely folded back to reveal strong forearms. He swept back his messy hair that had fallen in his eyes. He appeared younger than most of the people in the room. And he would probably fit in perfectly if he wasn't holding himself so still. He reminded me of a rabbit freezing up right before it darted. I estimated I had another thirty seconds before Prof. Em scurried away.

He glanced around, his eyes latching onto mine, and then, only then, did he smile. I felt a spark between us, a jolt of energy that made me want to conquer the world, and I couldn't help the grin on my face. I shouldn't read too much into it. He was just relieved I was finally there, and he could get out of this awkward situation. Although I found it funny that he did this torture to himself by arranging to meet here instead of in his office. I tried to contain the giddiness I felt as I slipped into the seat across from him.

"Mr. Evans," he said formally. "Thank you for meeting me here."

"Call me Maddie. And I think I'm supposed to call you Reid."

He shuffled uneasily, folding the corner of his tie, and then unfolding it again. Was he nervous? "I prefer you called me Prof. Emerson."

I grinned at him. "That's not what my text message says. Should I read it?"

"No..." Then he obviously could tell I was joking because his shoulders relaxed. He laughed. It was the first time I'd actually heard him laugh. I liked it. A lot. More than a lot.

"I don't text very often," he said with a small smile.

"Really? I couldn't tell."

"The only one who texts me is Gal. I mean, Prof. Ramon. The only other person would be my brother..." The smile slipped from his face, leaving a frown, and it broke my heart a little. There was a story there. A sore that had scabbed over. I wasn't going to pick at it. I didn't like it when people picked at mine.

"Prof. Em it is," I said brightly. "What are we discussing today?"

He gave me a small, grateful smile. "If there's something you need help with, just let me know. Otherwise, I thought we could go over that question you had in my office and explore it more in-depth."

"Sounds perfect," I said. Even though the thing I wanted to explore more in depth was him. Everything from the freckle on his neck and the too-tight chinos he was wearing to the story behind why talking about his brother upset him.

"Are you going to open your book?"

"Yes, sorry." I pulled my book out of my backpack and turned to the page he mentioned. We talked about trees and fungi, then moved on to arguing about the role of conservation in society.

"You have to get along with people," I said. "There's no other way. We're the middleman between nature and the human race. We keep the balance."

"But it shouldn't be a negotiation, Maddie. This is science, not a car dealership. If people would listen and do what's necessary, we could save the planet. Do you know how many species go extinct every single day?"

"You're preaching to the choir, Professor. I'm just saying, part of our job is to convince the public that it's in their best interest..."

"And if that doesn't work? Tradeoffs? Begging?" he said with more passion than I'd seen from him in a while.

"Whatever it takes."

He laughed, shaking his head. "I'm not sure I agree with your methods. But I can see your point. So I'll allow it."

"Allow it?" I leaned forward, and he moved toward me in response. "We're not in class right now, Professor," I said. "You're not the boss of me."

Before he could respond, and I felt like it was going to be a hell of a good response, we were interrupted by a blonde student wearing a Badgers T-shirt that surely must have been in a child's size. She also wore skintight jeans and a confident smile. She seemed too sure of herself to be a freshman but not bored enough to be a senior or grad student. Maybe a sophomore?

She hugged her books as she smiled at my professor. "Prof. Emerson," she said in a breathy voice. "The lecture series you did on climate change and its effects on the biosphere was brilliant. I loved every minute of it." She peeked up at him from beneath her lashes.

"Thank you, Miss..."

"Taylor. Daphne Taylor." She gave him a hopeful smile.

"Ms. Taylor. It's an important topic."

I wanted to roll my eyes and tell her to move along. This professor was not interested in her lady parts. And he certainly didn't need the academic equivalent of a gym bunny. And if he did need one of those, the part was already filled. By me.

But he didn't push her away. He talked cordially to her and even seemed excited about her interest. He wasn't embarrassed by the attention at all. *Huh.* He had no idea she was flirting with him. At all. Was the fact that she was female the reason he didn't notice her interest? It was a theory. And as a scientist in training, it was one I felt compelled to test.

Thankfully, she didn't stay long after that, and we went back to studying. We were in our own little bubble. It was safe because we weren't alone. But the white noise of people talking and laughing around us made it feel intimate. As if we were sharing this moment.

Prof. Em asked more questions, and he acted interested in my answers. He quizzed me on facts that weren't debatable, and I enjoyed debating them anyway. It drove him crazy, if the way he gestured wildly and raised his voice all the while grinning at me like he couldn't believe I'd challenge him was anything to go by. In the classroom, when he lectured, I had trouble focusing. But here with him so close, I could feel the heat radiating off his body, and I could smell the fresh clean scent of what was that? Lilac? Okay, never mind. I was also distracted here. But I was still getting more out of it, and maybe it was our back and forth. He asked me questions and then checked to see if I knew the correct answers. I felt myself falling into that old familiar pattern that started when I was five and my dad left us. I became the perfect boy. Just ask my teachers. My desk was organized. My grades perfect. If I was the best in everything, my mom didn't have to worry. I didn't try to impress my dad. At least, not that I'd admit to. No one could live up to his idea of perfection.

And now, I wanted to impress Prof. Em. Show him that I was perfect. That I could be perfect. For him. And I absolutely hated that part of myself. The part that craved approval like a damned puppy.

Was this why I never let anyone close to me? If they got to know me, the real me, they might leave me, too.

I took a deep breath and focused on the colors in Professor Em's rainbow tie: yellow, red, green, orange, and blue. I counted each color. Twice. Five of each and perfectly symmetrical. I approved of this tie. The tightness in my chest eased, and I noticed the Wonder Woman emblem at the bottom. Did he wear this one for Professor Ramon? Students called her Wonder Woman because her name matched the actress who played the superhero. But she also seemed to fill the role without any problem. She was a strong woman, short but fiery. Not many people would mess with her.

"Maddie?"

The touch of his hand broke through my thoughts and warmed me. I glanced down at his hand on mine, my breath stuttering for another reason and aware that he had just broken two of his own rules in a matter of seconds. He jerked his hand away.

"You seemed lost," he said.

"Sorry. Just distracted."

"Oh. Okay."

I could tell by the sad look in his eyes that it wasn't. I pushed back on the need to make it better. To fix everything and take away his pain. I was his student. Nothing more, no matter how much I wanted it. I needed to remember that. But I also couldn't stand the thought of him thinking he was boring me.

"I really appreciate you meeting with me. This has really helped me understand the material."

"So, I'm not distracting you?"

"No," I started but then noticed the glint in his eyes. He was teasing me. I remembered my confession in his office. "Well, those pants are a little tight. But I wouldn't change it for anything, so I guess I'll have to live with it."

A light blush started at his neck and moved its way up his cheeks. I wanted to follow that trail of pink with my tongue. What would his skin taste like? Would it be hot to the touch? Taste slightly salty from the day? And why, oh why, couldn't I kiss those lips?

He sat back suddenly, the scrape of his chair loud in the room, and I remembered where we were. Had I embarrassed him? I couldn't risk a look. Because more than anything, I wanted to pull him in my lap and kiss him senseless.

"Reid. So glad to see you out of your office." The man was older, probably around thirty. Good-looking with a quick smile.

"Brad," Prof Em said. "It's nice to see you again." He stood up and shook his hand.

"What have you been up to?"

"Nothing new. Teaching. The usual."

"You should let me take you away from all that. Make a day of it... Hang out."

Reid considered this with a tilt of his head. "Maybe when things settle down."

Brad's confident smile slipped just a bit, and he glanced over at me.

I nodded at him, and he turned back to Prof. Em, who had settled once again into his chair.

Brad patted him on the shoulder. "I'll let you get back to it. It was good to see you again."

I watched him leave with a sigh of relief. Brad was a professor. I'd seen him somewhere before, but I couldn't place it. And for some reason, I wanted to punch him, which would not help me retain my spot in the graduate program. I glanced over at Professor Em. He skimmed the book, probably trying to come up with more questions to stump me. That was when I realized just how clueless Dr. Reid Emerson really was.

"Oh my God. You don't even know."

"What?" He glanced at me, his brow crinkling. "What are you talking about?

I leaned forward. "You. I'm talking about you, Professor. You. Have. No. Idea."

"I have many ideas, actually."

"You've been quizzing me this whole time. Now it's your turn to be quizzed."

"I don't think I like the sound of this."

"Tough. Get used to it. It's happening."

He barked out a laugh. "Okay, Mr. Evans. Quiz me."

I had to take a second because my body took that as the innuendo it wasn't.

"Mr. Evans?"

I held up a finger, thought of soil and sewage and invariably disgusting feet, and took a deep breath. "Okay I'm ready. Are you?"

"I'm not sure what's happening. I guess I'm ready."

I sat up straighter, using the teacher voice I didn't really have. "Since we've been sitting here, how many people have flirted with you?"

"With me?" His eyes narrowed, and the amusement on his face turned to suspicion.

"It's not a trick question," I said. "Not at all."

He glanced at the table, nodding like he was seriously trying to figure it out. "Well," he said finally. "I always feel like you're flirting with me. So, I guess...one?"

I made a buzzer sound. "Wrong answer."

His blush turned a deep red that resembled complete mortification. "I...I guess I misunderstood," he said. "I should have gone with my initial response. Zero."

Oh hell. He misunderstood. Of course he did. I shook my head. "No, you big nerd," I said, going for a light tone. "Obviously, I've been flirting with you this whole freaking time. I try to stop myself, but I just can't. You're just so damn cute."

The red blush faded to a light pink, and he couldn't meet my eyes, but the small smile on his face that he couldn't hide gave me joy.

"It's my turn to teach you something, and it's even based in biology."

He narrowed his eyes again. "Am I going to hate this?"

"I honestly have no idea," I said. "But here goes. While we have been sitting here, there have been four people who flirted with you."

"No way. I was here, remember? I would've noticed."

"Obviously, not. Number one, me. Duh. Number two, Daphne."

"Who?"

"Ms. Taylor."

He thought back. "What? No. She's just a student."

"That has no bearing on what we're talking about. I didn't say you were interested in her. I said she was flirting, and you didn't notice. I thought at first it was because you weren't interested in girls or women, which is an assumption on my part. And that was why you didn't notice."

He didn't respond to that. He watched me carefully, probably weighing the evidence in his head.

"Then we got to the third person. *Brad.*"

He smiled like he knew I was wrong on this one. "Brad is a fellow professor. He wants to hang out as friends."

"How can you be so clueless? He was asking you out."

"No, he wasn't. He's not even gay," he said. His smile faltered. "I mean, I don't think he is?"

I took a sip of my soda, letting the moment sink in for him. Letting him replay the whole exchange and probably every other exchange he had with the man. Professor Em was a genius. He probably remembered everything.

After a few minutes, he glanced up at me, confusion in his eyes. "Do you really think he was flirting with me?"

"Absolutely. And he saw me as a threat."

He laughed. "Really?"

I pressed my hand against my heart as if he'd struck me. "Ouch."

He shook his head slightly. "I mean, you're gorgeous, of course, but you're my student..."

I wanted to make fun of him some more, but I got caught up in the fact that he called me gorgeous.

"Stop doing that," he said, avoiding my gaze. "You're making me uncomfortable."

I realized I was biting my lip and daydreaming about him calling me gorgeous while he kissed me. Yes, I know this wasn't the appropriate place for that fantasy, but I got distracted.

He stared my mouth for a second before turning away and swallowing.

I started to tease him, but he was staring at his hands, all amusement gone from his face. "How do you do it?" he asked.

"What?"

He shrugged one shoulder. "People are so complicated. How do you know all this?"

"The question is, Reid," I said gently, "why don't you?"

He sighed. "I'm a fast reader. You probably could've guessed that. I have an almost perfect memory. But the one thing I don't get, no matter how many books I read, is people. I remember my senior year in high school, I tried to make friends. Intellectually, I was smarter than all of them combined. I'm not being arrogant here. It's just a fact."

"I have no trouble believing that."

"But socially, I was awkward," he said with a sad smile. "I didn't hit puberty until I was a senior."

His admission startled me, but I tried to keep my reaction from showing. Because of course he graduated high school very young. I mean, he was my age and a freaking professor.

"What about college?"

"Who wants to date someone still considered jailbait?"

"And those who did want to date you..."

"Creeped me out."

Again, something I'd never thought about. I wanted to ask him about his brother. About why he didn't help him. I was irrationally angry at the man I knew nothing about. And I didn't want to bring it up and bring back the sad look on his face.

"But Reid, you're an adult now, and everyone here is an adult." I didn't want to say this, but I knew it needed to be said. "So why not take Prof. Brad up on his offer?"

"I didn't realize it was an offer."

"And now that you do?"

He shrugged again and leaned in just a little closer. "There's so much I don't know or understand. And everyone else is confident and sure of themselves. I mean, look at you, Maddie. You're popular and charming. Everybody loves you."

It didn't feel like a compliment. It felt like I was lumped in with everyone else who'd ever rejected him or made fun of him. And I didn't like that at all. "I'm faking it," I said. I couldn't believe I was admitting this to him. Something I hadn't even shared with Rae.

He tilted his head, and I felt like he didn't believe me. That wouldn't do at all.

"I'm serious, Reid. Look at me."

He'd been avoiding eye contact. Something he did a lot when he was embarrassed. But his eyes caught mine.

"I'm not always confident. A lot of times I feel insecure. I found that if I pretend that I know what I'm doing, then sometimes other people believe it, and I can believe it too." I looked down at my soda, watching the bubbles float to the top. I twirled them around, getting them riled up, matching the bubbles swirling inside me. "And honestly there's still a part of me..."

"What?"

My turn to shrug. "A part that thinks that someday people will realize I'm not that great after all." I didn't look at him. I couldn't. I'd just admitted to the one guy I really liked, and my professor, that I was a complete fraud.

10

REID

I usually avoided the student center. Not because I was a professor, but because I didn't care for crowds. And it was always crowded. Hence it was the perfect place to meet with Maddie.

But my plan backfired. All the people surrounding us, and yet it felt like we were in our own little cocoon. It made no logical sense, but I couldn't deny it was true.

I certainly confessed more than I wanted, and Maddie gave me a glimpse of him that I didn't think he showed many people. The idea that this charming, popular, *exciting* man felt as insecure as I did... Well, maybe not as insecure as I did. I took insecurity to a whole new level.

Maddie having a chink in his persona, this person I built him up in my head to be, made me feel like I could breathe. Maybe I wasn't a complete loss when it came to people. Maybe there was hope.

"I can help you," Maddie said, leaning closer. "Teach you."

"Like you did with social media?" Why was I pushing him away? Everything I wanted was within my grasp. Quite literally. His hands were next to mine on the table. I tried to swallow my fear, but it stuck in my throat, choking me.

He smiled and touched the back of my hand lightly. Could he see through me? Most likely.

"Every time I brought up the words Twitter or Instagram, you asked me to recite the scientific order: Kingdom, phylum, class, order, family, genus, species."

"I only did that once."

He smirked, and I wanted to kiss the smug look right off his face. "Because you didn't appreciate the mnemonic device I used to remember it: Kinky people can often find good sex."

"What's your point?" I was having difficulty keeping our conversation straight. All I could think about was what it would be like to kiss him.

"Is that really what you want me to help you with?"

"What?" Did he read my mind? Or was it apparent? Oh, God. It probably was.

"Social media? Is that really what you want me to help you with?"

"You asked me for my help, Maddie." I had to regain control. "I'm your professor."

"But we can help each other." His hands were close to mine. Within reach. But was I brave enough to touch him?

All the moisture in my mouth dried up, but I resisted the urge to down my glass of water. My hands felt shaky. "What did you have in mind?" I finally asked.

He smiled that smile. The one that seemed to put a everyone in a trance. Or maybe it was just me. "You teach me about tree stuff—"

I started explaining that it wasn't stuff. Trees, forests, were imperative in the ecological foundation of life. But he shook his head at me with such fondness, it stole my breath, along with my words.

"And...I'll teach you about flirting."

I sat up straight, moving my hands to my lap, and stared at him. "Absolutely not. That's not appropriate for a student and professor to—"

"I'm sorry. Not *flirting*. Social cues. It is a part of social sciences."

He was stretching it a bit, but the excitement in his eyes and the smile on his lips were almost too much to resist. I pushed back my anxiety at the thought and took a sip of my water. "I guess, maybe."

"Flirting will be included in our lessons."

I opened my mouth to protest, but he held up his hand.

"Professor Em, it's important for you to know if someone's flirting with you, especially if it's a student. That way, you can nip that unacceptable behavior—unless it's me, of course—in the bud."

"You present a compelling argument." It was difficult focusing with the way he watched me. And that trigged a memory of something he'd said when we had our first meeting. Was it only a couple of days ago? "Am I no longer a distraction?"

"Excuse me?"

"Wasn't that the point of meeting? I mean, besides helping you catch up. Your plan to get tired of me so you could focus." Saying the words out loud bothered me, but it usually didn't take long for people to get tired of me. Or tired of dealing with me. I often didn't realize I was being annoying until it was pointed out or they just started finding a way to not be around me.

He opened his mouth and then closed it again. Was he afraid of hurting my feelings? Screw that. I needed to know.

"Do I annoy you?"

"What? No."

"I want the truth."

He gave me a lopsided grin. "I mean, you can be irritating, but in a cute way."

I noticed he didn't answer my first question, but I didn't want to push it. Getting more involved with Maddox Evans was a mistake. But what if he could teach me the mysteries of social interactions? I'd been labeled as possibly autistic when I was younger. Labeling things was what we did as humans to understand our world. But sometimes labels just put people in a place where others expected them to stay. In the end, the reason this was difficult for me didn't matter. Was I going to continue using it as an excuse to keep people at arm's length? To push Maddie away? Absolutely not.

I finally nodded, not trusting my voice.

His face lit up, illuminating the world. My world. "This is going to be amazing," he said. "I'm going to make up this whole teaching plan. It'll involve flashcards and memory aids..."

"I have a perfect memory," I reminded him. "Please don't neglect your studies."

He rolled his eyes. "You're cute and all, Prof. Em, but there's no way I would jeopardize my acceptance into grad school. Besides, the only class I'm struggling in is yours. You do realize we can't do this in your office? There will be field trips."

Panic fluttered in my stomach. Or was it excitement? "What do you mean?"

"We need people. We can start in your office, but we'll have to interact with actual people. Do you think you can do that?"

I leaned back and crossed my arms. I felt offended, but I shouldn't have. I didn't like people. Or being around people. Or dealing with people. Or any kind of social interaction that involved...people. I combed my hand through my hair. What was I getting myself into?

"Don't worry. I'll run everything by you first."

I didn't quite believe him, but I did enjoy the spark in his eyes as he talked about it.

"And meanwhile, you come up with a list of the things I need to know in your class."

"It's called the syllabus. And you already have it. I'm not giving you anything more than what the rest of the class gets."

"After everything I'm doing for you?"

My heart sped up, and my mouth was suddenly dry again. Was this a quid pro quo thing? Had I misread him?

"I'm just kidding, Professor," he said. "Maybe you can give me some questions I have to answer to show I understand the material. Or have me write a paper or essay. I'll do whatever you want."

I tried to ignore how much my body liked that idea. Of Maddie doing anything I wanted. When had I become like this? I didn't think of myself as a sexual person. Not really. And yet Maddie—my student, I had to remind myself—brought that out in me. And now I was agreeing to spending more time with him. And not time studying. Time with him in a social setting, talking and flirting. *This is how careers ended.*

But it was also a chance for me to finally feel like I was alive.

As we packed up to leave, something he'd said struck me. "Who was the fourth?"

"Fourth?"

"You said there were four people flirting with me."

He smiled and nodded at the table next to us, where a guy was scrolling on his phone.

I crossed my arms. Now he was just making stuff up.

He pulled me toward the door, probably so the guy wouldn't over-hear us. "He did everything in his power to get your attention, and you never even noticed."

"Like what?"

"He kept turning toward you, dropping things, sighing. Loudly. It was becoming annoying, actually."

I still wasn't sure I believed him, but I did enjoy listening to him talk.

"I can't make fun of him," he said once we reached the door. "I feel his pain. I've done everything I can to get you to notice me."

"One difference," I said with a smile. "You succeeded."

He followed me outside with a grin on his face. We stopped at my Vespa.

"This is your scooter?"

"Yes." I prepared for the inevitable ridicule.

"She's a beauty."

I blinked back my surprise. "Do you want a ride home?"

He immediately retreated. "No, thanks."

"Don't trust me?"

"That's not it," he said, a wicked grin on his face. "I don't trust myself."

Oh. *Oh.* Both of us on my bike with his arms around me. Not a good idea at all. I could feel the blush on my face. Could I get more awkward? "I wasn't suggesting—"

"I know. I'll see you later, Professor."

"WHAT'S UP WITH YOU, EINSTEIN?"

"Don't call me that. And nothing."

Gal grabbed my shoulders and stopped me from gathering my stuff to go home. She never got physical. And she always respected my boundaries, at least physically. Mostly. I stared at her hands, and she let go.

She had a knack of knowing when something was going on with me. But that didn't mean I was ready to share.

"Come on, cupcake."

"Don't call me that either."

"It's frustrating," she said, moving my pens so I had to stop and look at her. "You're full of energy, but I can't tell if you're ecstatic or terrified."

"Can't I be both?"

She let go of my things and watched me for a moment.

I sighed, crossing my arms. I was ready to be done with this inquisition.

"That's it, isn't it? You're going to see him again."

"Gal," I said. "Sometimes it's better if you don't know everything."

"That is never true."

I picked my book bag off the desk and finished stuffing my papers in it. It wasn't that I didn't want to talk to her. I needed to talk to someone. But I wasn't sure I could do it without telling her everything. And I hadn't figured out *everything*. I wanted to figure *that* out first.

"Just be careful," she said as she tapped me lightly on the cheek. "I like having you around."

I hugged her. A quick blink-and-you'll-miss-it hug. It shocked us both.

"Must be serious."

I shook my head, brushing my hair from my face. "Not serious," I said. "Just confusing. I promise when I figure it out, I'll tell you all about it."

"Even the sexy details?"

"Not that there will be any of that, but I thought you weren't a big fan of penises. Or hearing about penises."

"You are so wrong, Professor Innocent. I love me some cock." She smirked at my shocked face. "I just prefer there's no man attached."

"Ew."

She swatted me on the shoulder. "Look up the word pegging. And then we'll talk."

"Ew squared. Exponentially. Please stop."

"You brought up penises. Not me. Must be on your mind."

Before I could come up with an answer, she winked and started to leave. I loved that girl.

"Just remember, Reid. If you decide to play in the rain, make sure to wear a raincoat."

"It's sunny out... oh." She wasn't talking about the weather. My face heated up as I tried not to think about Maddie or penises or raincoats. She laughed at my discomfort as she headed out the door.

The excitement and panic returned, crawling through my body and electrifying it. This was it. The beginning or end of my life as it had been for the last twenty-two years. Was I going to sink or swim? I didn't know. There was only one thing I was sure of. I was in way over my head.

11

MADDIE

The next several days, I did what I had to do. I went to class, aced my tests, didn't blow anyone up in my labs, and pretended like everything was fine. Rae didn't buy it. But what was I going to tell her? *I'm teaching our professor how to flirt?*

Professor Emerson and I were meeting after his last class finished at five. He didn't want to wait until next week, and meeting on the weekends seemed too casual. Only Prof. Em would think meeting on a Friday night was acceptable and not date-like. The guy was adorable. And I was in so much trouble.

I tried to convince my body it wasn't a date, and no sex would be involved. Of course, it wasn't happy about that since my last hookup had been months ago. And my body was reminding me of how unusual that was at the most inappropriate times. Like when Professor Em reached up to the top of his bookcase to retrieve his book on the trees of North America. Or hearing him laugh at something I said. Or his deep sexy voice when he said my name. Ugh.

"Maddie? Is everything okay?"

I willed my body to just shut up already. I was quite aware of our problem. Prof. Em watched me with concern, or was it nervousness in his eyes?

"Yeah. I'm good," I said. "I'm surprised you're okay with this." I nodded toward the restaurant directly in front of us.

"You said there had to be people. And we have to eat. I mean, biologically speaking, it's important—"

"I get it," I said with a laugh. "At least we shouldn't run into anybody." We were south of Springfield, closer to Nixa and completely away from the campus. Not that we were hiding. Or sneaking around. Or risking everything for a few minutes of ... what? I had no clue what this was. But nothing could have kept me away.

"Have you been here before?"

Professor Em shook his head. "Gal said they had amazing food."

I didn't say what I was thinking. Most people had heard of Lambert's Cafe, even if they hadn't been there before. Why would Professor Ramon have suggested it? Maybe the same reason I was doing this. To get our clueless professor out of his comfort zone.

Once we were seated and the waitress had our drink orders, I looked over the menu. It was a typical diner serving American food with a touristy feel to it. Tables were in sections like a labyrinth, and a wooden Native American Indian stood guard inside the reception area.

"I probably should warn you—"

"Heads up."

We both looked up in time to see a roll heading straight for Professor Emerson. He ducked, and it hit the person behind him.

I bit back a laugh. "I think you're supposed to catch that."

"How about you?" The server motioned to me, and I nodded.

I caught the roll and offered it to Professor Em.

His gaze bounced from me to the server and back to me. I broke the bread in half and put one part on his plate while I munched on the other.

"What's happening here?"

I tapped at his menu where it clearly said Lambert's Café, Home of the Throwed Roll.

"I didn't think they meant literally."

"Professor Ramon didn't mention it?"

"No. She didn't. We will be having words about this."

I wanted to watch that conversation unfold. "It's one of the reasons I was surprised you suggested this place."

"Is there anything else I should know about?"

"I mean, you're all about the animals. I would have thought you were a vegetarian."

He tilted his head. "Glad I could exceed your expectations."

"No, that's not what I meant."

"I'm kidding." He touched my hand and then quickly removed it.

I missed it immediately. In fact, if he wanted to touch any part of me, I would be fine with that. My body perked up at the thought.

"I'm a biology professor. The cycle of life is a part of nature. Life and death. I don't agree with killing animals just for fun. But for food and clothing." He shrugged. "It's all a part of it. I don't judge the mountain lion for killing a deer."

"So, we're all part of it. Just following our animal instincts to eat... hunt... to mate."

I said it just to see the blush on his face. And it was so worth it.

"Yes, well..." He reached for his water and almost knocked it over.

"Although," I continued, "I suppose mating is another thing that shouldn't be done just for fun. Nature has its reason. Procreation."

"You're deliberately trying to provoke me."

"Is it working?"

"Not at all. There are many instances of homosexuality in nature. Making it a completely natural response to our basic animal instincts."

His words were calm and measured, but the bright spots on his cheeks and nervous flutter of his fingers gave him away. The waitress appeared again, apologizing for keeping us waiting, and took our orders. We ordered the main courses. Most of the sides they brought by for anyone to try.

"I've been thinking about what we should do," I said as soon as she left.

His eyes widened, and he swallowed audibly. "Maddie..."

I leaned closer. "Your lessons," I said. "Remember? Social cues?"

"Of course. I thought…never mind. Go on."

I ignored the urge to pull him across the table and kiss him. That would be totally inappropriate, and it would probably freak him out. Plus, the whole boundaries thing we needed to preserve.

I took a sip of my soda. "Most of our communication is nonverbal—"

"Stop." The playfulness in his smile had vanished. Off to a great start. "I'm a genius. I don't usually point that out to people, but I do feel it's necessary in this instance. I don't need you to explain nonverbal communication to me. If I wanted that, I could have read a book on it. Again."

"I think we need some ground rules," I said, leaning away from him to give him space. "I don't know what you know or don't know unless I ask. And you can't get upset every time I try to explain something. But I'll do better about asking instead of telling."

"Fine. And I'll try not to take it personally. Which might be difficult. I hate not knowing something."

"Welcome to my world, Professor."

"Go ahead," he said, taking a deep breath. "I'm ready."

"You act like you're about to get a flu shot. There are many parts to nonverbal communication. Eye contact. Facial expression. Body movement and posture. Gestures. Voice. Touch. And space."

He nodded along, but he also bit his lip like it would keep him from interrupting me.

"On their own, these are mostly self-explanatory. But that doesn't make interpreting them on the spur of the moment any easier. Some are obvious, like when someone is angry. They might glare at you, scowl, stand over you with their fists clenched. Their voice might be loud or sound low and dangerous. They might get into your space, not caring about boundaries, and lord help you if they touch you. It's probably going to be a punch, right?"

"Yes." He was smiling again, so I took that as a good sign.

"But there are several of these that can be taken in different ways. In fact, it's not unusual for people to misunderstand what someone is feeling or trying to convey. There are thousands of rom-coms out there exploiting that fact. Does she love him? Or does she hate him? I've been thinking about it, Reid—I'm sorry, I can't keep calling you Professor Em while we're having a nice dinner."

He waved for me to continue.

"I have an idea why this is so difficult for you."

"I already told you."

"Let me finish. You don't seem to be having any difficulty understanding me. You can tell when I'm joking—mostly— and when I'm upset. And I'd venture to say you can tell when I'm flirting with you."

He fidgeted with his fork. "Yes, well, you are fairly obvious about it."

I touched his hand to stop his movements. "So was Brad. I'm not kidding about this, Reid. That guy was pouring it on."

A male server came by with black-eyed peas, corn, and green beans. Once we had the ones we wanted, the server moved on to the next table. Reid hardly looked at him, focusing on the food on his plate.

"What was he wearing?" I asked between bites.

"Who?"

"The server."

"Clothes?"

I shook my head. He confirmed all my suspicions. Our main course arrived, halting our discussion for a moment. I retreated to my side of the table, but I couldn't be too sad about it. The food smelled amazing. I loved a good steak and fries. We ate in silence for a while with Reid sneaking glances at me when he thought I wasn't looking.

He finally took a sip of his water and sat back with a sigh. "That was good."

I agreed completely.

"So, your theory."

"It's simple, really. The main part of being able to understand social cues is to pay attention."

"I pay attention."

"You are a genius." I said, throwing his words back at him. "And have a near perfect memory, but it has a flaw."

"I don't know what you mean."

"When I was in middle school, I was a fast reader. I thought just by reading the words, I would somehow know everything there was to know about the American Revolution. What I soon realized is that reading the words didn't do me any good if I didn't put meaning to them."

He still looked lost.

"Reid, *you're* not even looking at the 'words.' Let alone assigning meaning to them."

"Not true."

"What color shirt did our waitress have on? I'll give you a hint. It's the same as every server in here."

His eyes flickered up briefly. "Red and black."

"Easy one since that's the uniform colors. What color was her hair?"

"Blond. I think."

"She had brown hair, but it was a lighter brown, so I'll let you have that one. What color were her eyes?"

"I don't know," he said, toying with his menu. "I don't think most people notice that."

"What color are my eyes?"

He didn't even glance up. He continued studying the table. "Ocean Blue. But darker when you're wearing the Henley..." His eyes flew to my face. "I mean...I've known you more than just a couple of minutes."

"No judgement. I'm just trying to point out that you have the capacity to read social cues, Reid. You just need to learn how to get out of your own head. Look at me."

His eyes reached my face.

"Keep looking at me. Notice my facial expressions." I smiled, and he couldn't keep the smile from his face. "You asked me how I did it. How I got people to like me. It's easier than you think," I said, never wanting to look away. "You just pay attention to them like they are important."

"Is that what you're doing?" he asked quietly. "Paying attention to me so I'll think I'm important?"

"You're different." I let my gaze move to his mouth where it wanted to be, before returning to his face. "You stole my attention the moment I first saw you in your black dress pants and Zelda tie, and you've entranced me ever since."

"Maddie, are you flirting with me?"

"I've moved way past flirting."

"What comes after flirting?"

I shut my eyes breaking the connection. "You're killing me."

"How about dessert?" Our waitress was back with her cheery smile. "Do you boys want to try our caramel fudge brownie sundae?"

I started to send her on her way so I could get back to Reid, when the man in question surprised me and our waitress by looking her in the eyes.

"Can we get one of those with two spoons?" He glanced at her nametag. "Deloris?"

"Why of course, honey," she said, patting her apron for her pencil, which was still in her hand. She was clearly flustered at getting Reid Emerson's full attention. "I'll be right back." She left without writing anything down.

"I think we're going to get our ice cream for free," I said with a grin. "I hope you use your powers for good."

"Brown. Her eyes, I mean. They're brown."

"I don't even know what to say."

"I can't believe it was that easy," he said, leaning toward me. "Is that really all it takes?"

"Not always." I chuckled at the look of awe on his face. "But you'd be amazed at how much people just want to be seen. And I didn't even get to the part about saying their name. You're a natural."

"No. I'm not. But that did feel good."

Deloris returned with our ice cream and our check. As I suspected, she didn't add the ice cream. Reid pulled the check out of my hand before I could stop him.

"I'll get this."

I didn't fight him for it. Sometimes you had to pick your battles. And I thought the next one might be a big one.

"You make a good teacher, Maddie," he said as he took a bite of his ice cream, enjoying it more than was necessary. Enough that my cock thought it was time to play. Or maybe it was the way he said my name and told me I was good. My cock was a slut for praise.

"Tone it down a little, Professor, unless you want the attention of all the patrons and half the staff of Lambert's."

"Just half?"

I stared at him, my mouth practically hitting the floor. "Who are you, and what have you done with my sweet innocent professor?"

"Oh, he's in here. Just tired of always being so innocent."

He said it matter-of-factly. Not seductively. My body was not good at reading those cues because it was totally on board with helping him with that problem.

"Sorry, that lesson is advanced, and we are still working on the basics. Once you're done molesting your dessert, we will be moving a few doors down."

"Aren't you having any? She brought two spoons."

"I'm full." I didn't share food. It was another rule I had. But that wasn't the reason. I needed him to be done with his ice cream before I embarrassed myself. Seriously, did there need to be so much licking involved?

"What are we doing next?" he asked between bites.

"Going to a place with more people so we can put your abilities to the test."

He stopped with the spoon almost to his mouth and narrowed his eyes. "What place?"

"It's actually called Three Doors Down."

"The gay bar."

"Yes."

He stabbed his ice cream with his spoon and pushed it away. "I'm done."

"Excited to get started?"

"Read my cues," he said, crossing his arms and frowning at me.

"I know you don't like crowds, but we need people to test this out. And not just a waitress with a soft spot for nerdy geniuses."

"This never ends well for me, Maddie. Can't I just ride the high of my success for a few minutes or days or years?"

"It'll be fine. I promise."

"There's no way for you to know that."

"Do you know how I know?"

"How?" He still had a pout on his face, like I was making him dissect a raccoon. Except he'd probably enjoy that.

"Because I'm going to be right there with you. Do you want to have a signal in case you really want to go?"

"Yes. Good idea. If I get overwhelmed and need to leave, I'll give you the signal."

"Which will be...?"

"Me. Heading for the door."

I sighed, taking his arm, and leading him out.

"Fair enough."

12

REID

"I DON'T UNDERSTAND why we're here?"

Maddie smiled. "We talked about this. Working on your social cues. Do we need to work on your memory?"

"The music is so loud we can't even talk to each other."

"It's not all about talking," he said.

"Ha ha."

When Maddie had returned with our drinks, he sat beside me instead of across from me. I was surprised but grateful. The amount of people, mostly guys, packed in the bar was intimidating. And having a layer of protection in the form of Maddie reassured me.

He leaned a little closer. I tried to ignore the way my pulse jumped at his nearness. "It's all part of my plan."

"Which plan?"

"My plan, dear professor, to help you feel more comfortable. It's all about experiencing new things."

I pushed my hair behind my ears and took a drink of the beer I'd just ordered. "I've been to a bar before, you know."

"A gay bar?"

"Yes," I said. "With Gal." Despite the loud music and awkward situation, I was enjoying myself. At least I was up until the moment I outed Gal. Not that she hid her sexuality, but I wasn't sure the students knew. Thankfully, Maddie didn't seem to notice.

"I really love this band. You know this song?" He moved to the music, tapping his hand and even singing the words.

I didn't know the song, but I liked watching him enjoy it. "No."

He flashed me a bright smile and sang even louder.

I'd never been a big fan of bars or clubs. There were too many people. And at times, it felt like nothing more than a meat market. Most guys were probably okay with that. Maddie had probably been okay with that. It just wasn't me. I didn't mention that to Maddie.

Although the music was loud, we could still hear each other, and that was a good thing. I enjoyed having Maddie lean in closer so I could hear him. His breath on my ear was both heaven and torture.

"See that guy at the end of the bar? He's waiting for someone, and they're late."

"You're guessing. There's no way you could know that."

"A skeptic. Aren't you a scientist? Just look at the facts. What do you see?"

"He's dressed nice," I said.

"He should be. He's trying to impress someone. Probably the first or second date."

"He's looking at his watch."

"Yes, but that doesn't necessarily mean anything. People have all kinds of things on their watches these days. He could be texting or reading an email. But," Maddie said, touching my shoulder as he leaned in closer, "he keeps looking around like he's trying to find someone. His leg is shaking. Again, some people just shake their legs. It's not always a nervous habit, so don't assume. But when you add everything together..."

"You get a first date or a blind date?"

"You are correct."

"What about that guy?" I asked.

A cute guy, about twenty-five, shifted restlessly at the bar. He glanced at people often but never let his gaze stay too long. At times he looked like he might need to throw up. His eyes darted back and forth to the guys pressed together on the dance floor. He wiped his hands on his pants and then downed his drink in one go.

"First time in a gay bar?" I guessed.

"Very good," Maddie said. "Maybe he's questioning or just wants to know for sure whether he's really gay or not. It's possible he could be bi or pan, but I suspect he doesn't really know yet."

"Poor guy."

Maddie tilted his head. "You really are just a good person, aren't you?"

"As opposed to a not-so-good person?"

"Do you want to dance?"

"Not a chance."

"Worth a shot."

We sat close together so we could talk as we continued analyzing people. Maddie was scary good at this stuff. The first guy's date finally showed up, and he sagged in relief. I was sure he was getting stood up. Maddie started betting with me on who could profile people better. But I knew not to take that bet. The baby gay got hit on quite a bit. He always said no.

"I feel so sorry for that guy."

"You know you guys aren't the same." Maddie shifted so he was facing me.

"You're right. We're not. Don't think that just because I'm hesitant to make social connections, I don't know what I want. I'm gay. I know exactly what I want." It would've been better if I hadn't been looking Maddie straight in the eyes as I said it. The moment stretched, growing in intensity. Or maybe it was the alcohol talking.

"Should we invite him over?"

"Who?" I'd only had two beers. That was usually my limit, to be honest, but I wasn't exactly following. Maybe it was Maddie's closeness and the spell I seemed to be under whenever I was near him. I couldn't think of anything or anyone else.

"The new guy. He looks a little terrified."

"Oh, sure." I didn't really want to have a third person with us, not only because I didn't want to share Maddie with anyone but because I didn't feel comfortable around strangers. But wasn't that the whole reason we were doing this? It wasn't so I could get closer to Maddie, my student. He was helping me become more socially competent. Maybe he was just a good guy. Had my world been tainted by my view of popular kids and jocks I'd known over the years? Had I slapped everyone with the same stereotypical label and missed that there could be good things about them? That Maddie had good things about him? I was beginning to believe that.

"I'll be right back."

I watched him approach the guy and get rejected. But that didn't stop Maddie. I knew it wouldn't. He would use his charm and convince the guy to join us. Which was exactly what happened.

"This is Henry. Henry, this is Pro—I mean Reid."

He had a shy smile and shaggy brown hair. He was cute. Maddie told him we were both at the university without giving any details. Which was smart. It wasn't like we were hiding, but we didn't need to advertise it either.

"So, Henry," Maddie asked. "What's your story?"

He shrugged and took a drink of his beer. "I just moved to Springfield. I'm thinking about going back to college next semester. I've been out for a few years. Just stuff...life. So what are you guys going to do? School's almost done, right?"

He thought we were both students. I glanced at Maddie, letting him take this one.

And he went with it. He talked about his last year. About grad school. About what he wanted to do when he was totally done. It took the pressure off me to answer, but it also made me realize something.

Maddie had talked about going to Alaska, but I didn't realize his dream was to live there.

Would he return to Missouri at all? Maybe to see his family but probably not often. Why did it matter? We weren't together. My students came and went all the time. But I felt like we were becoming friends, and the knowledge that he wouldn't be around made my heart ache. I tried to keep up with the conversation, but I'd lost my focus.

"Let's dance," Maddie said, looking at me.

What was he thinking? I already told him I wouldn't dance. "You guys go ahead."

I didn't like the thought of Henry and Maddie dancing together, but I had no right to have an opinion on that.

"It's none of us or all of us," Maddie said. "Leave no man behind."

Henry seemed nervous but excited as he glanced at the crowd of guys dancing.

If I didn't go, he wouldn't get to go either. Did Maddie plan it like this? "Fine."

It turned out better than fine. The alcohol, the music, and Maddie, gorgeous as ever. I couldn't resist any of it. The nervousness eased away. Even Henry seemed to be having a good time. And he started having an even better time when the guy next to us started dancing with him. It wasn't a formal announcement; he just pulled him away. Then Maddie and I were alone.

"Having fun, Professor?"

"Yes," I admitted. "Especially since this is supposed to be tutoring."

"But who's tutoring who? I'm just teaching you to have fun, and you're an A-plus student."

"I have an excellent teacher."

Watching the other couples dance, which was mostly them grinding against each other, would have normally embarrassed me. But now it just gave me ideas I didn't need. I glanced at Maddie. He had a glint in his eyes, like he knew what I was thinking. Did he know that I liked it? That I pictured him and me doing the very same things? These guys were doing more on the dance floor than I had ever done in the privacy of my own home. I wanted to change that. I wanted to change that with Maddie. But he kept his distance. Was it because I was his professor? Or did he just not want me?

Sometimes, Maddie would get close and say something in my ear. It was usually about the other dancers or things he'd noticed, but I didn't care. As long as it brought him closer to me.

At one point, he excused himself to go to the bathroom, and I felt like I held my own while he was gone. I continued dancing, although I never let other guys get close. If I was going to have anyone grinding against me, it was going to be Maddie. Not some faceless stranger in a gay bar. When Maddie came back, I noticed a change immediately.

It wasn't overly apparent. He held his body a little straighter, and his smile was tight around his lips.

"I'm getting a little tired, Reid. Are you ready to go?"

I wasn't ready. I was having a good time. But I could tell there was something wrong. A reason he wanted to go. We went to say good night to Henry. I was hesitant about interrupting him. He was making out with another guy. But that didn't bother Maddie.

"Henry," he said. "We're going. You can join us if you want or stay."

I wanted Maddie to myself. I didn't really want anyone tagging along.

"I'm doing fantastic," Henry said. "You guys go on."

Maddie held my hand as we threaded ourselves through the crowd. I realized then that it was more than just wanting to say goodbye to Henry. He wanted to make sure he was okay. Give him a way out. He intentionally left the impression that Henry had come with us. This guy was such a sweetheart. How could I have ever believed he was a self-serving jerk? I'd been totally wrong about him.

The cool air on my face felt amazing after the stifling heat of the club. We laughed as we walked down the street, enjoying the ambience of the smaller town.

"If you're ready, I can call an Uber."

I tightened my hand in his. "Let's walk a while." A small brick wall a couple of feet off the ground lined the sidewalk. I jumped up, walking on it like I was on a tightrope, still holding Maddie's hand.

"I wish I could fly free like the butterflies. Catch me, Maddie!" And then I threw myself at him.

He caught me in his arms and swung me around, before placing me on the ground. We laughed, standing close to each other. Maddie tucked a stray hair behind my ear. "Reid," he said, his voice soft and warm. "Why don't you ever let anyone see you like this?"

I studied the brick sidewalk and lifted one shoulder up, my giddiness gone. "I have," I said. "It just never worked out for me."

"Yeah?" He leaned forward, tracing his thumb across my cheekbone. "It's working now." His voice dipped impossibly low, and I felt it all through my body.

He leaned closer, his breath caressing my mouth. I shouldn't kiss him. But I couldn't resist. "Maddie," I whispered. Right before our lips touched —

A horn blasted, jerking us apart.

"Our Uber is here."

So much for kissing Maddie.

We shuffled into the back of the car and gave him both our addresses. The moment was over, but it solidified what I'd already suspected.

I wanted Maddie Evans to be my first kiss. My first everything. And the fact that he was my student seemed completely irrelevant.

13

MADDIE

"I WANT A NEW BEST FRIEND."

"You can check the freshman dorms. I hear there's plenty of people there looking for besties."

Rae glared at me with a tilt of her brightly colored head and her lips pursed. She meant business. "It's been weeks, Maddie. You've given me nothing."

"Two weeks. And I don't know what you want from me." That wasn't true. I knew exactly what she wanted, but I wasn't willing to give it to her. Two weeks ago, to the day, was one of the best nights of my life. And for a hot second, I'd almost got to taste to Reid's lips. But that night, I also got the wakeup call I needed. I'd seen my professor, Mt. Surly, at the gay bar. Not that we were doing anything wrong. But Reid and I both had too much to lose. He wanted to keep his job, and I didn't want to get kicked out of school two months before graduation. And I had grad school to think about. I'd been accepted, but that didn't mean they couldn't kick me out for inappropriate behavior or some such crap. The smart thing to do was to quit seeing Reid completely except for in the classroom. I didn't usually do the smart thing, including this time. But I did limit the time we spent together to office hours in his office with the door open and occasional study sessions in the student center. We also met once on the quad, but it felt more like a date, so it didn't happen again. I didn't explain it to Reid. He would worry needlessly. But I think he understood that we needed to keep it more professional.

"You're uninvited to my birthday party."

Rae and I were hanging out at our favorite place, the Coffee House. I sipped my Chai Tea, and she gave me the evil eye.

"It's your birthday? You're having a party? I'm invited?"

"No. No. And yes. But I'm only inviting you to my nonexistent party so I can uninvite you."

She was sulking, and it was kind of cute. "Childish Rae. I don't want to go to your stupid nonexistent party anyway."

She leaned forward. "Come on, Maddie."

"Prof. Em's been really helping me. I'm doing better at focusing in class. My other studies are not in jeopardy. Everything is wonderful."

"But aren't you breaking your rules? It's been over three times. Over a dozen times." While she talked, she rearranged the sugar packets and mixed them in with the sugar substitutes. She put pink in with the blue and added yellow. Then she decided she didn't like it and mixed them all together. Some might see this as a sign of her being nervous or needing something to do with her hands, but I saw it for what it was. She was messing with me. When she was finished, she smiled proudly and put her hands in her lap.

"Rules are meant to be broken," I said, ignoring the condiments. "Cliché? Yes, but also true. I see this as growth. I'm around someone I enjoy spending time with and not getting bored. Kind of like hanging around with you. Except you're annoying."

"Whatever do you mean?" She smiled sweetly at me. But I could see the challenge in her eyes. She was waiting for me to break.

I glanced at the mixed-up packets. It didn't make sense. Why would someone want to do that? But it wasn't hurting anything, so I could ignore it. "How are your classes going?" I asked.

"Pretty good. I mean, my Forest Ecology professor has been in a really good mood lately. I think he must be getting some. Thoughts?"

"Nice try," I said. But Reid *had* been in a good mood lately. Was she right? Maybe he got in touch with Henry. I mean, they would probably make a good couple. My heart rejected that thought right away.

And for a second, she had distracted me. But only for a second. Then my eyes returned to the sugar containers. I blew out a breath and gave in, putting them all back into their proper places.

"Oh, I'm sorry, did that bother you?"

"Not really. But what if someone sits here and they have diabetes? And they accidentally used sugar instead of sugar substitute? It would be all your fault, and I couldn't let that happen. Especially since you only did it to bug me."

She laughed. "But you're so easy to bug."

"Ha ha."

Her eyes locked onto something behind me. "Oh, this should be fun," she said. "But don't turn around."

"What?" I started to look when she gave me her sternest glare. Which, to be honest, wasn't really that stern. Don't get me wrong, Rae was a badass, no doubt, but she didn't scare me. Mostly.

"Hi." Reid sounded breathless like he'd ran all the way to the Coffee House. And maybe he did. Surely, it wasn't because he was nervous to see me. Not when we saw each other almost every day.

"Reid—I mean, Prof. Em, what are you doing here?"

"Coffee," he said, pointing at the barista pouring coffee into a cup.

"Yeah, of course."

"Would you like to join us, Professor?" Rae sounded excited, and I kicked her under the table. She grinned, still not looking at me. "We'd really like you to join us. Isn't that right, Maddie?" She finally glanced at me, a mischievous glint in her eyes.

She knew what she was doing. I couldn't push Reid away. It wasn't that I didn't want him to sit with us. I just didn't want prying eyes and to do something stupid in front of Rae.

Reid's face lit up, which made me suddenly glad she'd suggested it. Anything to put that smile on his face was worth it, even if Rae used it later against me.

"I'll get my coffee and be right back. I mean, you guys aren't leaving, are you? Because if you are, that's okay. You can go ahead and go. I mean, I can just take it back to my office...."

I held up my hand. "We're not leaving."

"Good. I'll be right back."

"Well, lookie here. This is going to be so much fun."

"Don't you have something better to do? Maybe mix up the patient charts in the pediatric ward at the hospital."

"Nope. I'm right where I want to be. Spending time with the cute professor and watching you squirm. Two of my favorite things."

And really, it wasn't that bad. Reid sat next to me. I knew he would. Not because he preferred me, although that was probably true, but because he knew me. He was always a little uncomfortable around other people.

Reid did surprisingly well, and as his mentor, I felt proud of his progress. He asked questions about Rae's classes and stayed engaged in the conversation. He also did a little nervous chattering thing, but on him, it was so damn cute. I honestly wanted to spend every moment with him, and it was starting to scare me.

Occasionally, someone would stop by and say hi. They didn't seem at all surprised that there was a professor sitting with us. Of course, Reid looked our age. Because he *was* our age. Unless they were from the biology department, they might not even know he was a professor. A guy from Rae's sociology class stopped by and chatted with her.

"Is he or isn't he?" Reid said, after he was gone.

"Is he or isn't he what?"

I started to explain, but Reid beat me to it. He seemed to be enjoying himself. "This is a game that Maddie and I play. He's helping me with social cues. So, the question is...is he or isn't he flirting with you?"

"First of all, no, he wasn't. Second, cute little game. You're just so imaginative, Maddie."

"Why, thank you, Rae, but you're wrong. He was flirting."

"That is one for and one against, so I guess Prof. Em is the tiebreaker here. What do you say, Professor? Is he or isn't he?"

"Well, let me think," Prof. Emerson said, as he straightened the sugar containers until they were side by side. A guy after my own heart. "He looked at you more than he looked at us, but that was probably because he knew you. His eyes did seem to widen a little when he looked at you. The tone of voice and the inflection on your name makes me think that he *was* flirting."

"Whatever. You guys are ganging up on me. Okay, my turn. What about the barista? He keeps looking over here, so either *one*, he's hoping we leave because it's getting crowded, and he needs a free table, or *B*, he's interested in one of us, or *third*, he's looking out the window because he's worried about his car."

Prof. Em turned to me, his mouth open. "I don't know what to say."

"She does the mixing-up thing to drive me crazy. She knows I hate it."

"Well, yes," he said. "That did bother me, but I'm also wondering if she's got insider information or just a very good imagination."

"We're all scientists here," Rae said. "We can test this."

"I'm the only actual scientist here."

"Okay, but Maddie and I are scientists in training. We have a theory. Let's test it."

"How do you propose we do that?"

"Don't ask," I said. But it was too late. She was already waving the cute barista over.

"Hey, guys, did you need something?" He glanced back over at the counter, but his coworker had it covered.

I wasn't sure how she was going to do it. Was she going to flirt with him, or did she want us to flirt with him? How else could she figure this out? But I should have known the answer.

"We have a bet going."

"We don't have a bet," Reid said.

"She's crazy," I agreed. "No bet."

"A bet?"

And now he thought we were making fun of him. Great. We had to find a new coffee place.

But Rae wasn't deterred. Rae was never deterred. "You keep looking over here, and we were wondering if you were *one*, interested in me, or *B*, interested in one of these two cutie pies, or *thirdly*, if that is your car out there, and you're worried somebody might mess with it."

I wanted to slink down under the table, but Reid had grabbed my leg and was squeezing it. I couldn't figure out why until I looked at his face. He was trying so hard not to laugh. I felt giddy. Not sure if it was sharing this moment with Reid or the fact that all my brain cells were focused on his hand, so close to where I most wanted it to be.

"Have you guys been drinking? Or... no judgments." Poor Sam. At least according to his nametag. "Because I've got work to do."

"Can you just give us a hint?" Rae was relentless.

"I mean, honestly, one," he said, ticking off the answers with his fingers. "You guys are all attractive, but I have a boyfriend. And B, I ride a bike to work."

"You guys are driving me freaking crazy. Stop doing that. Pick one."

Sam ignored my rant. "If you guys aren't going to order anything, I'm going back to work."

"Wait a minute," Reid said, surprising us all. "Why do you keep looking over here? That's really all we wanted to know."

The guy looked down at his feet and lifted one shoulder before glancing back up. "I had biology with you, Prof. Emerson, and you're my favorite teacher by far. I was just surprised because I'd never seen you in here before."

"Oh." Reid's face got a little pink as he twisted his coffee cup around on the table. "Thank you, Sam."

Sam nodded, smiled at us all, and walked away.

"That's so cute. You're my favorite professor, too."

"Thank you, Rae," Reid said.

"You're okay."

He looked up at me in surprise.

"Kidding. I'm pretty fond of you, too, Professor Em." Reid wasn't comfortable with flattery, but I wasn't sure if that was the reason he was embarrassed. "This your first time here? I'm surprised."

Reid laughed. "Are you really? I don't usually bother with things like going to get coffee when I have coffee in my office. I also don't like social situations where I have to talk to people. And ordering coffee is actually talking to people. I don't even like ordering out because I have to...talk to people. That's why I order the same thing from the same place all the time."

"Then I don't get why you're here."

Rae rolled her eyes at me. I knew what she was insinuating, but she had to be wrong. Didn't she?

"You told me it was a great place to get coffee, and I was hoping you'd be here."

I would never get used to how blunt he was sometimes. No games. No pretending. Even though we were supposed to be pretending. He looked at me, and I felt like we were the only ones there. The urge to pull him in my arms and do what I should have done a few weeks back was overwhelming. I wanted to kiss him so much.

"Sorry, guys," Rae said, waving her hand between us to get our attention. "I need to interrupt before you both combust right in front of me. Plus, we're in a public place where there's lots of students, so you might want to do this thing you got going on somewhere else. Anywhere else. Also, he is."

"He is?" Reid tilted his head in confusion.

"That was meant for Maddie. Aren't we still playing the 'is he flirting with you or not' game? Because if we are," she indicated the two of us, "then he is." She pointed at Prof. Emerson just so I didn't misunderstand her, or maybe it was so Reid wouldn't misunderstand her.

If I thought Reid was going to deny it, I was completely wrong.

"Oh, he definitely is," Reid said. "And he also wants to know if you would go out to dinner with him tonight."

"Reid—I mean, Prof. Emerson. We should probably keep it professional."

"He'll be there."

"Rae, I can speak for myself."

"If your answer wasn't immediately *oh hell yeah,* then you obviously need someone to speak for you."

"Perfect," Reid said. "I'll meet you at our favorite restaurant around six-thirty. It was nice seeing you again, Rae." He gave us a smile, waved at the barista, and left the coffee shop.

"You have definitely been holding out on me."

"Rae, he is my professor."

"I'm not saying you have to fuck him now. But you *are* graduating in a few months."

"I don't want to mess anything up for him."

"Maybe you should let him worry about that."

"Maybe."

"But one thing is for sure—you need to stop holding out on me and tell me everything that happens."

"Not everything."

"Maybe not everything, but I want a fairly detailed stat report on how the evening goes. For science."

"And if I don't?"

"Well, let's just say I know how to make your life miserable. Mixed-up sugar packets and numbering systems will be the least of your worries."

"I'm glad you're my friend, not my enemy."

"You got that right. Just ask my last chemistry partner."

"What happened to them?"

"Let's just say some things are better left unsaid, especially if you like your eyebrows the way they are."

14

REID

I MUST HAVE LOST my mind. Inviting Maddie to dinner was pure insanity. What was I thinking? But that part at least was simple. I'd never felt this connection with anyone. Gal was a close friend, but this was different. I needed to be with him. Obsession described it best. It made no sense, and I liked things to make sense. But this thing between Maddie and I felt amazing, invigorating, almost magical. And maybe it was built on lust. I wanted him even if I couldn't have him. But it felt like more than that.

"Prof. Emerson," Professor Oliver said, sticking his head in my door. "I wanted to get updates on your grants for your research projects and where you are with each for the department meeting tomorrow."

"Why? I usually give those directly to Dean Albin."

"He asked me to gather them." He shrugged, as if it was no big deal. But something about his posture gave me the feeling that he wasn't being truthful. I was doing better figuring out body language, but some things still eluded me. Even if I couldn't figure it out, I knew I couldn't trust Oliver. I'd never trusted him.

"I'm still working on getting them together, but I'll let you know when they're done."

He smiled, and it reminded me of a shark. Something predatory.

And then his smile widened as he turned to leave. As if he'd gotten the best Christmas present ever. "Mr. Evans. Can I help you with something?"

I resisted the urge to push my fellow professor out of the way. I wanted to protect Maddie, which didn't really make sense. He could protect himself. It's not like Prof. Oliver was really a threat.

"I just need to turn something in to Prof. Emerson. But I can wait until you're done."

Oliver glanced from me to Maddie. "Oh, I'm done."

Once he wandered down the hall, Maddie came in and started to shut the door.

"Leave it open," I said, low enough it wouldn't be heard in the hallway. Maddie nodded his understanding and walked over to my desk.

He wouldn't look at me. Was he canceling for tonight? It was probably for the best, but my stomach felt like it had lead in it.

"I have you scheduled for tomorrow, not today," I said. I was sure he knew that, but I couldn't figure out how else to get him talking.

"I know. I wanted to give you these." He dug through his bag and pulled out some papers, handing them to me.

The assignments I'd given him. "There's this thing called email. You should try that."

He smiled and picked up the tiny rake in my Zen garden. He wiped away the swirls Gal had left in the sand. And he still wasn't looking at me. "I didn't think this was an official assignment."

I understood what he was trying not to say. I'd given him a couple of short essays just to help him understand the material. I looked them over and glanced up at him. "You're right. I can't give you extra credit for these. But I'm impressed. You know the material."

"Maybe we could discuss them... later."

He said the words low, so they didn't travel. They sparked excitement in me. He wasn't calling off our dinner. It was not a date. We were not dating. I couldn't say that right now, but I could make it clear later when we had dinner. Which sounded a lot like a date.

"Are you okay?"

My face heated up. Just thinking about it being a date made me think of all the possibilities. Our near kiss flashed through my mind. I was in so much trouble. But I didn't say any of that. "I'm fine. Are we still good for...later?"

His eyes finally found mine, and a smile brightened his face. "Absolutely."

"Reid, do you know what that asshat did now?"

We both turned to stare at Gal, whose mouth had dropped open. She stared at me, then Maddie, and back at me. She waved her hand. "Sorry. I didn't mean to interrupt."

"No problem," Maddie said. "I'm on my way out. I'll see you... later."

After he left, Gal stared after him. Then she turned to me with a huge grin on her face. "Later?"

"Gal."

She ignored me and the warning in my voice as she shut the door.

"You don't have office hours today." She plopped down in the chair and stretched out her legs. Her shoes plopped to the floor.

I couldn't see her feet, but I'd heard that sound often enough to know. And then I *could* see her feet because she placed them on top of my desk.

"Gal, that's disgusting."

"My feet are clean," she assured me. "Answer the question."

"You didn't ask a question." I shuffled the papers on my desk. I had things to do, and she would just make me late—I stopped, catching her eyes over the top of the papers. Maddie's papers. I held up my hand.

"What?"

"I need you to go to dinner with us."

She stopped wiggling her toes and tilted her head. "That doesn't sound like an invitation. More like a command."

I leaned back in my chair, no longer able to face her. "I invited Maddie to dinner."

"A date?"

I kept my face down, but I could hear the excitement in her voice, and I needed to squash it. "No."

She moved her feet and leaned on my desk, waiting. It didn't take long for me to crack.

"Maybe. I don't know."

"It's not like this is the first time, right?"

I glared at her. "That was different. He was helping me."

"And now you're helping yourself. Way to go, Reid."

"No. I'm not…"

"Wait." She stood up and walked around the desk. "Am I the third wheel?"

"No."

"The buffer?"

I hesitated. "Maybe."

"I'm actually okay with this," she said finally. "I'd love to watch you fall harder for our boy."

"I didn't fall for him—"

She held up her hand. "I'm talking now."

I rolled my eyes.

"But if you guys are going to be all lovey-dovey, why do I want to be there?"

"Good food?"

"Eh." She tilted her hand back and forth.

"Good food and keeping Prof. Oliver off my ass?"

"Creepy wanker," she said. "Sold."

Lambert's Café was busy, which seemed to be a regular occurrence. Maddie had a table already and was drumming his fingers on the top when we arrived. His eyes seemed to light up when he saw me and then dimmed a little as he glanced behind me. I probably should have mentioned I was bringing someone. As we approached the table, I realized my dilemma. Should I sit next to Maddie? That was where I wanted to be. But I wasn't sure I was brave enough for that.

Or maybe across from him. And then a second later, it was out of my hands.

"Scooch." Gal motioned for him to move over as she sat beside him. I wasn't sure if I was grateful or not. Okay, I was grateful. I sat down on the other side of the booth.

"Hey, guys," Maddie said. "Good to see you."

"Hope you don't mind I tagged along, Maddie," she said, smiling at him as she grabbed some peanuts from the bowl on the table. "Reid knows how much I love being assaulted by my dinner."

I almost corrected her. I didn't need her to take the heat for me. But when I looked at Maddie, he smiled. He either got it or didn't care as long as we were together. I tried to keep the goofy smile off my face, but I knew I failed when Gal cleared her throat.

"Nope. We are not doing this," she said, waving her hand between the two of us. "You guys can get all mushy after I'm gone. This place has alcohol, right? Because I need a drink."

Maddie's face turned pink. "Professor Ramon..."

"Gal."

"Gal...I'm not. I mean we're not..."

She looked between us, raising her eyebrows. "Seriously?"

Why did I think she would behave? "Gal. Be nice."

"Maybe this wasn't a good idea," Maddie said. "You guys are my professors and—"

"I'm not your professor, Mr. Evans. I was your professor your freshman year when you got the highest score possible and then some in my Biology II class."

"You remember that?"

"How could I forget it? You were so bored in my class that you frequently hit on your fellow students just to have something to do. I think you were the reason five percent of my students switched classes within the first add-drop period."

"How was I to blame?"

I watched the two of them, wondering if I'd have to break them apart at some point.

"I couldn't prove it, mind you, but I heard enough whispered complaints. You slept with some and didn't call them back. And the others wished you would have slept with them."

"Gal."

She turned to face me and must have realized what she'd said. Or maybe it was the thunderous look on my face.

"That's it. I'm out." She stood up to leave, but Maddie stopped her.

"You're not wrong, Professor...Gal. Please don't go." He was watching me, studying my face. "That was me up until the beginning of this semester."

"You've suddenly changed?" She crossed her arms and stared him down.

I didn't get it. Up until five minutes ago, she was on team... Raddie? Meid? Now I was making up couple names?

Pathetic. The point was suddenly she was not in favor of Maddie, and it didn't make sense. Was this outrage staged? I wasn't proficient at this stuff yet, but I did know my best friend, and something was off.

"Gal," I whispered. "Sit down so they can take our order." I nodded at the server behind her.

She slid back in her seat. I didn't dare look at Maddie. What could I say?

The young man in red suspenders and matching bow tie took our order and quickly left.

"I don't think I've changed," Maddie said. He fiddled with the straw in his tea. "I think I was searching for something." He gave a shrug of one shoulder and then glanced up at me. "And now I'm not."

"Good enough." Gal smiled like she'd won something. "Ground rules. We need 'em. You," she pointed at Maddie, "call me Gal. No professor nonsense. And Reid, lighten up. Now where are those hot buns?"

Maddie laughed. his eyes lighting up, and my heart swooned.

Thankfully, the waiter came by with the pass-arounds of black-eyed peas, macaroni and tomatoes, fried potatoes and onions, and fried okra.

Gal, as much as she protested, got the rolls for everyone. She had a knack for catching the server's eye, and he'd throw a roll to her. She caught it like she'd been playing baseball or some other sport I never played all her life. And maybe she had. I needed to ask her. I knew from the last time we were here that Maddie had no problem catching...oh dear god, now that was in my head. I shook that thought free, hoping without hope that it wouldn't scorch through to my face. No such luck.

"Something you want to share with the class, Reid?" Gal asked.

I shook my head, not daring to speak. Trying not to squirm in my seat, I willed my body to calm down. I pictured Professor Oliver storming into the room and demanding an explanation. My body reacted accordingly, and I sighed in relief.

The food was delicious. I had one beer. Only one. I needed to stay focused. Gal and Maddie kept the conversation going with anecdotes on their college years. But before I could get depressed that my experiences didn't match theirs, they'd draw me out—they seemed to take turns at it—and I'd end up telling a story or two.

"And tell him about the time you..." Gal cracked up, unable to do more than sputter out a word or two. "Library...card...freshman."

I smiled. It wasn't that funny a story, but now Maddie was laughing, and he hadn't even heard it yet. "I went to the campus library to study. It was late, and there was a group of..."

Gal giggled some more, and I stared at her. "Gal."

She covered her mouth and motioned for me to go on.

"It's not that funny," I warned him. But I kept going. "There was a group of guys wearing football jackets at a table, and as I walked by, they called out to me."

"Oh boy." Maddie bit his lip and shook his head.

"I almost ignored them, but I was afraid they'd get louder. And it was the library," I said to Gal and Maddie. "You don't yell in the library."

Gal nodded, a little more under control.

"So, I went over and asked if they needed help with anything."

I paused, remembering how humiliated I'd been by the experience at the time. Now it was just a funny story. When had that happened?

"What did they say?" Maddie asked, his eyes wide.

"The leader," I said, using air quotes, "asked me if it was past my bedtime and to make sure I had my library card on me."

"Reid..." Maddie wasn't laughing anymore. He looked like he wanted to beat up some football players for me, and it warmed my heart.

But this wasn't one of those stories. Not really. I smiled. "I glanced at the name stitched on his jacket to the book in his hand and said, 'Thank you for your concern, Mr. Colman. But you should probably focus more on the exam we're having tomorrow in Intro to Biology.' I heard the girl behind him whisper, 'Told you,' as I walked away."

"Wait. You were their professor?"

"Teaching assistant. It was only a few weeks into the semester, and I hadn't led any lectures or labs at that point. But I was at every class. They just didn't notice me. There were over a hundred in the class, though, and to be fair, I looked twelve."

"Tell. The. Rest," Gal said, trying to not laugh and failing.

Why did I tell her this story in the first place?

"There's more?" Maddie glanced at Gal and then me.

"The professor had me run the next class. I think he went golfing. As students finished, they brought their exams to the front and dropped them off. The football player hovered after depositing his paper. 'I'm sorry, Professor,' he said. Probably worried I'd fail him. I told him it wasn't a problem, but he might want to spend more time studying and less time on hall duty since we weren't in high school anymore."

"That's my favorite part," Gal sighed.

Maddie reached over and squeezed my hand. And for that moment, I let him.

15

———

MADDIE

HOLDING Reid's hand in public was risky. I knew that. I just couldn't help myself. Hearing his story, everything he had to go through, and yet he was the strongest person I knew. Gal suddenly jumped up. I had a hard time not thinking of her as Prof. Ramon. Even in class, she'd always been a hoot.

"Well, boys, I gotta go."

Reid let go of my hand and turned toward his friend.

"What? Why?" He sounded nervous. Was he afraid to be alone with me?

"I got a hot date," she said.

"I don't believe you."

"This isn't about you, Reid," she said, turning her phone to face us. "It's about her." On the phone was a picture of a gorgeous blonde. I wasn't into women, but even I could tell she was hot. And under her picture were a couple of messages I absolutely should not have read. The first said, *What are you doing?* And the second one said, *Hopefully you. Give me a minute.* Last message read, *You have thirty.*

"So yeah, time for me to go. Maddie, can you give our professor here a ride home?"

"Absolutely."

"But... But..."

She tapped him on the cheek a couple of times. "You've got this."

And then she was gone.

Reid's gaze flitted around the room, looking everywhere but at me.

I sighed. "Do you want to go?"

"Yes," he said, quickly.

"Oh, okay." I didn't look at him as I grabbed the bill. Before I could get too far, he took it out of my hands.

"I've got this," he said. "Remember, I asked you."

He squeezed my hand, and I looked up at him. He leaned a little closer. The sounds of the restaurant—the chattering of patrons, the clink of dishes, the shouts of the servers—made it difficult to hear at times. And I certainly didn't mind getting closer.

"I don't think it's a good idea for us to be seen together alone."

That made total sense. I nodded and gave him a smile, although it felt weak.

"So, we just need to make sure," he continued, "we're not seen."

Oh. I smiled. "Gotcha."

After we went up to the counter and paid, I led Reid to my car. The days were starting to get longer now, and the sun setting over the fields burst across the horizon as if they were painted on. Tonight, anything felt possible.

As we headed back into Springfield, I realized I didn't know where we were going. I lived in the student apartments, so we certainly weren't going there. I'd never been to Reid's place, but it felt like a step too far. Which was crazy, considering my whole plan had been to seduce him in the first place. I was no longer sure that was a good idea. Not because I didn't want to, but because it seemed too risky. There was more at stake. I was afraid someone would find out. But I also wasn't going to throw away this opportunity to spend time with Reid.

"I have an idea," Reid said. "Take the next left."

I turned, following his directions, and we arrived at the last place I expected. Nathaneal Greene National Park. The place was massive.

I'd been once or twice, but it was impossible to see everything. For labs we usually went to the Woodlands conservation center.

"I love this place," Reid said, holding my hand as we strolled through the Botanical Gardens.

We met a few people as we walked, but not as many as I expected. "It's quiet."

"It's busier when the Butterfly House is open," he said. "And the Japanese Stroll Gardens. They're beautiful. I'd love to take you there some time."

I ignored the voice in my head that talked about an expiration date on our time together. I needed to just enjoy the time we did have.

Reid pointed toward some beautiful flowers. "The azaleas are beginning to bloom. Next month, irises, peonies, and roses will be everywhere."

He bent down and picked up a rock from the garden. Butterflies and ladybugs were painted on its flat surface. He handed it to me.

"This is cool."

"You can take it if you want."

"Really?"

"Local artists hide them in the garden so people will find them. You can keep it or hide it, again, for someone else to find."

"Let's hide it," I said, grabbing his hand.

The joy on Reid's face was infectious. We searched for the perfect spot, and after finding it, we hid it behind some irises. "I hope whoever finds it gets as much out of it as we did."

"Me, too." He pushed my hair back behind my ear, lightly touching my face with his thumb, and for a moment, I thought he was going to kiss me. But then he moved away and pulled me down the path.

We stopped in front of the Rosen Butterfly House. It was shaped like a greenhouse but with netting instead of glass. "We're here," he said.

"It's closed."

"I thought you were adventurous?"

"I doubt Rae or Gal would bail us out of jail, Reid."

His eyes sparkled as he pulled out a lanyard and held it up. "I have connections."

I followed him in. Inside it seemed bigger than it had from the outside. Plants in pots surrounded the perimeter. Red bricks covered the floor, and the middle section held trees and plants.

Reid gave me the tour, spouting off facts about the different plants and types of butterflies.

"Is there going to be a quiz later?" I asked, threading my fingers through his. "You have all this knowledge. It's humbling."

"I have a confession," Reid said. "I volunteer here. My mom took me to a butterfly park when I was four. That was when it happened. I fell in love with nature...and science. And if I can help a child get that spark." He shrugged, but the gesture held weight. "I love watching their faces light up. It's a beautiful moment. It gives me hope—what?"

I tried to hide my smile, but I couldn't. Reid helping a child discover science was seriously doing things to my heart. "You're beautiful...and good. How are you real, Dr. Emerson?" I kissed his hand. "And I suspect you like butterflies more than people. Adult people," I qualified.

"Of course," he said. "Most adult people. But maybe not all."

"Really? Tell me more."

He pulled me close. "That feeling I get when I'm in the forest, in the middle of nature, and everything feels right? I get that feeling when I'm with you."

I touched his face. His cheeks were warm, but the rest of his skin was cool from the night air. "Can I kiss you, Reid?"

"Yes?"

I was focused on his lips and almost missed the hesitancy in his voice. I could tell he wanted me. Was he afraid of getting caught? "Is that a question?"

He closed his eyes, and I waited for him to gather his thoughts. But I didn't let go. Not yet. I didn't want to lose this connection. What if I never got another chance?

"No," he whispered. "I just have...never..."

He started to pull away in embarrassment. I could feel it in the way his body tensed up and his blush darkened.

"It's okay. I've got you." I rested my forehead against his. "Do you want to kiss me?" Thankfully, his response came much quicker this time.

"Yes." There was no question in his answer. "You're a good teacher, Maddie. Can you show me how?"

Oh. Fuck. He was going to kill me. I wanted to ravage his mouth and some other caveman bullshit, but I had to be gentle with him. I ordered my dick to stand down. It didn't listen, but it did give me a moment to get myself together.

"Unless…"

I heard the uncertainty in his voice. In my attempts to keep myself under control, I hadn't answered him. Time to remedy that right now.

"Please," I whispered, before touching our lips together. I kissed him softly. My body roared back to life. I kept myself in check as I brushed our lips together again and again.

"Oh," he sighed, returning each sweet kiss. We made out for a few moments. Closed mouth kisses that increased in intensity until we were both panting.

"More, please."

"Are you sure, Reid?"

He nodded, his eyes bright and full of longing.

I kissed him again, biting his bottom lip to taste more of him.

Reid wrapped his hands around my neck and pulled me tight against him. He opened his mouth, inviting me in. I couldn't stop as I slid my tongue in, and then we were kissing for real. It was awkward and sloppy and wonderful. Reid had no finesse but he kissed me harder. He trusted me enough to not care if he messed up, and that was intoxicating. This was what sex with Reid would be like. Hesitant at first and then trying anything and everything in his thirst to know more. My cock ached to be closer, preferably without clothes. In his ass or mouth…at least just skin to skin. My need was taking over. My resolve breaking. I had to regain control.

"Reid," I said, pulling away.

His lips followed mine, lost in the new experiences. He whined, rubbing up against me, his cock hard against mine. Oh, holy hell. He wasn't making this any easier.

"We're in public, Reid."

"No one can see us."

"I want you so much," I said, and he whimpered. "But..." I tried to pull back again. This time he let me.

"But..." His lips were swollen, and he tried to catch his breath. He looked debauched.

"I think we need a place more private."

"Yes. Okay." He nodded. "Yes."

"But not tonight."

Reid pulled back, and his eyes shuttered. I could almost see the old shields going back up. The ones that stopped him from doing this before. With anyone. I knew it wasn't from lack of potential partners.

"Well, then, I guess..." He raked his hand through his hair.

"Whatever you're thinking is wrong."

He laughed. It sounded self-deprecating. "You don't know what I'm thinking,"

"No. but I can guess." I reached for his hands and was gratified when he didn't pull back. "This is biology, Reid."

A flash of hurt shuttered through his eyes.

"No. I don't mean biology as in us..." God, could I mess this up any more?

But at least now the hurt was gone, replaced by a furrowed brow.

"It's like Biology 101. Would you teach your freshman students about advanced plant physiology?"

"Of course not. So many high school biology classes aren't adequate. Students come to us completely clueless. Introducing those concepts would overwhelm them and...*oh*."

"I'm not saying you're clueless." I kissed the palm of his hand. "But I want you to learn basic light energy conversion before we jump into the more intricate chemical processes."

"You're so romantic." But at least he was smiling. "Can we still do the kissing thing?"

"I think we should," I said. "Right now, I'd put you at an A-minus. I think we can do better than that."

"If I practice?"

"Exactly right."

"You're a good teacher, Maddie," he said, kissing me again.

My heart melted all over the butterfly displays. How was I going to survive this?

"But I hope you're willing to give extra credit. I'm probably going to need it if I want to get that A-plus."

I wrap my arms around him. "Let's start with less talking and more doing."

"Yes, sir."

Reid was a fast learner. It didn't take long for him to reach that A-plus level. Not long at all.

16

———————

REID

I ARRIVED at the Coffee House on autopilot. My mind buzzed all night like a swarm of bees searching for nectar. My emotions jumped from excitement at my first kiss to fear that I was too emotionally invested. What if Maddie didn't feel the same? I couldn't worry about that right now, though. I had a class of fifty freshman waiting for me to enlighten them, when all I wanted to do was find Maddie and kiss him again. Or sleep. And then more kissing.

Coffee was a necessity at this point. I needed focus, and I wasn't above taking a drug to get there. Caffeine was my drug of choice. The only one I was okay with using.

But as I stood in the back of the line to order, I noticed Maddie and Rae with some other students. They were laughing, and Maddie pushed the shoulder of a cute guy standing next to him in a letterman jacket. The guy looked familiar. He was probably in one of my classes.

Maddie had friends. Jock friends. He was popular. I knew this. But I couldn't stop the doubts invading my mind. Why would Maddie be interested in his geeky professor?

I tried to control my spiraling thoughts, but I'd been here before.

Was Maddie telling them about our kiss and my lack of experience? Were they laughing at me? My stomach churned.

Maddie wouldn't do that. He cared about me. But how many times had I been wrong? In high school and college when people pretended to be my friends and then laughed about me behind my back. And what about Maryville? I'd trusted another student, and he used me.

I deserted my search for caffeine. I couldn't handle coffee with my stomach in knots. And I couldn't face Maddie. Not with his friends there. As I hurried from the coffee shop, I thought I heard my name, but that was probably my imagination.

I could do this. I could get through my day without coffee and without Maddie.

My Intro to Forestry students couldn't get out of the lecture hall fast enough. The class hadn't been that bad. I lectured them on the abysmal essays they'd turned in last week. And then I gave them a pop quiz. I normally didn't do that to my students. I gave them plenty of time to study for my tests, but today, they were chattering like monkeys at a watering hole, and I'd had enough. Okay, so maybe they did have reason to rush out.

After gathering my things, I stepped out of the room and was immediately accosted by Gal.

She pulled me off to the side, out of the way of milling students. And out of earshot.

"What happened?" she asked, her eyes worried.

"Let go." I shook her hand off and glared. "I gave them a pop quiz."

"I don't mean in your—wait, you did what?"

"They needed a reminder."

"That you're an asswipe?"

"What? No. That they needed to focus in my class."

She studied me, a smile playing around her lips. "Something happened."

"I told you—"

"With Maddie."

"Oh. I don't want to talk about it."

"Was it amazing, and now you feel guilty? Or horrible and you feel guilty? Or," she said, grabbing my shoulders and facing me full on, "did nothing happen, and now you're even more sexually frustrated?"

I stared at her, unable to believe the words tumbling out of her mouth. "What? Why does anything have to have happened?"

"Besides the fact that you gave your students a pop quiz? Are we still in high school?"

Before I could answer she turned her phone towards me.

"What am I looking at?"

"An iPhone."

I crossed my arms and waited.

"Twitter."

"Gal..."

She scrolled on the screen. "Look at all these tweets about Professor Em and his mood swings."

I grabbed her phone and scanned the comments. What. The. Hell. "Don't they have anything more interesting to talk about?"

"First of all, this is complaining, not talking. Second, you have your own hashtag. #ProfEmHottie."

I practically threw the phone at her. "Make it stop."

"And the school encourages students to tweet to bring in potential students. But not so much about grumpy professors. Although those are popular too. Students love to hate Dr. Stark in the Psych department."

"Doesn't the school get upset?"

"As I said, it brings in more students. Why are you having massive mood swings today?"

"I don't want to discuss it."

"You're lucky I have a class. We will be discussing this later." She walked away but turned back before she reached the stairs and gave me the signal that she was watching me.

I wanted to confide in her. But how could I tell her why I was so messed up when I didn't even know? Shouldn't I have been ecstatic? I had my first real kiss, and it was amazing. Was it sexual frustration? That was a thing. Biologically, humans were driven to have sex like all animals, and while the main function was to procreate, there was also a need to claim that was biologically driven.

Analyzing it did me no good. I wanted Maddie. It was more than just being tired of being the only adult on earth not having sex. I was obsessed at this point. I couldn't think. And I now sympathized with Maddie's position when he first talked to me about his grades.

I could tell Maddie wanted me. The way he kissed me and held me. Even the way he stopped himself from going too fast. Although his initial rejection hurt, I'd been relieved we hadn't jumped into it. I needed time to think it through. And I had. All night. And the thing I realized was that I wanted him. I wanted to do this.

Sleeping with a student was against the rules. I didn't always go by the rules since they never seemed to apply to me. Not because I was too good for rules but because they were made for people who weren't like me. I had never fit into the boundaries those rules were made for.

And the point of this rule was so professors didn't take advantage of their students. There was an inherent power differential between professor and student. But I had no power over Maddie. He didn't need to have sex with his professor to get a good grade. The man was brilliant. He'd caught up on all his work and was back up to an A-plus.

Was my fear of going further from my own feelings of inadequacy? I couldn't really see Maddie sharing information about us. He wasn't the same as the popular kids I'd known throughout my life. But I couldn't shake the feeling of being played. I needed to talk to Maddie.

And I knew just where to find him. Not because I memorized his schedule. At least not intentionally. He'd mentioned his classes once, and my brain catalogued it like it did everything else.

Hanging outside of the Plant Taxonomy lab might not have been the brightest idea, but I couldn't go to his apartment. I almost texted him, but I was afraid he wouldn't answer. He hadn't texted me today at all. Mostly, I wanted to see his eyes when he saw me. Would they light up? Would he avoid looking at me?

Had I learned enough to be able to read him? Maddie had been easier for me than most. But what if he'd been faking it?

I pretended to examine the mural on the wall in the hallway. The beautiful red and orange colors of the autumn trees surrounding a lake usually captured my attention, but now I watched the doorway as students poured out of the classroom.

Professor Aubrey walked out of the lab and raised a well-defined brow at me.

"Reid."

"Delana." I nodded at her and tried to appear as if standing in the hallway waiting for a student was a perfectly normal thing to do. She gave me a small smile as she walked away, and I wondered if she'd been talking to Gal.

I noticed Rae coming out of the room first, her bright pink hair like a beacon. Maddie wouldn't be far behind. She smirked and grabbed Maddie's arm, nodding toward me. He glanced up, and a bright smile lit up his face. He tempered it quickly as others noticed me.

I stepped forward, my heart thudding wildly. "Mr. Evans," I said in my most *professory* tone. "May I have a moment of your time?"

Was I now making up words? What had this man done to me?

"Of course, Professor Em. I'll catch up with you guys later."

I walked the opposite way, knowing he'd follow. I found an empty lab, pulled him in, and slammed him against the wall. I followed with my lips, crushing them against his. He threaded a hand through my hair and pulled me closer. Everything fell into place. As long as I had Maddie in my arms, all my doubts disappeared. We kissed for a while, just enjoying the feel of each other.

Maddie pulled away, a grin on his face. "Hello to you, too."

"I missed you." I didn't even try to pretend. What was the point? I knew what I wanted.

"I love your enthusiasm, Reid, but we should probably be more careful."

I leaned my head against his. "I know. I'm sorry."

He squeezed the back of my neck. "Do you know how happy I am to see you?"

"Tell me."

His fingers trailed over the skin of my neck causing me to shiver. He rubbed his thumb across my bottom lip. "I dream about your mouth, Reid. The things I want to do to it. The things I want you to do to me."

"Like..." My body burned from the inside out. I wanted so many things.

Maddie gave me a quick kiss and shook his head. "I can't. Not here with all these dead things watching us."

I glanced around at the glass cabinets containing specimens. They were mostly birds and their eggs. I tilted my head at him. Did it really bother him that much? "They can't watch if they're dead. And you're a biology student. Is that really the reason?"

"No," he said with a laugh. "I don't want anyone to walk in on us. And..."

"And..."

He bit his lip and blushed. "There is a serious lack of symmetry in this room. The number of cabinets are uneven. It's throwing me off."

"You're adorable." The words slipped out before I could stop them. And then I said the words I'd thought about all day before I could change my mind. "I want to have sex with you. Tonight."

"Reid." His eyes burned through me. "Are you sure? I don't want you to regret anything."

His concern solidified my decision. Maddie was a good man. He cared about me. He wouldn't hurt me.

I kissed him. "I'm sure."

The sound of footsteps and doors closing in the hallway interrupted our moment. And reminded me we needed to wrap this up.

"I have class, but I'll call you later, and we can plan the details." Maddie flipped us around and pressed me against the wall. His kiss held heat and promise.

The memory of that kiss kept me going through my final classes and a meeting with the grant committee on my research project. I even found myself smiling at Professor Oliver when I passed by him, although he only scowled in return.

It wasn't until much later that my giddiness wore off. When I'd finished a hasty dinner of Chinese takeout without hearing from Maddie. And then even later, when I finally got a response. It wasn't at all what I expected.

17

MADDIE

I'D BEEN a people pleaser most of my life. Although it started with me wanting to take care of my mom after my dad left, it didn't end there. I realized early on I was good at reading people and knowing what they wanted. When you added in my slight OCD tendencies to try to make everything perfect, you ended up with an organized student and dutiful son. I wanted my mom to be happy. And eventually, she was. She married my stepfather, Harry. He seemed like a good guy, although liking him and trusting him not to hurt my mom were two different things. Trust wasn't something I did easily. But Harry proved himself by always being there for my mom and our family.

I didn't care if my dad was happy. A lie but one I held on to. Thinking about my dad's happiness led to unhelpful thoughts like if I'd been a better son, maybe he wouldn't have left us in the first place. I still had contact with him, but it was hard to enjoy visits when a seething rage tinged with self-doubt simmered just under the surface. My mom said I had a chip on my shoulder that was weighing me down. She was wrong. It wasn't a chip. It was the whole damn block.

Some people were good at playing a musical instrument. I was good at charming people. I knew just what strings to pluck or keys to play. I figured out what they wanted and used it. I gave them the attention they craved.

And I wanted people to like me. I needed it. If people liked me, didn't that mean I was worth it?

I'd always thought my three-date rule was about me getting bored, but I didn't believe that anymore. I didn't want anyone to get too close. What if they saw the real me? Not the perfect shiny thing I tried to portray, but the scuffed-up person not worth caring for. These thoughts mostly haunted me late at night or when I drank tequila.

But lately, I'd been having them all the time. Because of Reid.

I sounded manipulative. I wasn't. At least, I didn't think of it like that. It was more of a need. I needed to have people like me, and I had the ability to make that happen. Did I misuse it sometimes? I did. When you had your own little superpower, it was hard to be good all the time.

Had I used it to get myself out of a speeding ticket? Answer: yes. Had I talked my way into getting more points on an essay question? Answer: absolutely yes. But that was because I was right, and the TA was wrong. I might also have had a problem with failing. But who didn't?

This thing with Reid was different. Yes, I wanted him to like me. Yes, I wanted him to care for me. But more than that. I liked him. I cared for him. I couldn't say that about most people.

And the fact that he searched me out to make sure I knew how he felt caused little bursts of happiness throughout my body. Neurons fired haphazardly in my brain.

Reid had been having a bad day. I knew it. Everyone knew it. He was practically trending.

He never checked his Twitter. It was something he'd asked me to help him understand. I'd meant to, but we somehow never got around to it. And I knew he hadn't figured it out on his own because if he had, he'd be yelling at them to take it down. Everyone tagged him in their tweets. Like they were begging for his attention. I understood that completely.

I could always tell how his day was going by checking his hashtag.

Today, it was blowing up. I had waited to text him. I didn't want to pressure him or anything. He needed time to figure out what he wanted. But then later, when his hashtag blew up, I realized he was not doing well. Had he regretted everything? I decided to wait and let him reach out to me.

Surprisingly, that worked out well for me. Although the thought of him torturing himself all day wondering made me uneasy. But Reid had to figure this stuff out for himself. I couldn't figure it out for him.

I was on a high when I walked into my last class. Thoughts of Reid slamming me up against the wall, kissing me like he meant it, like he'd been doing it all his life, kept me going.

"Dude, Mt. Surly is in a mood today," José said.

I slipped into the seat next to him. "Isn't he always in a mood?"

I started to unpack my stuff, barely paying attention to my friend's chatter. I had more enjoyable things to focus on. Like tonight. And sex with Reid. How was I supposed to focus on Soil?

"No, you don't get it. He's in a good mood. It's freaking me out."

I stopped in the middle of setting up my laptop and looked up at the front of the class. The professor was whistling. Whistling. I glanced back at José.

"I don't think I've ever seen him in a good mood. It's terrifying. Like what does that mean for us?"

"The only thing that would make him happy is being able to fail the whole class," I said. Maybe that wasn't fair. I didn't know what made this professor tick. But not many students liked him.

José twirled his pen through his fingers. He only did that when he was nervous. "I don't know what he's up to," he said. "But I think we're about to find out."

We were on edge the entire class waiting for our professor to do something. But nothing happened. It was a normal class, which should have been reassuring but just creeped us out. We weren't the only ones, either. Throughout class, students sent each other confused looks and seemed restless. By the end of it, we were ready to escape.

"I don't know," José said as we packed up our stuff. "Maybe the guy just got laid."

"Maybe."

"Mr. Evans."

I almost made it out the door before he stopped me. I turned to face him. "Yes, sir?"

"Can I see you after class for a moment?"

I wanted to tell him no. But I knew that wasn't something I could do.

José's eyebrows crawled up his forehead. "You want me to wait for you?"

"No. You go on. I got this."

I did not have this. I had no idea what was going on, but I had an uneasy feeling in the pit of my stomach. I thought back to the times I'd ran into him on my way to see Prof. Em. I had to think of him of like that instead of Reid. I didn't want to mess up and call him that in front of Mt. Surly.

"Yes, Mt—I mean, Prof. Oliver?" I asked. "Did I do something wrong?" I'd almost called him by his Twitter nickname. I wasn't sure where it had originated from. Was it because he was as big as a mountain? Or surly as hell? Or both? He'd had the name when I started four years ago. Who knew anymore?

"Of course not, my boy." He patted me on the back, and I resisted the urge to get as far away from him as possible. "Just some things I wanted to discuss with you."

I waited, but nothing more came. Every few seconds, he would look up and scan the room and then return to putting things away into his bag. I soon realized he was waiting for the other students to leave.

If he didn't want witnesses, this couldn't be anything good.

Even though my back was to the room. I could tell when the last student left by the smile that crept up on his ruddy cheeks. He motioned to a chair. I didn't want to sit down. I didn't want to be there that long. And I didn't like the idea of him towering over me. But I sat down anyway.

"How are your classes going?" He almost sounded like he cared. But I knew better.

"Fine."

He nodded. "What about Prof. Emerson's class? Are you doing okay?"

Fuck. This was about Reid. I had suspected as much, but hearing him confirm it made me want to throw up. Not only at the thought that this could get Reid in trouble, but also anger. Anger that people couldn't just leave the man alone. Reid was a good person. He didn't deserve this crap.

"It's fine."

He nodded again. "I noticed you coming in for some extra credit."

I didn't like the gleam in his eyes. I didn't have to explain myself to him. It was none of his business how I was doing in Prof. Emerson's class. But I also knew getting into the graduate program could blow up if I failed this class. Even if I passed, Prof. Oliver was an Associate Professor in the department. I couldn't avoid it. I relied on him to not screw up my future.

"I was struggling with some of the material, and Professor Emerson was helping me understand it."

He shook his head, a smile on his face. "You know, Maddox...Can I call you Maddox?"

He didn't wait for my answer.

"In the four years I've known you—all the way back to when you were a freshman and in my Intro to Soil Conservation—I've never heard of you struggling in any class."

I shrugged, trying to be as nonchalant as possible. "Everybody has a weakness."

I knew I said the wrong thing when his smile widened.

"You are so right," he said. "Everybody does. Something I've noticed about Prof. Emerson is that he has a weakness for his young male students."

I scowled. I couldn't help it. "You make him sound like a pedophile. He's younger than many of his students." As soon as the words were out of my mouth, I realized how they sounded.

He grinned like a shark on crack. "So right again. I mean really, who could blame him? It would be hard to set those boundaries up when you're the same age as your students. When he first came here, I think many of the faculty questioned whether this was a good idea."

"Is this something you should be discussing with a student?" I asked, trying to throw his behavior into question.

"Normally, I wouldn't. But I need your help."

"I can't help you," I said. It didn't matter what it was. No way was I helping him do anything to Reid. Did he really think that would work?

Dr. Oliver pursed his lips together and tilted his head. "Lambert's Cafe is one of my favorite places to eat. A little pricey, especially for students, but I love their rolls. Very tasty."

My mouth went dry, and my stomach churned. I might throw up right there on Prof. Oliver, and that would not help my case at all. I had no doubt he wasn't just announcing his favorite place to eat. He'd seen us there. I hadn't noticed him, but that didn't mean anything. The place was always packed. And most of the time I'd been focused on Reid. But I'd had enough of innuendos.

"If you've got something to say, Prof, maybe you should just spit it out." It was risky talking to him that way. After all, he had the power to fail me. And would anyone even believe me if I told them about Prof. Oliver?

But I wasn't going to play his games. If he had proof—real proof—he wouldn't be bothering with me. He'd go right to the dean.

"You know, Maddox, I get it," he said, ignoring my outburst. "He was helping you, and it got late, and then you guys got hungry. It happens. I think the dean would even understand that. Maybe not the part where you went to a bar together. A gay bar at that."

I tried not to squirm. My hands felt sweaty, and I wiped them on my pants. I wasn't sure at this point why he didn't go to the dean, but maybe he hadn't been sure. I remembered seeing someone who looked like him. But I really hadn't thought Professor Oliver was gay. Of course, he could have been there with friends. Was there another reason he didn't get along with Reid? Maybe it had something to do with that.

"There's nothing going on between Prof. Emerson and myself," I said. "I'm not going to lie and say there was."

"Maybe not. But there could be..."

My mouth dropped open. "Are you encouraging me to sleep with my professor?"

His eyes widened as if surprised by my statement, but I didn't buy it. The smirk around his mouth told me otherwise. "Of course not. That would be wrong. But if Prof. Emerson did try something. I'm just saying—don't discourage him. See how it plays out."

"You can't be serious."

"Maddox. If he tries this with you, imagine how many other students he might have been inappropriate with."

I almost laughed at that. There was no way Reid was faking his lack of experience. And If he was, he needed to get into acting right away.

"Don't give me an answer now," he said, squeezing my shoulder and making my skin crawl. "Think about it. I know you have a lot going on finishing up your classes and preparing for grad school. That can be incredibly stressful. You should try to make things easier for yourself."

The implied threat hung in the air as he dismissed me from the room.

My legs felt heavy as I trudged back to my apartment. Rae and I had planned to meet after classes to talk about a group project we were working on together. But I couldn't do it. I couldn't face her. How would I explain my mood?

Thankfully, Atticus was out for the evening. I skipped dinner. It wouldn't settle right, anyway. Instead, I made myself a cup of hot tea, wrapped a blanket around me like a cocoon, and settled into the sofa.

This was all my fault. I started this whole thing not caring that I could ruin Reid's life. That I could ruin my own life. I'd been so focused on getting perfect grades. What did it matter now? I might not even graduate. Environmental Soils was only offered in the spring. If I didn't pass, I'd have to wait another year to take it. And say goodbye to grad school. I had enough to satisfy Professor Oliver right now. I could go to him and tell him everything that had happened with Reid. And that would be it.

But I couldn't do it. I'd rather fail first. My mom would be devastated. She'd worked so hard to make sure that I had everything I needed to succeed. I was letting her down. I couldn't even think about my dad or his disappointment in me if I failed. Worse yet, he'd say he thought it was too much for me anyway and this was probably for the best.

But worst of all was knowing that Reid was waiting for me. I wanted to see him more than anything. I wanted to be with him. I wanted to show him how wonderful we could be together. But I couldn't do that.

Professor Oliver would find out. Not because I couldn't lie and make it believable. Because I could, and it would be. But Reid couldn't lie worth a damn. If they asked him, he wouldn't even have to answer for them to know. And yes, we kissed. But we didn't have sex. That would be a whole lot worse in the eyes of the school and the dean.

I had to figure a way out of this. I had to. This was what I did; I fixed things. And this was my mess to clean up. I wouldn't get Reid or Rae or anyone else involved.

But I had to start by stopping whatever this was between us. I didn't want to hurt him, but I also couldn't tell him why. He'd try and fix it by challenging Professor Oliver and in doing so confirm everything he suspected.

I let the scent of Earl Grey tea calm me. It was the back-up to my usual Chai tea. I slipped a little cinnamon in it to sweeten it up. My phone buzzed with a text.

PROF. EM HOTTIE: *Is everything okay?*

I needed to end it right now. Tell him it was over. But selfishly, I wasn't ready. And I couldn't do it over text. And I definitely couldn't face him tonight, especially knowing that nothing would happen between us. Nothing would ever happen.

MADDIE: *Just tired. I'm going to stay in tonight.*

His reply came late. I wondered what he was thinking. Did he think I was blowing him off? I mean, I was, but did he think that?

PROF. EM HOTTIE: *Okay. Get some rest. I hope you feel better.*

And that was what brought on the tears. This man was so sweet and caring. Such a good guy. Why would anyone want to hurt him? I felt a burst of anger at Professor Oliver. I'd do whatever it took to help Reid.

And take Professor Oliver down in the process.

18

REID

I'D DONE IT. Stepped out of my cocoon and tried out my wings. I went after what I wanted. I didn't wait for Maddie to come to me.

It felt amazing to take charge and admit that my needs were important. That I was important. And it had paid off. Or so I thought.

Later that night, when I hadn't heard anything from Maddie, I gave in and texted him. He wasn't coming. And I wanted to take his reasons at face value. He probably was tired.

But I couldn't. It felt like he was pushing me away. I couldn't explain why I thought that. I wanted to spend time with him, even if we didn't have sex. I thought back to the lab and the way his body, hard and ready, had felt in my arms. He wasn't faking that. Maddie did want me.

Was it my insecurities? My lack of confidence when it came to all things social or sexual? Was I even reading the situation correctly? That *would* be a first.

I arrived at my Forest Ecology class early. Just in case Maddie wanted to talk beforehand. My heart pounded in excitement when he walked into the room. I tried to slow it down. Temper my expectations. Would he smile when he saw me? Would his face light up?

But he didn't even look at me.

As much as I tried to warn my heart, it wasn't prepared. Maddie had never ignored me. I had my answer. But I didn't have all the answers, or even any of the ones I wanted. Had Maddie suddenly decided he wasn't interested in me? That seemed unlikely. Did he realize he could do better? Did he regret the spur-of-the-moment impulse to say yes to my proposition?

I had texted him initially before class. Simple texts. *I hope you're feeling better. How are things going in Plant Taxonomy?* And the one I regret the most. *I miss you.*

He hadn't answered any of them. How did people do this? How did they go on dates and get involved in relationships? How did they invest their entire emotional stability on one person, just to be shredded? Destroyed.

After class, Rae started to walk toward me. I didn't know how I felt about that. Was she going to tell me something? Or was that pity in her eyes?"

"Rae," Maddie said fiercely in a low voice. She turned toward him, and they argued without saying a word. Finally, her shoulders sagged in defeat. She gave me one last attempt at a smile and followed him out.

That was that.

I somehow made it through the day. My brain took over, doing what needed to be done and letting my heart retreat in peace. But once I got home and had no distractions, I couldn't stop wondering what I had done wrong.

Was it worth it? Being with Maddie had been amazing. The kissing. Talking. Friendship. But was it worth the pain tearing me up inside? He gave me everything. And then took it all away.

I wanted to say I wouldn't do it again. But I couldn't regret the time we'd spent together even if it was over. And I felt like it was.

A knock at my door startled me out of my melancholy stupor. I put down the half-empty carton of mint chocolate chip ice cream. I'd seen it portrayed in movies as something that would help you feel better after a heartache. I doubted there was any scientific validity to it, but I was desperate. And I had to admit there was some truth to it. It didn't take away all the pain or even most of it, but somehow, it helped. As I headed for the door, I grabbed it again. Whoever was at my apartment could just deal with me sitting in my PJs and eating ice cream.

For a millisecond, maybe even less, I thought it might be Maddie. My heart rate increased, and hope bloomed before my brain even thought it was a possibility. Probably because my brain knew better, and I hated it when my brain was always right.

"What the hell is going on?"

I didn't respond to Gal. I just turned around and found my way back to my couch to continue eating my ice cream. I heard the door shut as she made her way into the room. And then she sat beside me.

"Seriously, Reid. What the hell?"

I hadn't told her anything, which I realized now was a mistake. It would been easier to explain in small bits rather than all at once. I didn't think I could do it all at once. My brain gave up the good fight and let my emotions take over. I didn't realize I was crying until Gal reached over and wiped the tears off my face.

"Is it that boy?"

I couldn't help but laugh at her calling Maddie the boy. I nodded.

"You want me to hurt him? I will."

I shook my head no.

"You want to talk about it?"

I again declined. But then, like the tears that fell without my permission, the words tumbled out of my mouth. I told her everything. Even stuff she probably didn't want to hear. Her face hardened, and her eyes glittered dangerously.

"That weasel," she said. "I can't believe he just blew you off like that. I knew he was no good."

"You encouraged me to spend time with him."

"No. I encouraged you spend time with anybody. Because, Reid, sweetie. You're a hermit."

"Not technically true. Hermits are— "

She held up her hand. "Stop being so literal. You know what I'm talking about. You close yourself off from everyone."

"Look what happened when I opened myself up. My heart got stomped on. Is this really your idea of a good time, Gal?"

She sniffed and crossed her arms. "Stop being so dramatic. And stop feeling sorry for yourself. Have you ever heard the saying 'you have to kiss a lot of frogs...?'"

"That's stupid. Kissing frogs doesn't get you a Prince Charming. I don't even want a Prince Charming. I just want a guy who's decent and doesn't make promises and then desert me."

"Let's go out tonight to the club."

"Fuck no." I gave her my best I'm-not-kidding-about-this look. Of course, it did no good.

"Come on, Reid. Get you right back on that saddle."

"Weren't you paying attention? I wasn't on the saddle. I was standing next to it. Wishing I could be on it. I didn't ride anything."

She held my hands, which was true friendship, or maybe she just didn't realize what she'd gotten herself into because they not only had ice cream on them, but snot from whenever I tried to wipe some tears away. She didn't let go or even bat an eye.

"We're going out tonight. I'm not taking no for an answer," she said in response to my immediate head shake. "If you retreat now, you might never try again. I'm serious. It's the only way to prove to yourself that this wasn't you. It was him. Whatever is going on, it has to do with him."

I shook my head again, knowing it was no use.

"So go fix yourself up and wipe that snotty nose. I'll put away this ice cream before you gain a hundred pounds."

"Gal." I wanted to sound stern, but it came out as a whine.

"I don't care if you dance with a guy. I don't care if you flirt with the guy. I just want you to see that there are other guys out there, and they are interested in you. Now that you're aware of social cues, thanks to what's-his-name, you'll be able to tell."

I didn't want to go. It would be torture. But God, she was right. Damn it to hell.

Gal gelled my hair into what she called bedhead sexy. I wasn't sure about that, but I thought I looked good. She even picked out my outfit. I might've fought on it, except at this point, I didn't really care. This couldn't end well. There were two possible outcomes. One—guys were not falling all over themselves to get to me, which would just reinforce how I felt. I wasn't desirable. That's the way I'd felt most of my life. The only time I'd felt sexy had been with Maddie. The second outcome was scarier than the first. Guys did pay attention to me. I might even find someone to dance with and actually enjoy myself. There was only one problem with that scenario that doomed the outcome. Whoever this mysterious guy was, he wasn't Maddie. But I was tired of feeling sorry for myself. Tired of sitting in my pajamas, eating ice cream, and binging Doctor Who. I needed a distraction. Plus, Gal wasn't going to leave me alone unless I did this.

The club was crowded by the time we got there. The lighting was down; the music was loud. The beer was cold. It fit right with my mood. I noticed several guys checking me out and smiling at me. It made me wonder how many times that had happened, and I just missed it. It took Maddie to wake me up, and now that I had the attention I'd been looking for, I didn't want it. I just wanted him.

"Nope. Nope. Nope," Gal said. "You are not going to sit on your butt while there are hot guys and hot girls out there for the picking. Get up out of that chair, Reid. We're going dancing."

I tried to sink into the booth, but it was no use. She grabbed my arm and pulled me up. Yes, she was that strong. But I also didn't fight her too hard. She led me to the crowded dance floor. Most of the bodies grinding against each other as they danced were male. I couldn't help but watch. No one seemed to mind. In fact, I got quite a few winks. I wasn't much of a dancer. I had always been a little gangly and awkward. Although that wasn't really true anymore. I sometimes forgot I was a grownup. Intellectually, I was mature. But emotionally, I still felt like a child. And I hated it.

Gal grabbed my arms and pulled me closer. I wasn't sure why. I certainly wasn't her type. But then she whispered into my ear, "You're doing fine. Loosen up. All these guys can't keep their eyes off you."

If this was a straight bar, I'd say they were all looking at her. My best friend was hot with a capital H. I couldn't dismiss the fact that in this gay bar, they might be looking at me.

And I was okay with them looking. I enjoyed it. Guys thinking I was attractive...cute. It was a new experience for me. But I wasn't enjoying it when a guy slid behind me and pulled me back against him. I could feel his hard dick harden against my ass as we swayed to the music. I was not okay with this. I had to do something to get away from his grasp. But then it wasn't necessary. He was suddenly gone. I'd seen Gal step closer out of the corner of my eye, but when I turned around, she wasn't the one staring the guy down.

My heart swooped. Maddie glared at the guy like he wanted to do him bodily harm. The guy put his hands up as if to say no hard feelings, and then he winked at me and walked away. I wasn't sure how to feel. Happy that Maddie was there? Or pissed that he thought he had a right to step in? I didn't like what the guy was doing, but he didn't know that.

He reached for my hand, but I pulled away, glaring at him. He stepped closer, holding his hands up, and leaned in.

"You looked like you needed help," he said.

I ignored the scent of him, my body suddenly aware that he was right there. I glared at him.

"I didn't."

"Reid, listen..." He seemed at a loss for words, so I let him have it.

"Are you following me? You can't do that, Maddie."

"No. I swear I wasn't. I didn't know you were here, until I saw that guy...well, until I saw you."

I realized that was much worse. If he was following me, then I was the reason he was here. If he wasn't here for me, what did that mean? Was he with friends? Or was he here finding someone to hook up with? His life seemed to be going on fine without me. That hurt way more than it should have.

"Are you here with someone?" I asked and then cursed myself for caring. Gal watched us from a distance, ignoring the cute girl dancing with her. I felt needy. Like a child. Everybody always trying to protect me. And I was so over it.

"No. I came by myself."

Why come to a bar by yourself unless you want to hook up? That thought made me feel like I was going to throw up the beer I'd been drinking. Worse, my eyes burned, and I blinked back tears. I wasn't going to cry in front of him. I wouldn't give him the satisfaction.

"I'm fine. You can go on and do whatever it was you came here to do."

His eyes widened. "Reid, I wasn't...I'm not."

"It doesn't matter why you're here, Maddie. Because I know why you're not."

I turned away from him, searching for Gal. I knew I couldn't hold it in much longer. We just needed to get out of there before I fell apart.

"Reid, wait." He reached for my hand. "Dance with me?"

Was he crazy? But my body responded before my brain could catch up. Just like that, I was in his arms. I wanted to lean in. Relax. Trust him. But the feeling of being played was like an old itch. Familiar. Was this all a joke? I didn't really believe he would do that, but the fear was impossible to ignore. I pulled away. I fought against the tendency to run. I was tired of running.

"Maddie, come with me," I said. "We can just talk."

I'd gotten better at recognizing the signs. The emotions on his face. The way his brow scrunched together said no before the words ever reached his lips. I wanted to be clueless again. I wanted to pretend I didn't understand. But that was the old Reid.

"I can't. I want to, but..."

"Just tell me why."

He closed his eyes, fighting with himself. "I can't."

All the hope I didn't even realize I had escaped my body, dissipating in the air like the scent of his cologne. "Goodbye, Maddie."

Thankfully, Gal was right there. I resisted the urge to glance back at Maddie as we gathered our things and left.

Gal didn't question me on the way home, and I was grateful for that. I'd put myself out there. And been rejected again. When would I learn? When would I realize Maddie didn't want me—not really? It felt like high school all over again. And I was just done.

19

MADDIE

Reid walking away almost broke me. I wanted to run after him and reassure him this was real. We were real. I wanted to beg him to hold on to me and never let go. But I couldn't.

I was doing this for him. But telling him that might have resulted in me getting punched. Reid wasn't a violent person, but I probably could have gotten him there.

Two sides of the same coin, my mama used to say. I could charm a certain roommate until they gave up the piece of cherry pie they'd been saving for later or push their buttons until they chased me out of the apartment building and locked the door while I wore nothing but my underwear. Same skills involved: paying attention. Telling them what they wanted or didn't want to hear. And making stuff up if you had to.

As a kid, I practiced on my sister. She was a teenager when Dad left and seemed less affected by it. Maybe that was why she was my favorite target. Now she prosecuted bad guys. I feel as if I helped prepare her for her career choice.

But I didn't want to charm Reid or lie to him. This was the most honest relationship I'd ever been in. Reid believed in me. At least he did. And for a hot second, I almost took him up on his offer to talk.

He would have understood. And then went right to the dean. Reid couldn't lie. He never learned or more likely had never wanted to. And he hated when people did it.

I couldn't have him going to the dean, confessing all. He would lose everything. I would lose everything.

Was I more worried about myself? I didn't want to get thrown out of school. Or fail. I didn't want to lose my spot in graduate school. I'd worked hard to get here. Would Reid have to move to another school? I couldn't let that happen either.

My plan was simple. Find something on Professor Oliver. That was the whole reason I was at the bar in the first place. I didn't expect to run into Reid.

Focus, Maddie. I needed to stop feeling sorry for myself. Do what I do best. Find out what made Professor Oliver tick, so I could destroy him.

Someone here knew something about him. I just needed to find it.

As I explored the club looking for my prey, I pushed thoughts of Reid out of my mind. I had a job to do. It had been stupid of me to ask Reid to dance. What if Oliver had seen us? It would have given him more evidence.

But it was done. And I didn't regret having Reid in my arms. I'd deal with the fallout later. I pushed through the crowded club, ignoring the flirty looks and occasional grabs at my ass. I scanned faces through the low lights and intertwined bodies. It wasn't easy. It was hard to tell where one person ended and the other began. Thankfully, no one cared if I stared at them. It was expected.

I heard him before I saw him. Even in a club, he was a hothead. Bitching at a guy who had bumped into him and spilled his drink. Mostly on his hand. The guy patted his hands with a towel and winked at him. Was it a pickup attempt? If so, it didn't work on the professor. He told him to fuck off. Loudly.

"Your loss, mate."

Oliver huffed and waved him away.

Maybe Prof. Oliver wasn't gay? Was he there just trying to get evidence against Reid? That didn't seem likely.

But then a twink slid next to him and batted his eyes innocently. The grin on Oliver's face was predatory. Bingo. Not that it really helped at all. But seeing him flirt with the baby-faced younger guy supported my theory that maybe Reid had rejected Oliver at some point. I discreetly took a picture, acting like I was taking a selfie. This guy could be a student. It was a longshot. But when gathering evidence, you never knew what you had until you had it. Jen taught me that. And the scientific method was based on testing everything. Controlling the variables. Gathering evidence and accounting for every possible outcome.

Their heads were close together, and the younger man touched Oliver every chance he got. It made me want to throw up. Or punch something.

Professor Oliver didn't deserve a moment of happiness. Not when he tried to blackmail a student to destroy the sweetest and best person I knew.

After thirty minutes of watching them flirt, I was almost relieved when they left together. I didn't have anything. I wanted to scream. I wanted to march over to Reid's apartment and confess everything. But I had to be smart about this. Figure out what my options were before rushing into anything.

I stayed for another half-hour asking around about the professor. No one really wanted to talk about Oliver, and I couldn't blame them.

The night was a bust. Worse than that. I had done more damage to this thing I had with Reid. The betrayal in his eyes broke my heart. What was he thinking? That I was like all the other guys who'd rejected him over the years?

Those thoughts played on repeat in my brain, making it impossible to sleep. What if I couldn't find anything on Prof. O? He expected an answer from me. My brain hurt. My heart hurt. My whole body hurt.

I felt alone. I couldn't drag Rae into this. What if Oliver targeted her, too? She wasn't in his Environmental Soils class, but he had a long reach in the biology department. I didn't want to underestimate him.

I had to do this on my own. Which wasn't easy when Rae realized I was hiding something. I should have skipped the coffee shop this morning.

"I can break you," Rae said, raising a pierced brow at me. It had a little skull on it, but I wasn't intimidated.

"Good to know. Thanks for the warning."

"Is it Prof. Em Hottie?"

"No."

"Okay," she said with a smirk. "I'll take that as a yes."

"Hey." I scowled at her as I sipped my tea.

"I'll take never for five-hundred, Alex."

"You've been drinking too much coffee. Maybe you should cut down."

"It's Jeopardy," she said. "I give you the answer, and you guess the question."

"Rae..."

She made a buzzing sound. "Wrong. The question is... When does Maddie give up a chance to talk about his favorite professor?"

"Ha ha." I lined up the condiment containers in a row, trying to ignore her glare.

"I'm not laughing." She pushed the container of sugar packets away from my nervous fingers.

"Something is going on. Professor Emerson has been...I don't even know how to describe it. He's not grumpy. I'd settle for that. He's...defeated. Maddie, did you defeat our professor?"

The emotion hit me before I could stop it. I'd learned how to hide my feelings at a young age. I didn't want to burden my mom with the devastation I felt after my dad left when she was dealing with her own grief. I was fairly good at it, but Rae had hit a nerve. I blinked back tears.

"Oh, honey," she said, reaching for my hand.

I shook my head at the concern in her voice and the pity in her eyes. I couldn't handle it. I needed her anger. I deserved it. I'd started this. It was my own actions that were destroying both our lives. I deserved her reproach, not her compassion.

"Maybe I had it backwards."

"What?" I sniffed.

She sighed. "I think Prof. Emerson broke you."

I choked back a laugh. "He definitely broke me. But that's not a bad thing."

Rae squeezed my hand. "It'll work out, sweetie."

"I wish I had your faith."

"Don't worry. I see the way that man looks at you. He's just as gone."

"Thanks, hon." I smiled at her as I reclaimed my hand, but I didn't say what I was thinking. As much as I wanted Reid to be gone for me, was it really the best thing for him? Wouldn't the best thing be for me to walk away and let him get on with his life? I just didn't think I was strong enough or selfless enough to do that.

And that was a problem.

20

REID

"I'm not in high school anymore."

"Get out of the car, Reid." Gal poked her head through the window to gripe at me some more. Not that I minded. Much. She was saving me from myself. And helping me stock up on groceries. We cleaned my apartment. Which I could've done alone, but I wasn't sure she believed that I would. I stepped out and shut the door. Gal had given up waiting for me. I ran to catch up with her as she made her way into Save Mart.

"I'm just saying, Gal. I'm not in high school anymore. I've got a PhD. Friends who love me."

"Now you're really pushing it."

I ignored her. "It's stupid to let my old fears haunt me. I don't know what's going on with Maddie, but he cares about me. I know it."

"I agree, but—and I can't believe I'm saying this—maybe give him some space. He's obviously going through something, and only he can figure it out."

"But it's killing me." As we stocked up on necessities, Gal replaced all my junk food with healthy choices. When had our positions reversed?

"Hey, I need those," I said.

"No one needs ten gallons of ice cream."

"At least leave me one. Or five."

"You can have two."

"Deal."

After shopping, we ate a light supper and watched a movie.

"You don't have to babysit me, Gal."

She leaned her head against mine. "We're friends. Deal with it."

I sighed. "I'm not in high school anymore."

"So you've said. What does that even mean, Reid?"

I shrugged. "I shouldn't still feel this inadequate."

And despite my protests, she wrapped her arms around me and pretended I didn't have tears running down my face.

Monday morning came way too soon. I wasn't ready for it.

Gal met me for coffee. Not at the Coffee House. At the Starbucks that was out of the way and less likely to have a certain student in it.

"I know what I want."

"I hope so. We're next in line."

"Not the coffee. In high school I didn't know what I wanted."

"Well, you were, like, twelve, so…"

"I was fourteen when I graduated."

She grabbed my hand, and I realized I had been mangling my tie. "Your point?"

I waited until we had our coffee and sat down at a table. "When he started ignoring me, I worried Maddie didn't really want me."

She scoffed. Loudly. The older couple at the next table glared. Obviously, they weren't morning people.

"Sorry," she said with a quick smile.

"But now I think it's some stupid reason. Like he thinks I don't know what I want."

"What are you going to do about it?"

"Go with what works."

"I like the sound of that."

MONDAYS WERE MY BUSIEST DAYS. I tried to focus on my classes. It wasn't fair to my other students not to give them my full attention.

It worked. Partly. Right up until Forest Ecology. My eyes strayed to Maddie a few times, but he never noticed. He focused on the book or his laptop. Or Rae beside him.

He had on black jeans and a button-down green shirt. He looked good. When had he stopped wearing T-shirts to class?

"Remember, for lab tomorrow, we will be testing the samples we collected last week."

As Maddie started to leave, I raised my voice. "Mr. Evans, can you stay after class for a moment?"

He took his sweet time getting to the front of the classroom. Was this his way of being defiant? Or did he dread being around me? *No time for that, Reid. You can't chicken out now.*

"Did I do something wrong, Prof. Em?" he asked when he was finally in front of me.

I waited for the stragglers to leave the room. Rae was one of the last ones. The door shut behind her with a thud.

"Maddie..."

"I'm sorry about Friday night."

"Which part?" I had rehearsed what I wanted to say, but I wanted to hear this.

He held his hands up. "Everything."

"Pushing me away?"

"Yes."

"Not going home with me?" This I said a little quieter. I was afraid of the answer. The clock on the wall, an archaic thing, clicked the seconds away.

"Yes."

"Now's your chance to make up for it."

The silence in the room tore at my soul.

"Reid..."

"No. You don't get to do this. Telling me you're sorry for pushing me away, while pushing me away."

"I'm sorry."

"Not good enough," I grabbed his shirt and pulled him closer. I leaned in, absorbing his scent, his warmth, his being. My heart thudded in my chest. I couldn't look at him. I wasn't that brave. My anger had deserted me, leaving me exposed.

"Do you want me?" I whispered, half afraid of his answer.

His breath brushed across my skin. "It's not that simple."

I needed to be closer, to touch him. I rested my cheek against his. I felt giddy with want. Intoxicated by his nearness. I tilted my head, tracing a path across his jaw with my lips until we shared the same breath. "It could be."

"Please, Reid..."

I knew in that moment he would surrender if I kissed him. But I needed him to close the distance between us.

I needed him to choose me.

And then he was kissing me, and it was frenzied and needy and hot as fuck. His hands grabbed my hips and pulled me against him.

"I shouldn't...We..." His voice broke as I sucked on his neck. He leaned his head back, giving me access.

"I'm done waiting for you to figure things out, Maddie," I said between nips on his skin. "I know what I want." I leaned back against the desk and pulled him between my legs. "Tell me to stop if you don't want this."

"Fuck, Reid."

Emboldened by his reaction, I claimed his mouth again, kissing him with more enthusiasm than finesse, but if Maddie's moans were anything to go by, he wasn't complaining. I threaded my fingers through his as I kissed him. Once I had his attention, I moved his hand to my cock and almost passed out in pleasure at the sensation. *Oh, fuck.* "Feel this?"

"Yes," he said breathlessly.

"We're taking care of this, tonight." I pressed his hand against my erection. God, I wanted him so much.

He squeezed, and I almost came right then. "You want me to show you where that goes?" he said, sounding like my Maddie. "Because I have some ideas. And if you're exceptionally good, I might even grade you on a curve."

"A curve?" My mind decided to stop working.

"This curve," he said, stroking me through my pants. "And the fine curve of your ass." He slipped his hand down the back of my pants and squeezed my ass cheek.

I whimpered. I didn't think I could wait another minute. Maybe we could just do it right here. Right now.

"I have to go," he said reluctantly. "But I'll be there tonight, Reid. I promise."

BUT IT WAS a promise he couldn't keep or that I even wanted him to. Because once I got back to my office, the dean called me into his.

I still hadn't completed the grant information he wanted, but he waved that off.

"A concern has been brought to my attention about you and one of your students."

"I don't...understand. Where's this coming from?" I could barely get out the words. My lunch. Dinner. And ten gallons of ice cream threatened to come back up.

And that's when I realized Professor Oliver was in the room.

"A student has come forward," Oliver said. "You've gone too far this time, Emerson."

"I don't believe you." I tried to push down the panic in my chest and the bile in my throat. This couldn't be happening. Not again.

"This isn't my doing," he said. "The boy will tell you himself, Dean Albin." Oliver handed him a piece of paper.

The dean glanced at it and then back at me. "Maddox Evans."

The room dissolved around me, going black. I clutched the edge of the dean's desk to keep from passing out. "This...it's not true."

I wasn't good at lying, but this wasn't a lie. It couldn't be true. Maddie would never betray me. I could still feel his lips against mine.

"Of course, you'd deny it," Oliver said. "Just like Maryville..."

I wasn't violent, but at that moment, I understood why some people were. I detested Oliver. Calling him a worm would be an insult to worms. At least they served a purpose.

"Stop." Dean Albin glared at Professor Oliver until he retreated into his corner. "This is not Maryville. I want to be sure we have all the facts straight before we jump into anything. But I do think it's a good idea, Reid, to have someone else take your classes for the next few days."

"Am I suspended?" It felt like the last time. Being accused. Only this time, there was actual truth to it.

"No," the dean said, staring at Oliver. "Not yet. I want to get the facts straight. So, take a few days off while we do that. None of this will be made public." He again gave Oliver a stern look and then turned to me. "Until we have those answers, absolutely no contact with students, especially Mr. Evans. Do you understand? I'm serious about this, Dr. Emerson."

I wasn't sure how I got home. As soon as I'd collapsed on my couch, I got a call from Gal. I almost didn't answer.

"Reid," she said in a rush of words. "Is everything okay? You left early."

"No." I choked out the word, barely holding it together.

"I'm coming over..."

"Gal? Could you do something for me?"

"Yes, Reid. Anything."

"Bring more ice cream?"

21

———

MADDIE

T HE DAY STARTED SO PROMISING. Reid taking charge of his life, of his body, of us was so fucking sexy. I couldn't resist him even though I should.

But thoughts of seeing Reid naked flew out the window when I met with Prof. Oliver. I'd planned to tell him there was no way I could do that to Professor Em. In fact, that was exactly what I did tell him. But it didn't matter.

"It's done," he said.

"I don't understand. What's done?"

His oily smile disgusted me and filled me with apprehension. "The dean has been informed about a complaint from a student about Prof. Emerson."

My pulse sped up. Did he find someone else? It had been my fear all along. If I didn't go along with his scheme, he would just find someone else. I didn't think he'd tell me, but I had to ask. "What student?"

"You."

My chest felt tight, and it was difficult to breathe. I had an over-whelming urge to punch him in his smug face. "I never agreed to that."

He crossed his arms and stared down at me. The threat flared in his eyes, but his voice was calm, almost nonchalant. "You didn't have to. I did it for you."

"I'll deny it…"

"There are plenty of people who've seen you together. And *you* can deny it, but can your professor? Slow dancing at the gay bar doesn't seem school related. Go ahead. Refute everything. I have pictures."

"We're just friends," I said, trying to think of anything to stop this train wreck from happening.

"Which is still inappropriate between a student and their professor. So deny it and go down with him or meet with us on Friday and tell your side of it." His stance shifted subtly. Less aggressive and more pitying. He stepped back, his head cocked to the side as he studied me. "I've another picture to show you."

He scrolled through his phone, his chest puffed up and his smile triumphant. Whatever it was, it wasn't good. He handed me the phone. "You're the victim here, Maddox."

The picture wasn't of me and Reid. I didn't know the other guy in the picture, but I immediately disliked him. Because he was sitting in Reid's lap with his arms around him, nuzzled against his neck. Reid's arms were around him, and he was staring at him with his mouth slightly open. Was his expression one of surprise or of awe? For all my talk of reading social cues, I had no idea. Had Reid been lying to me this whole time? My body felt heavy, and I needed to get out of the room so I could process this without anyone seeing my breakdown. But I wasn't giving Prof. Oliver the satisfaction of knowing he'd gotten to me.

"What is this?" I asked.

"This is why Professor Emerson had to leave his last school. This young man was his student. Did you know your professor didn't even fight the allegations against him?"

Every ounce of happiness fled my body. Replaced by that increasing heaviness. One I recognized. It was the same feeling I had every time I talked to my dad. The feeling of being… betrayed? Used?

Discarded. That was the one. And maybe Reid hadn't discarded me yet, but how did I know he wouldn't? Everything he'd said was a lie, just like with my dad.

"This is your chance, Maddox. Save yourself. While the dean may not throw you out, he most certainly wouldn't let you get credit for Emerson's class. Then you wouldn't graduate. Goodbye grad school. But if you help me with this, I'll do everything in my power to help you."

"I don't know," I said truthfully. My thoughts jumbled together with memories of Reid and me walking through the park hand in hand. His first kiss. Was that even true? And the butterfly house. His laugh. The way he looked at me. Was it all a lie? I didn't think so. I couldn't believe that. But everything was twisting together, and I couldn't think. The headache starting behind my eyes was going to be a doozy.

"You have a lot to consider," he said. "But Friday at one, this is happening. With or without you. Oh, and your precious professor has been relieved of his classes this week and has been ordered to have no contact with any of his students, especially you."

I wanted to go to Reid despite my concerns. He must have been devastated. But I also wanted to scream at him for not being completely honest with me. This was what happened when I broke my rules.

Instead of going home and hiding away like I wanted, I did what I always did. I worked my ass off. Maybe they would throw me out or take away my credit for Reid's class, but I would do all the work to prove that I deserved the grades I had. I would ace every test I took. Even in Environmental Soils class. Especially in Environmental Soils class. I had no doubt Professor Oliver would find some way to screw me over if I didn't help him. But that didn't mean I had to make it easy for him.

Over the next couple days, I avoided everyone, even Rae. But that didn't last long. During Forestry lab, she cornered me. "Spill it."

I studied the jar of fungi in my hands before glancing back at her. I raised a brow in question. "This?"

She rolled her eyes. "Spill your guts, Evans."

"Didn't you get enough of that when we dissected that racoon last quarter?"

Her lips tightened like she was contemplating murder and hiding my body.

"Violent," I said. "You're in a mood."

She pointed toward the front of the class where Professor Ramon glared at everyone, her nostrils flaring. "According to Twitter, Prof-EmHottie isn't teaching any of his classes because he..." She had my full attention now, and by the smirk on her face, she knew it.

"What?" I didn't think to check social media.

She scrolled through her phone, taking her own damn sweet time, and finally found what she wanted. She held it up to me. "He had a family emergency, apparently."

I sighed with relief, returning to my work to avoid talking about it. Like that would work.

"But I'm not buying that."

I tested the sample and then wrote down my findings, trying to ignore her.

"Maddie," she said grabbing my hand. "What is going on?"

"I don't want you to get involved."

"Too fucking bad. Professor Ramon keeps glaring at you like she'd gladly stuff you into one of those specimen jars."

I'd noticed that. I wanted to ask her how Reid was doing. But that was dangerous. Especially with the way she was holding that knife. She was using it to cut roots, but I suspected that wasn't what she wanted to use it for. I covered my lap protectively as she pierced me with her stare.

Rae returned to her own work, but not before whispering, "You're going to tell me. I don't care about your stupid rules."

And that's how we ended up in my apartment eating pizza and trying to strategize.

"You should have come to me sooner, Maddie." Rae took a gulp of her strawberry soda—her favorite drink besides coffee.

I nodded not trusting my words. How could I explain that trusting others was not something I did easily? I'd always taken care of my own shit. It wasn't that I didn't trust other people. I didn't *want* to trust other people. That way I didn't get let down. Which was exactly what was happening now.

I wanted to confide in her, but that voice in my head, the same one that said I could have been a better son, held me back.

"I'm here for you, Maddie," she said, taking my hand.

And she had been there through this whole thing with Reid. And we'd been friends for years. I could trust her. I silenced the voice in my head and prepared to spill my guts.

I sighed. "Professor O asked me to report Reid for..." I couldn't say the words out loud.

But I didn't need to. Rae filled in the blanks. "How did he know?"

"I think he guessed at first. And he wanted me to make something up if nothing had happened. He said he could find someone else."

"Bastard. But I don't understand. You didn't report Professor Em." She stated it as fact, not as a question, and I could have kissed her.

"No. I told him I wouldn't. But he kept pushing me. When I went back and told him I wouldn't and couldn't do it, that there was nothing between us..." I shrugged in defeat. "He told me he saw us at the club slow dancing."

"Oh fuck. You went to the club with Prof. Em?" Her eyes were wide like she couldn't believe my stupidity or my daring.

"No." I rubbed my eyes. I was so tired. "I'm telling this all wrong. I can barely think. God, Reid must be freaking out." But did he believe what they were telling him? "I can't contact him. It's killing me."

She leaned in closer, putting her arm through mine. I was lucky to have a friend like her. She was right. I shouldn't have pushed her away in the first place.

"What happened at the club?"

"I was trying to fix things. I went to the club to catch Professor O doing something—anything wrong. I needed some leverage. But Reid —Prof. Em—I need to think of him that way, so I don't mess up. Anyway, he was there." I explained everything then. I was all in. If I was going to trust her and accept her help, she needed to know everything. It was risky. The more people who knew about Reid and me put us both at risk. But it seemed a little late to worry about that, so I told her about Professor Emerson cornering me and asking me to be his first. It hurt remembering the picture Professor O showed me. Everything between Reid and I could be a lie. That didn't matter anymore. I loved him. The thought stopped me. Had I already fallen for my professor? I'd never felt this way about anyone. And I'd broken every single rule I had.

"Maddie?"

"Huh?" I glanced over at her.

"You stopped mid-sentence," she said. "What's that about?"

She was talking about my pause, but my cheeks felt like they were on fire. I couldn't tell her what I was thinking. If I was going to tell anyone how I felt, it was Reid.

"Sorry," I said. "Where was I?"

"Professor Em thought you were looking for a hookup that *wasn't* him."

Thankfully, she didn't call me out for not answering her first question. "I did not say that."

"Like that matters. I can read you like a trashy romance novel."

"That's a little disturbing, Rae. He asked me to leave the club with him," I continued. "But I couldn't. I needed to see if Professor Oliver was there. It was stupid of me to dance with him. But I wanted... I needed that connection." My eyes started tearing up. Fuck. I turned away, wiping at my eyes.

"Oh, hon. It's going to be okay. Professor Emerson knows you wouldn't do this."

"You don't understand. People have pretended to care about him all his life and then..." I shook my head, trying to push back my emotions. They served no purpose right now. I needed to be clearheaded.

"So how do we beat this asswipe and save our professor?"

I shook my head. "I don't know. What if others have seen us..."

"Others have seen you."

"And what if they tell Professor O?"

"Not possible."

I squinted at her. "Why do you say that?"

"Twitter. Have you seen it lately?"

"I told you I was afraid to look."

"Everyone loves Prof. Em. He treats his students like they're human beings. He cares about them." She held out her phone. I scrolled through his hashtag. There were no mentions of inappropriate behavior. No speculations. Just an outpouring of support for Prof. Emerson. My heart swelled. But Reid would never see this. He never looked at his Twitter feed. He didn't know how much his students loved him. And suddenly, it was clear. I stared at Rae, thinking again of kissing her in gratitude.

"There has to—Maddie, are you having an aneurysm?"

"No. But I do have an idea. It will take the both of us, and it still might not be enough."

"We're throwing out all your rules?" Her face lit up with exhilaration. I understood her elation. Doing something, anything, even if it didn't work was so much better than just hoping.

After hours of plotting and getting a plan together, I called my mom. I couldn't avoid it any longer.

I didn't tell her everything, but I did tell her there was a possibility that I'd have to do another semester or even go somewhere else for grad school.

"Maddie, do what makes you happy. You work so hard to please everyone else. Just do what's right for you. That's what's important."

At least I was by myself so no one else saw the tears falling down my face. "Dad may not see it that way." I tried to keep the sadness out of my voice, but I wasn't successful.

"So? Fuck him."

"Mom—" I almost dropped the phone. My mom never cussed.

"I think you're wrong about your dad. But it doesn't matter. It's your life, not his. He made his choices. And they were his, Maddie."

My throat tightened with emotion. If she was here, she'd already be hugging me.

"Honey, you've always been harder on yourself than anyone else. Remember that time you grounded yourself for getting an A-minus?"

I could almost see the fond smile on her face. I felt homesick. I could really use a hug from my mom right now. "Thanks, Mom."

"Any time. Just remember you don't have to be perfect at everything. We all make mistakes, and sometimes the best things come from those."

I thought about her words long after the call. Could I do this? Could I allow myself to fail? But I could. Because the only mistake I couldn't come back from was letting my Prof. Em Hottie down.

22

———

REID

How did I end up in the exact same spot I'd been three years ago? Trusting someone who could destroy my career?

But this was different. I wasn't as innocent this time. I had done what they were accusing me of. Almost. I hadn't used my power over a student. It wasn't like that. But the school wouldn't see it that way. All they would see was the contact between Maddie and me.

I hadn't slept with Maddie, but I wanted to. I was guilty of that in my heart. Was that why Maddie didn't follow through with our plans? Was he trying to protect me?

Or himself?

As much as I wanted to believe Maddie wouldn't intentionally hurt me, I couldn't forget all those years of being played. People pretending to care about me and then using it against me.

The banging on my door mirrored the banging in my head. I'd barely gotten out of bed for the last couple of days. What was the point anyway?

Someone else was teaching my classes. What if I had to leave? Would I even be able to go to another school? The banging continued, and I realized whoever was at my door wasn't leaving.

Was it Maddie? It would be stupid of him, and yet I couldn't help the hope that flared in my chest.

"It's me, you idiot. Open up."

Of course, Gal.

I opened the door but didn't wait for her to enter before I crawled back into bed. I didn't care if she followed me. Hugging my pillow tight, I rested against my headboard.

"Oh, Reid..." She was looking around, and I realized what she saw. My normally neat room was trashed. Laundry on the floor. The trash can almost to the point of overflowing. Papers I had tried to work on but discarded were scattered on my desk. I waved my hand, dismissing it all.

Gal crawled into bed with me. "Want to talk about it?"

"No."

She nodded as if my answer was expected.

"I think he wanted to ask about you."

"Gal," I said, trying hard not to cry.

"I know what guilt looks like."

"And he didn't look guilty?" Hope spiked in my chest. Maybe this wasn't Maddie's doing.

"No, he looked guilty as hell."

I slumped down. Of course he did.

"But he mostly looked worried. He watched me all through your class."

"I can't believe they put that on you..."

"I volunteered. At least for the upper-level classes. I let Oliver, that snake—I know he's behind this. I let him take your freshman classes."

I rested my head on her shoulder. "Thank you."

She frowned, looking worried. But I didn't dare ask.

"I think he cares about you, but I still blame him."

"It's not his fault," I said. "I knew better. We both know this wasn't the first time."

She turned to face me. "Tell me about Maryville."

I'd never given her the full story. I'd been too ashamed. But it didn't matter now. So I told her about Kyle. How he'd struggled and needed my help. "I thought that was what he wanted. We were around the same age. I was struggling with insecurities, and I may have inadvertently given him the wrong impression."

"Bullshit."

I shrugged. How did I know? Maybe it was just a bunch of crap. "Then one evening, I was helping him after hours—"

"At your place?"

"No." I shook my head. "Even I knew better..." Then I had to stop. Did I know better? What about Maddie?

"And?"

"We were at my office. I shared it with others, but they were gone. And he became affectionate."

"What does that mean, Reid?"

I didn't want to say the words out loud. My mouth was dry. I hated talking about this stuff, especially what happened in Maryville. I was so ashamed. I didn't look at her as I answered. "I'm not sure. Suddenly, he was in my lap and kissing my neck. I didn't know what to do. I was so focused on him and my body's inappropriate reaction to having a guy in my lap for the first time ever..."

She squeezed my hand. "It's not your fault, Reid."

"I didn't realize he'd taken a picture until the dean at Maryville showed it to me."

"Why did he take a picture?"

"He was failing. I tried to help him, but it was too little, too late, I guess—"

"He came on to you?"

"I guess? He was flirting, but I thought that was his personality."

"Poor sweet, innocent, dumb Reid."

"Hey."

"So, when you wouldn't sleep with him for a better grade, he tried to blackmail you?"

Heat creeped up my face. "He said he'd tell if I didn't change his grade."

"But you didn't."

"No. So, he turned me in."

"This isn't the same. You know that, right? I don't think Maddie's doing that."

"I agree. He's going to get hurt in all this. Unless he says it was one-sided, he could lose his grade in this class. But I don't see him pulling a Kyle and trying to blame me."

She leaned against me. "What are you going to do?"

I sighed. "Tonight? More ice cream. Tomorrow? Clean my apartment. And then clean up the mess I made of everything."

"Anything I can do to help?"

"Yes," I said, unable to look her in the eyes. "Tell me about class today. What did he do? How did he look?"

"Fine. I'll do it. But only because I know he couldn't have done this. If I thought he was responsible at all, I would help you burn his memory and maybe his body."

"Comforting. I'll keep that in mind."

I GATHERED MY PAPERS, my courage, and my self-respect and headed to Hudson Hall. Gal had offered to meet me ahead of time for coffee, but I didn't want to see anyone or talk about it anymore. I just wanted the whole thing over. A sense of homeostasis, everything coming together for this moment, pushed me forward. If homeostasis was successful, life goes on. If not, an organism is destroyed. Whatever happened happened. I couldn't worry about it anymore.

But this wasn't Maryville. Then I had taken the outcome as inevitable. How could I challenge it when they had a picture? I was a child playing an adult role then. Not intellectually. Obviously, I was smarter than most of them. It was a fact, and they all knew it. But emotionally, I was still a teenager. But I wasn't playing anymore. This was my career. This was my job, and although spending time with Maddie, kissing him, wanting more, crossed the line—the facts were there—the implication that I was using him was incorrect.

But it was the only conclusion the school would come to with the facts they had. I would tell the truth. I never took advantage of him. I was helping him. He was helping me. And if it came down to it and Maddie outright said that we had a romantic relationship, that we kissed, even if he said we planned to go further, I wouldn't deny it. I didn't think he'd do that, but he had a lot riding on this.

I dressed as professionally as I could. At first, I picked out a boring dark blue tie that sat unused in the back of my closet. Was I just playing at being an adult? My youth felt like the tie, a burden around my neck. It was the one variable I failed to sufficiently adjust for in my life. But I had to accept that part of me. The whole was bigger than the sum of its parts. I was more than just my brain, and my youth, and my curiosity. Maddie was the one who taught me that.

I pulled off the tie and exchanged it for the one with science symbols and equations on it. This was who I was. I wasn't hiding that part of me. If the school didn't like it, and they probably wouldn't, I would go somewhere else. Do something else. If I was teaching or doing research in some capacity, I would be fine.

But I was less sure on whether Maddie would be in my life. No matter what happened, it seemed impossible for us to have a future. If I had to find another job, he would be here moving on with his life. And if things worked out. If neither of us had to go, he would still be a student in my department, at least for the next few years.

Worrying about that wasn't productive. My focus needed to be in the present. Everything depended on this meeting.

The elevators to the fourth floor slowed to a crawl. No sign of Maddie. And while that was a good thing, I missed him. I missed seeing his face. The way he looked at me as if I was someone special. But he did that with everyone. Wasn't that what he'd told me? A small part of me couldn't let go of the feeling that Maddie had charmed me, done all of this, just to ruin me.

But none of that mattered. Even if it hadn't been real for him, it was real for me. Maddie had given me so much. He'd helped me see the world in a different way. He helped me connect the two parts of my brain that were at war with each other every day. I would be forever grateful to him. Would I be devastated? Yes, but not the same way as I was after Maryville. This time, I would stand up for myself. My relationship with Maddie wasn't wrong. No matter what they said.

Would my perspective change if Maddie accused me of taking advantage of him? Maybe. Probably. But I'd worry about that if it happened.

Although physically impossible, the elevators seemed to suddenly speed up, getting me there before I was ready. The doors popped open into the lobby that had been part of my life for the last three years. Anxiety spread like invading ants. I balled my hands to keep them from shaking, but I couldn't do anything about my wobbly legs but stride into the reception area like I belonged there. I hoped that was still true. I hated starting over. Adjusting to a new life and new people was torture.

Posters covering the walls of the hallway varied, some announced upcoming events or chances for students to study abroad, and others were more about saving the planet and the effects of climate change. Some were familiar. Some I noticed for the first time. Did they change them? Or had I been in my head and just not noticed? Probably a combination.

I didn't head to my office. Would it be my office much longer?

"Hey, Dr. Emerson." Ben welcomed me with a bright smile, but then his gaze shifted away. I recognized that thanks to Maddie. Ben knew something was up. He might not know specifics, but he had more information than just the cover story given to everyone else.

"I'm here to see Dean Albin."

"Yes," he said. "Let me check and see if he's ready for you."

I didn't know what to do with myself as he called the dean to announce my arrival. Should I sit in the visitor chairs? It felt strange to be in the lobby waiting and not in my office. At least there wasn't anyone else around to see my humiliation.

"Go right in," he said, smiling again. He seemed genuine and supportive.

The ants were gone, replaced by butterflies, and I pictured emerald swallowtail butterflies and their colorful wings as they invaded my stomach. This was the moment. I took a deep breath in, forcing the butterflies out.

"Thank you, Ben," I said with a smile.

He stared at me with wide eyes before recovering with a quick nod.

Was it that unusual for me to thank someone? Or smile? Or maybe interact with them at all?

As I walked into the dean's office, Professor Albin held out his hand for me to shake. This was more formal than we usually were, but maybe he wanted to put distance between us? His gray hair hung in a long braid down his back. The dean glanced at me over his glasses. I was struck by his resemblance to a certain headmaster. His gaze was not unkind, and I relaxed a little.

"You know Professor Oliver." It was said as a statement, not a question, but it was still formal like we didn't work together every single day. Seeing my nemesis put me on the defensive, and I could almost hear Captain Kirk's voice in his head. "Shields up, Scotty."

We nodded at each other, not shaking hands. He loomed in the back like a dark cloud on a sunny day, ready to ruin everything. "Should we have someone in here taking notes?" he asked.

"This is not a formal review hearing. I've explained this to you already, Professor Oliver."

"I don't understand where this is coming from." It wasn't a lie. I had no idea what he had on us. "So I admit to being a little confused."

"Understandable," he said. "Let's all take a seat, and I can explain."

I sat in the chair in front of the dean's desk. Oliver was in the back. I didn't feel comfortable with him behind me, but there wasn't anything I could do about it.

"As I mentioned when we met at the beginning of the week, there are accounts that you're having an inappropriate relationship with one of your students, Maddox Evans."

It didn't sound like a question, so I didn't feel the need to answer it.

"Today's meeting is to determine if there are any reasons to take this further. Professor Emerson, I'd like to hear from you about your relationship with Mr. Evans. And then Professor Oliver will have a chance to explain his concerns. But I'm warning you," he said to Oliver. "I want facts and evidence. Not just rumors or innuendos. If I find that there's anything concerning, we will have a full review."

His gaze returned to me for the last part, and I tried not to squirm in my seat.

"Do you understand, Professor Emerson?"

"Yes, sir."

"I have witnesses—"

"This is not a hearing, Professor Oliver."

"Students, I mean. And they want you to know their concerns."

I pushed away the panic that threatened to overwhelm me. Maddie? Or someone who had seen us together? And students. More than one.

Dean Albin waved Oliver back, and then nodded for me to continue.

I twisted my hands in my lap, trying to remain calm and look confident. "Mr. Evans is a bright student who does well. He came to me after class one day and asked me to help him because he was struggling, and it was unusual for him."

"Did he say why he was struggling?"

I hesitated. I certainly wasn't mentioning Maddie's attraction. That wouldn't be helpful to anyone. "He said it was for personal reasons."

I'm sure he'd mentioned that phrase once or twice. So technically, I wasn't lying. I was skating the edge, though, and it made me uncomfortable. I didn't like deceit. But just like the golden tortoise beetle changed its color to protect itself from predators, subterfuge was sometimes necessary, and scientifically, at least, I was okay with it.

"Proceed."

"We met in my office a couple of times. I gave him extra assignments to assess his knowledge. They did not influence his grade at all. It was just to help him understand the material better."

"Why didn't he go to the other students for help?" Oliver snapped out.

I glanced over at him. "That would be a question for Mr. Evans, not for me. If a student requests my assistance, I help them. There are some professors who don't do that."

He crossed his arms with a huff.

"You'll have your turn, Professor Oliver." The dean gave him a warning look.

When he didn't say anything further, I continued, "We met a few times in the student center and outside because Mr. Evans felt claustrophobic in the office."

"Your relationship never crossed the line?"

I wouldn't make a good golden tortoise beetle. I couldn't lie convincingly.

"Professor Emerson?"

I—again—gave him half of the truth. "Mr. Evans noticed I was struggling with social cues. That's something I've never been good at."

"Are you autistic?" Oliver rose from his chair and started to move closer.

"That question is not appropriate." The dean motioned for him to sit back down.

"I'm not, as far as I know. But I've never been tested."

"You didn't have to answer that."

"I know. But whether I am or not doesn't change anything. Mr. Evans suggested helping me understand social interactions. That's why people saw us together. When others would interact with us, he would test my knowledge and challenge my reasoning. It was beneficial, but I realize it was also inappropriate. Mr. Evans is my student. I'm supposed to be teaching him, not the other way around."

I had to stop talking because thoughts of what Maddie had taught me and promised to teach me flashed in my head.

"I want to mention this as an aside. Professor...Reid. I think this has been the first time you've looked me in the eyes for more than a second without prompting. Whatever Mr. Evans has been doing is working."

"But it's not appropriate—"

"Sit down, Paul," he said, sounding exhausted. "You will get your chance."

A burst of happiness warmed me. I was better. Because of Maddie. "Thank you, Dean Albin. I think it was Mr. Evans's way of thanking me for helping him."

"Do you really expect us to believe any of this?"

The dean stood, glaring at him. "Do you want to wait outside?"

"No, sir."

I tried not to show how happy it made me to see Oliver chastised. Did that make me a bad person?

The dean returned to his seat. "Was he ever at your apartment?"

"No, sir."

"Were you ever at his?"

"No, sir." I was glad that we'd never taken that step so I could answer truthfully.

He glanced over at Oliver. He'd remained standing in the corner, like a petulant child. "I'm interested to hear what evidence you have."

Oliver glanced at his watch. He'd done that a few times already, and I'd also noticed him watching the door.

"Where are the students you mentioned?"

"They're late."

Again, I wondered if it was Maddie or someone who had seen us at the club or almost kissing on the sidewalk. Why hadn't we been more careful? I tried to school my features. Use my inner beetle to portray my calmness. I slipped my hand in my pocket and took out my smaller geode. I used it as a worry stone. It calmed me. And it reminded me of Maddie in my office stroking that very rock.

"I saw them together myself at Three Doors Down, the gay club downtown," he said and then turned to face me. "You were slow dancing. What was Mr. Evans teaching you then?"

Dean Albin's eyes widened as he glanced from Oliver to me. This was bad. Unbelievably bad.

"Professor Emerson? Is that true?"

What could I say? My golden beetle had fled, leaving me exposed. I swallowed. But as I opened my mouth, not knowing what was going to come out—a lie or a confession—a knock interrupted me.

Oliver opened the door. Maddie. And he looked amazing. I drank in the sight of him like a fish needing water to breathe.

"My witnesses are here." Oliver stood straighter, a wide smile on his face. "Mr. Evans and...you brought your friend?"

Maddie stepped forward, revealing Rae. What was going on? I wasn't the only one wondering, if the Oliver's eyes bugging out was anything to go by.

"Who is this?" he asked.

"I told you about Rae."

"*Ray* is a girl?"

Rae put her shoulders back. "Excuse me?"

He waved his hand. "Never mind. Let's get on with this."

Dean Albin welcomed them, even going over to shake their hands. The man was pure class. I hated that I was about to disappoint him.

Maddie didn't look at me, not even for a second. I couldn't keep my eyes off him. When the dean was talking to Maddie, Rae narrowed her eyes at me. Right. I needed to play it cool. I was getting better at reading her signals.

My heart pounded. This was it. The moment. I rubbed at my chest right underneath my tie, trying to ease the pain.

As everyone settled back in their seats, Maddie shifted on his feet. He slipped his hands into his back pockets, then brought them out again and crossed them. This occurred several times, as the dean explained that this wasn't a hearing. Almost the same speech he'd given me.

Was he nervous? I wasn't sure. I didn't think I'd ever seen him nervous before. He always conveyed complete confidence, even when he didn't feel it. All that had shattered. What did his nervousness mean? Was he nervous for me? Was he nervous for himself? Or was even his nervousness an act? Or maybe he was worried about his grades and planned to confess. Dark circles under his eyes suggested that, like me, he'd had trouble sleeping. Rae put a steadying hand on his back. Just a slight touch. It seemed to work. He took a deep breath and smiled.

"Mr. Evans? You understand that I can meet with you and Miss Watson in private if you wish?"

"No need, sir," Maddie said. "We know how important it is to tell the truth. And...Professor Emerson needs to hear it from us."

Oliver practically danced with glee.

The way he glanced at Professor Oliver made me wonder if the bastard had threatened Maddie. Was that why he was helping him? I didn't want to put Maddie in the position where he had to choose between his future and me. I stood up so suddenly my chair fell over. Everyone looked at me.

"Oh, sorry." I picked the chair up and rubbed the stone in my hand one last time before putting it back in my pocket.

"Professor Emerson?" The dean narrowed his eyes in confusion.

"The students don't need to say anything," I said, glancing over at Professor Oliver. "I'll tell you anything you want to know."

23

MADDIE

Rae gasped behind me. I tried not to show any emotion, even though I was freaking out inside. What the hell was Reid doing?

Professor Oliver put his hand on my shoulder to guide me forward, I wanted to shake it off and yell at him. How could he be so happy about someone else's misfortune? I glanced at Dean Albin, expecting to find him glaring at Reid, but instead he was watching Professor Oliver, his head tilted as if he was seeing something for the first time.

I held my hand out to Rae. She gave me the folder we'd brought. We had a plan, and Reid wasn't going to fuck it up by being noble or some other bullshit.

"But I have all the evidence you asked me to bring, Prof. Oliver. Don't you want to see it?" I didn't look at Reid. I didn't want to see the betrayal in his eyes. I also wasn't sure I could hide my true feelings from anyone in that room.

"Yes, yes. Sit down, Professor Emerson. Give the students a chance to talk."

I risked a glance at Reid, against my better judgement. He was ignoring Oliver and watching the dean, who nodded at him. I bit my lip to keep from smiling at that.

"Continue, Mr. Evans. Tell Dean Albin how Professor Emerson had been treating you."

"I was struggling in his class," I admitted. "And I went to him for help."

Oliver narrowed his eyes. "And?"

"And..."

"You said there was inappropriate contact?"

"Yes."

Out of the corner of my eye, I saw Reid flinch. I hated putting him through this. "I admitted to Professor Emerson that I was having difficulty focusing because he was..." Was I really going to say this out loud?

"Yes? Go on."

I glanced back at Rae, and she nodded in encouragement. "I mean, he's kind of hot, you know. It's distracting."

The room fell silent. Reid stared at me with his mouth open. I looked away as quickly as I could.

"Did Professor Emerson take advantage of you?" the dean asked.

"No. In fact, he told me that first day that any contact like that between us was inappropriate and would not happen. He was very upfront about it. Not that I asked him for that. But he just made it clear. He said things weren't always clear, and he wanted to make sure I understood." That wasn't exactly how it happened. Reid had blurted out that he wouldn't sleep with me. But it was close enough.

"Is this true?" Dean Albin asked Reid.

"Well, yes."

"These were the personal reasons you mentioned earlier?"

He sighed. "Yes."

Reid hadn't told him everything. He'd tried to protect me. And probably himself, but still.

"But there was more," Professor Oliver said. "Tell him what happened next."

"Prof Emerson helped me. He gave me extra credit. I mean, not that I got credit for it, but extra work to do. And I did that, and it helped me focus. I was able to get my grades up, which I'm very thankful for. That's it, I think."

Professor Oliver scowled and pointed at Reid. "Look at his Twitter account. They call him ProfEmHottie."

"Do they?" The dean turned to him.

"I was unaware of this until Professor Ramon showed it to me. I wanted to close the account right away, but I was told I had to keep an official account open. I've never used it. I don't do social media."

"Surely there's something inappropriate on there."

Dean Albin sighed. "Show me."

Professor Oliver pulled up Twitter and showed him his phone.

The dean scrolled through. "All I see are messages of concern for hashtag ProfEmHottie." He glanced at Reid. He was blushing adorably and biting his lip.

"All wondering if you're okay and worried you might be sick. I don't see anything of concern. I mean, there are some comments from the students that aren't appropriate, but I can hardly blame him for how he looks."

Professor Oliver pointed at Rae. His face flushed with color, and his eyes looked a little wild. "You said there was something inappropriate."

"Oh, you should hear the things Rae says about Prof. Emerson."

"I'm embarrassed," Rae said. "But can you blame me? He's cute. But I'm sorry to objectify you, Professor. I know you are a person with a brain and feelings, and it was wrong of me. I'm glad I had this opportunity to apologize."

She didn't look sorry at all. I had to look away. She was pouring it on pretty thick, and I almost lost it.

"I forgive you, Rae," Reid said.

She nodded and stepped back.

"This is ridiculous. Give me those papers." He ripped them out of my hands, glancing through them. Oliver's face got progressively redder and redder as he skimmed through the documents.

"Hand them to me," Dean Albin said, glaring at him. Oliver let out a huff and thrust the papers at him. He glanced through them.

"These are all statements from the students saying what a great professor Dr. Emerson is."

"Really?" Reid furrowed his brow and bit the bottom of his lip in that adorable way he had.

I'd been afraid to look at him. Afraid I might break down. Afraid that everyone could see how much I missed him. Needed him. How much I wanted him in my life. I couldn't let him confess. I couldn't let Oliver win. But I couldn't resist now. I needed to see his reaction.

"You asked me to get as much evidence as I could on Prof. Emerson and his contact with his students. I tried. This is what they said." Rae had given me the idea to go to the other students. We asked them to write a letter of support for Prof. Emerson. We didn't tell them what it was about, just that he was having a hard time. Just as we had thought, no one said no. They all loved him. He was always willing to help anyone. He treated them like they were equals—colleagues. That didn't mean he let them get away with anything. Reid was good at teaching. He was awkward as hell in almost every other aspect of his life, except when he was in front of a class. His passion shone in his eyes. He loved sharing his knowledge.

The dean glanced at Reid, and his eyebrows raised. "Just to read a few...Professor Emerson is the best professor I've ever had. When I get something wrong, he doesn't make fun of me. He seems to understand why I came to that conclusion, and he explains where I messed up."

He pulled up the next one. "I love Professor Emerson's class. He's hot but also wicked smart, and he knows his stuff. During labs, he really shows us what we're doing wrong. Prof. Emerson is young, and when I first took this class, I thought he was too young to be a professor. I didn't think I'd learn anything. In fact, I'm ashamed to say I called him Doogie Howser. Not that anybody knew who that was. But it used to be my mom's favorite show."

I bit back a laugh. Danny was in our forestry class and hilarious.

"But the truth is, it made me realize that it doesn't matter how young you are. It's what you know and how you act. And how you treat people. Thanks, Prof. Em."

I glanced over at Reid. His mouth was slightly open. He looked shellshocked. Did he not realize how much the students looked up to him? How much they cared about him? Evidently not.

"They're all like this," Dean Albin said. "Glowing reviews on what a great professor you are. I'm confused what's going on here, Professor Oliver. I thought you said you had evidence."

"I'm confused, too," he said, his voice getting louder. "What is this nonsense?"

I glanced at the dean and then at Professor Oliver. I tried to convey nervousness, a fear of upsetting them, and an innocence I lacked. "I'm so sorry, Professor. I know you wanted me to get evidence against Professor Emerson, but I couldn't find anything." I wrung my hands together and let my head hang down. "I know you said I should just go ahead and sleep with him. But I..."

"What?" That came from Reid and Dean Albin.

"That is not what I said." Professor Oliver tried to look shocked, but unfortunately for him, he wasn't as good an actor as I was.

"No. You're right. You said that if nothing happened to go ahead and *encourage...*" I said, using actual air quotes to make my point, "Professor Emerson. You were sure that he would do it. I'm sorry, Professor, but I couldn't. He is my professor. I realize my grade was riding on this, and you'll probably fail me and keep me out of the graduate program..."

"We're done here," Dean Albin said, standing up abruptly. "Mr. Evans, Miss Watson, you can go. We'll let you know if we need any further information. And rest assured your grade is not in danger."

"Thank you, sir," I said. But I didn't want to leave Reid. I needed to make sure he was okay. Rae grabbed my arm and pulled me out. I'd never seen the dean so angry before. He'd always been kind, like a sweet grandfather. As we closed the door, we could still hear him. His voice raised.

"As I see it, Professor Oliver, you have two options."

I wanted to hear what those options were, but Rae pulled me along with her.

"Let's get out of here while we can. You can check on lover boy later," she said under her breath, soft enough that only I could hear.

"Thanks, Ben," she said as we reached the front desk. She gave him a smile and a wave. The smile was a little on the flirty side.

I could've told her that was useless. The boy was gay. We even had a short thing once. Of course, it only lasted two dates. But they were a good two dates. He winked at me when I walked past him.

Rae hit the down button on the elevator. Rather aggressively. The plan was to go to the Coffee House, getting coffee for her and tea for me. I severely needed something. We'd been too nervous to drink anything this morning. Once we were in the elevator and going down, Rae put her hands on her hips and glared at me.

"What?"

"Did you sleep with Ben? And is every guy in this school gay?"

"Maybe...okay, yes. And sadly no."

She smacked me on the stomach. "Just once I want a hot guy who likes girls. Is that too much to ask?"

I opened my mouth to say something, but her warning look shut me up.

Then her face softened. "Everything's going to be okay."

"I'm not sure about that," I replied. Just because we weren't getting into trouble didn't mean it was going to be all right. I was still a student. Reid was still a professor. We still weren't going to be together. I had gone way past my three-day rule, but that didn't matter anymore. I loved Reid. I would do anything for him. But he didn't need to be tied down to me when he just discovered how great things could be. He had options now. And he might think I was the one he wanted, but would he still think that in two months? Two years?

"What's going on in that head of yours?"

I shrugged.

"Coffee, pastry, and then you're going to tell me."

"You're so bossy. Did you ever think that maybe that's why you can't get a date?" I regretted my words as soon as I said them. Mostly because she *accidentally* stepped on my toe. It hurt like hell. I hobbled after her to our coffee shop. It probably wouldn't have hurt so bad, but she had on little ankle-high boots that looked cute with her dress but should also be classified as a deadly weapon.

Once we settled in our usual table by the window, I took that first fortifying sip of tea. I sighed in relief.

"Now tell me what's going on."

I groaned. She never forgot anything, and that reminded me of Reid. I wondered how he was doing.

"Maddie, talk to me."

"I'm fine."

"Really? Because the label on your cup is not facing outward, and you didn't even notice."

"Quit messing with my shit." I sighed. "There is nothing wrong with wanting to have the opening right in front of me."

"No. But you always adjust it so the label is facing out."

"I haven't done that in a while."

"Because you give the baristas an extra tip if they put it on right. I saw you whispering to Sam the other day. But enough about you and your strange little habits. Tell me why you and Reid aren't going to live happily ever after."

"God, Rae. You know why."

"No, I don't, and neither do you. You can't predict the future."

"I was his first kiss." I thought back to the photo. Was I really his first? But he couldn't have faked his lack of experience. I was at least one of his first.

"So?"

"I might even get to be his first guy or lover or whatever." I didn't want to talk about this in the middle of the coffee shop.

"Again, so?"

"So, I've had years and years of dating to find the right guy. I know what I want. I know what I like. How can he know? He hasn't had any experience at all."

"Sometimes, you just know."

"In the movies or books, but not real life."

"What about you? Didn't you know?" She crossed her arms, challenging me.

Okay, I kind of did know. At least my heart knew even before my brain caught up. "That's different."

She raised an eyebrow. She was good at this talking without talking. She could've probably taught Reid a lot more than I did.

"I'm just saying. What if he decides he wants to experiment? I don't think I can take that."

"So let me get this straight. You're going to cut him loose for his own good, make both of you miserable, because someday he might leave you and make you miserable. Sounds like to me you're just ready to be miserable."

"It sounds stupid when you put it that way."

"I'm not saying you're wrong, Maddie," she said. "I don't know what's going to happen. But it's not fair for you to decide this on your own."

I covered my face with my hands. "I know."

"All his life Reid has been treated like he's not emotionally mature, like he doesn't know what he wants. If you treat him like that, you're taking away all the progress he's made. You're saying it was all for nothing," She pulled my hands down. "Present your side and see what he says."

"I didn't think of it like that." Reid deserved to make his own choices in life. He might break my heart later, but for now, I needed to enjoy being with him while we were together. "What about the fact that I'm a student, and he's a professor?"

"You definitely can't do anything until after you graduate, that's a given. But after that? You'll figure it out. Together. Now, put a smile on your face, honey. You won. And there's somebody here you might want to see. But don't turn around."

I rolled my eyes. No chance of me obeying that order. I glanced behind me. Reid was walking in the door and searching until he found me. Our eyes locked, and a surge of affection, excitement, relief...It all poured out of me at once. I couldn't help the goofy smile on my face.

He walked over to us. "Can I join you two?"

"I was just about to leave, but—" Rae turned to grab her purse.

"No," Reid said, "Please stay."

She stopped and stared at him in surprise.

"I think it's best if the three of us were...you know."

He was right. It would look better. The three of us talking might still look suspicious, especially after this morning. But not as bad as if Reid and I were alone.

"Okay, cool." She sat back down and tapped her fingers on the table.

I might have believed she felt awkward about the whole thing if I hadn't noticed the twinkle in her eye. She was enjoying this way too much.

Reid got his coffee and sat down across from me. He smiled, kicking his foot against mine under the table.

Now, I felt awkward.

I had no idea what to say.

24

***

REID

Going to the Coffee House was a mistake. But I needed caffeine. I felt exhausted from all the worrying I'd done and yet excited about what had happened in the dean's office.

But it wasn't the coffee I was here for. I'd gone almost four days without seeing Maddie. Four long days and that was too many. I needed to talk to him. Part of me worried that he wouldn't want to see me, but the minute I stepped into the coffee shop and found him, a bright smile lit up his face. My heart felt like it was about to burst. I wanted to hold him. Tell him how sorry I was to put him through this. Instead, I invited myself to sit with them and insisted Rae not leave us alone. I didn't care if Professor Oliver walked in and saw us all there together, like we somehow planned this. If he'd had anything solid, he'd have presented it. And the fact that he tried to push Maddie, sweet Maddie, into doing something with me just to get evidence. It was on my mind and the first thing that came out of my mouth.

"Was Professor Oliver the reason you didn't want to...you know?" I waved my hand around.

Rae stared off in the distance, pretending not to listen.

He nodded. "I need to teach you how to lie because you suck at it.

And I knew you wouldn't be able to deny anything and be believed. And while the things we did were bad, doing other stuff would have been worse."

I could have sworn that Rae rolled her eyes, but I was trying to focus on Maddie.

"I didn't want you to get into trouble. What happened after we left?"

I tried to keep the smile off my face. Act professional and all. But it was impossible with the memory of what happened and Maddie sitting close enough to touch. "Dean Albin basically told Oliver to drop everything, just let it go. Of course, he hadn't wanted to because he was sure there was something there. The dean said if he pursued it, then I had every right to file an ethics violation since he basically encouraged a student to sleep with me. He said that's not what happened. I told him that things weren't always what they seemed. I'd said…"

"Wait," Maddie said stopping me. "You said that?"

"Yes. I told him I didn't understand why we had to have this animosity between us and that I was done playing games. If he didn't like me, he could either deal with it or move along."

"Well, look at you. Growing a pair."

I studied my hands, smiling, and trying to will away the blush on my cheeks. I was still nothing like that beetle, but I was getting better at protecting myself. Standing up for myself.

"Rae, do you like Linkin Park?"

We both stared at Maddie like he'd gone insane.

"They're okay."

"Can you suffer through them for ten minutes or so?"

"Probably."

Maddie fished his earbuds out of his backpack, fiddled with his phone, and then handed the earbuds to her. She rolled her eyes but put them in. He pressed a button, and she waved her hand.

"Woah! Too loud. I'd like to keep some of my hearing."

He grabbed her leg, laughing.

"What?"

"You're shouting."

They both started snickering, and I covered my mouth to keep from giggling like a little kid. Maybe it was the relief of being done with everything. Or the joy in seeing Maddie and knowing he was happy to see me.

Rae put her thumbs up, indicating the volume was perfect.

Maddie placed his hand on the table off to the side, like he was going to grab mine and thought better of it. He leaned closer. Rae nodded like she was listening to us, even though nobody was talking yet. It wasn't perfect.

"I missed you," Maddie said. "I wish I'd been honest with you from the start, Reid. I should have trusted you, but Professor Oliver…"

I shook my head. "It's fine. I get it."

"Honestly, I was afraid of what you might do, if I told you."

"I don't know what I would've done. Challenged him, probably. And confirmed everything in the process."

He raised his eyebrows.

"I might have told him to stop threatening my guy."

"Your guy, huh?"

"Hopefully, soon to be my guy."

"It's too late for that," he said. "I'm already there."

"I want to be with you, Maddie. But I think that would be tempting fate."

Maddie nodded, but the smile faded from his face. I realized he misunderstood.

"I mean if we did anything now." I dragged my hand through my hair. Why did I always get my words tangled up when I needed them the most? "I don't think we should do anything until after you graduate."

"And after graduation?"

"I've been thinking about this a lot."

"You have?" he asked, peeking at me from under his lashes.

"I have."

Rae nodded at us, still acting like she was interacting with us. Anybody watching us would have been able to tell. Maddie and I only had eyes for each other. I hoped the dean and Professor Oliver didn't show up. It would've been better to do this somewhere secluded, but it would be riskier being alone with him.

"What did you come up with?" he said, prompting me.

"I won't be your professor. And I won't be your advisor, so you won't be teaching any of my classes. We have different specializations. I deal with trees, and you're focusing on plants and agriculture."

"True."

"And it's not as strict at the graduate level. Students and professors can be friends. They hang out more often. If you're not in my classes or my TA, I think we're good."

"But they'll think we were together all this time."

"We can take it slow. Or we can say we got to know each other better over the summer. Honestly, Maddie? I'm pretty much past caring, as long as I get to have you."

A sigh interrupted us. I glanced over at Rae. "Sorry," she said. "There was a song change. You guys are so sweet."

Maddie shook his head at her, indicating she needed to keep listening to her music.

"What about texting?"

"I think that would be okay," I said.

"Calling?"

"Maybe a little riskier."

His voice got low. "Sexting?"

I took a sip of my coffee to give myself a chance to calm down. My face burned as if it was on fire.

Maddie laughed. "I'm just teasing," he said. "I know you're probably not ready for that."

"We'll have to see." I didn't want him to think I wasn't open to that because I was. Oh, I was so open to that. But maybe not until he passed my class and got his final grade.

I kept my voice low. "I can't wait to hold you again."

He glanced at Rae. Her head bobbed, and her foot tapped. She was rocking out. Was she still listening to Linkin Park?

"I can't wait to touch you."

"You gotta stop," Maddie said. "Because in a few minutes, I'm not going to care about my grades or my diploma or grad school. I won't care about anything but getting you naked and underneath me."

I closed my eyes at the images he described. I deserved that. I brought that on myself. "Sexting is probably out because it will leave evidence. But phone calls are good."

"Yeah." Maddie said. "I still have a lot to learn. And sometimes remote learning is the best."

"We can do that."

Rae removed the earbuds and handed them back to Maddie. "I've got class," she said. "So, I gotta go. Either go on without me or get a move on."

"You better go, too, Maddie."

"Okay, but I'm giving you a heads up. Tonight, I'd say about nine or ten o'clock, I'm going to have a tree emergency. That material we're trying to learn is really *hard*. I might need you to *ease into it* for me."

"Ease?" I said, unable to resist teasing him. "Maybe I need to *pound* it into you."

He closed his eyes. "Oh, fuck. Why did I start this?"

"You guys are too hot to handle, and I have class. How am I going to get through Professor Aubrey's class now?"

We finally parted ways outside the coffee shop. I wanted to kiss Maddie, but I resisted. Graduation was too far away.

I had five missed calls from Gal, so I headed to where I knew she'd be. In the science lab from her last class, cleaning up.

"Don't you have TAs to do this?"

"I like it," she said. "And I knew you wouldn't want to talk in the office in case Oliver was still there. All you said was that everything went okay. I want details."

"Fine. But only if you let me help."

We scrubbed out beakers, cleaned the counters, and straightened up the room. It was amazing that one class could do this much damage. And although we had janitors who did the overall cleaning, instructors were supposed to make sure the lab was clean and ready for the next class. Including restocking supplies.

I caught Gal up on everything. She laughed and seethed and then sighed.

"I told you it would work out."

"You didn't have any way of knowing."

"I know that Oliver is all talk and no brains. And he was just pissy because you rejected him when you first came here. You could have let him down gently instead of ignoring him."

"I didn't ignore him."

"Honey, you ignored everybody. I was just persistent."

"True. You really think that's it?"

"I do. I've seen some of the looks he gives you sometimes. And he's jealous students don't like him, and they love you."

"I can't believe so many of them stood up for me." It made my heart hurt in a good way. "All I wanted to do was teach and make a difference in this world. Help my students and show them how amazing science can be. And be accepted for who I am. I'm grateful they wanted to help me."

"Maybe you should tell them."

"You mean in class?"

"No."

"How would I do that?"

Gal drummed her finger against her chin. "If only there were a social media site or something that everybody was on, and they could all see what you were saying at once."

"I've never used that Twitter."

"It's not called *that* Twitter or *the* Twitter, just Twitter. Here, let me help you." She took my phone, tapped an app I had never opened before, and pulled it up. "See? This is how you compose a tweet. All you have to do is write what you feel and then hit that button right there, and it will post, and everyone who follows you will see it. And we add the hashtag, and everyone following your hashtag will see it. They don't even have to be a follower."

"I don't think I have *any* followers."

"That's where you're wrong. You have many followers."

She showed me a number I didn't really believe. But I typed out a few words thanking them for their support and that it meant a lot to me, and I hit tweet. "What now?"

"Give it a minute," she said, putting the glass jars away and drying off her hands.

Suddenly, my phone went crazy, beeping all over the place. "What's happening?"

She shrugged. "I changed your notifications so that any time Prof-EmHottie gets a hit, it will ping."

"I still don't get it." I scrolled down to where it said there were over a hundred little hearts already. "What's that?"

"That means they liked your tweet." She pointed to the screen. "And that means they retweeted it. Have you honestly never looked at Twitter?"

"It's overwhelming. So many people at once."

"Look at all the replies you have."

The replies were from mostly students as they responded to my message. Some saying thank you. Some saying they had my back. Even one girl asking if I would marry her. "Is this normal?"

"For everyone else? It's not. But for you? And people like Keanu Reeves? Yes."

"Who?"

"I can't believe you. Google is your friend. Are you going to see Maddie again?"

"After he graduates. I'll see him in class, but otherwise, no."

"That's like a month away."

"I know. But he's calling me tonight. He may have a science emergency."

"Are you guys going to have phone sex?"

"Gal..."

"It's a good idea. Get to know each other before you *get to know each other*."

I laughed, shaking my head. "Thank you," I said. "For standing by me through all this and being my friend before I was trending."

"Wait. You do know about Twitter."

"I've heard of trending before. Now don't get me wrong, I don't really know what it is or how you do it or where it goes but..."

She pulled me into a quick hug. "One last piece of advice."

"Last? Can I record you saying that?"

She smacked my shoulder. "One last piece of advice," she said again. "Don't fuck this up."

I laughed. "There's a good chance I will."

I FINISHED GRADING ALL the final essays. I'd wanted plenty of time between the final paper and the test, so people were prepared.

"Why don't you just do an online test like everyone else?" Gal had told me when she dropped off the stack of papers.

"They were supposed to email the essays," I said, shaking my head. "This happens every year."

She had shrugged. "It's because they know you'll take them like this."

I finished them up as fast as I could, trying not to think of Maddie calling me later. I mean, what if he didn't? What if he was studying and got tied up or a number of things that could happen? I wasn't sure if I wanted them to or not. I wanted to talk to him, but I was nervous. I had been excited about the idea of phone sex. What if I said the wrong thing? Being hesitant about touching someone was a lot different than silence because you didn't know what to say. I worked myself up into a mess of anxiety. I tried to focus on my book. I'd been in bed about an hour earlier than normal. Who was I kidding? I never went to bed this early. But I wanted to be ready, no matter what time he called. I didn't want to have to get ready after he called. And what if he called early? I banged my book against my head. *Idiot, stop.* And then the phone rang, and a picture of Maddie at the butterfly camp came up on my screen. "Hello?"

"Hey, Reid."

"Hey." I settled on the bed and took a deep breath.

"You sound nervous. We can just talk, okay?"

"No. I mean, I want to. I just…"

"Why don't we start with talking? If that leads somewhere, great. And if not, honestly, Reid, just getting to hear your voice is good enough for me."

I hugged my pillow against me. "How was Plant Taxonomy class?"

"Frustrating. All I could think about was you and…talking to you tonight."

"I'm sorry?"

"No, you aren't," he said, sounding amused. "I can hear in it your voice. You like driving me crazy."

I was glad he couldn't see me blush. "True," I admitted. There was a pause, and I wished I could see his face. "Maddie?"

He sighed. "I didn't want to do this over the phone."

"Are we still talking about phone sex?" I tried to joke. "Because in person is definitely better."

The line went quiet. Again. He wasn't talking about phone sex. It was something bad. "Are you breaking up with me? Not that we're officially together. I mean—"

"No. We are together. It's not that."

"We're not talking about sex, either."

He huffed out a breath. "We need to talk about something. I almost brought it up at the coffee shop, but there were a lot of people around."

More silence.

"It's harder to read social cues when you're not here. You're making me nervous. Did I do something wrong?"

"I'm not sure you've been entirely honest with me. Professor Oliver—"

"He's a jerk. And he's out to get me."

Maddie laughed, and it eased some of the anxiety I felt. I rubbed at my chest. My stomach churned. I felt like I might be sick if he didn't talk to me soon. But did I really want to know?

"He is an asswipe." The amusement drained from his voice. "Oliver had a picture. It could have been photoshopped—"

"Damn." I wanted to scream. "How did he get that?"

"You don't deny it?"

"How could I? I told you about my last school and the student...I didn't mention the picture, but I honestly didn't think it was important."

"Reid," he said, his voice softer. Maybe he wasn't as mad anymore? "It's not the picture. It's the way you looked in the picture. You're holding him in your lap and looking at him like..."

Some of the tension left my body. Only some because he saw the evidence and came up with his own conclusions. Would he believe me? "You need to brush up on your social cues if that expression on my face looks like anything other than pure shock. He literally jumped in my lap. And..." I sighed. I'd have to really explain my reaction. "Imagine it, Maddie. An eighteen-year-old boy-man who'd never even touched another guy before suddenly had this attractive guy in his lap, moving around. My body reacted. I'm not sure I could have stopped it. Was I tempted? For a half-second, maybe. I was technically his teacher, but I didn't have my doctorate yet. After it came out, I was able to finish the program, but the plan for me to stay as a professor went out the window."

"I'm sorry."

"The only reason Dean Albin even knew about it was because I told him."

"Wait. You told the dean? It wasn't in your records?"

"I wasn't a professor yet. And it wasn't part of my transcripts. I had several professors who wrote glowing letters of recommendation."

"Still, you told him?" He seemed stuck on that point.

"I didn't do anything wrong. I was naïve and if I'd fought it, I probably could've stayed."

"I'm still caught up on the fact you told him when you didn't need to."

"If I hadn't told him, the first person he'd have heard it from was Professor Oliver. I have no idea how Oliver dug that picture up."

Maddie was quiet for a while, and I wasn't sure what to say. Would this change anything?

"It wasn't that you might have been with this guy. Or that he'd been your student. That would be hypocritical of me at this point," he said. "You told me I was your first..."

"You were my first. My first kiss...my first everything. And I'm looking forward to doing so many firsts with you. Maddie. No matter what happened with Kyle, the truth is that was all him. He wasn't my first anything because I didn't participate. It had nothing to do with me."

"I kind of feel sorry for the guy. I mean, you are distracting and hard to resist."

I laughed. Even though I didn't believe any of that. Maddie had even showed me the Twitter feed, trying to explain more about it. It wasn't that difficult. I just preferred to pretend it didn't exist. Seemed easiest.

"So," Maddie said, "you've never had phone sex?"

"Talking on the phone gives me hives."

"This, I need to see."

"You're the exception. Other than you, I hate phones."

"Until we can do this in person, these phones are our best friend."

The butterflies took flight in my stomach again. Were we really going to do this? "So, we're... talking?" I hated being awkward, but it seemed to be my default setting.

"We could video chat, but I think we need to work up to that," he said. "What do you want, Reid?"

Did I even know what I wanted? Video chatting was appealing. I wanted to see him. But I was nowhere near as gorgeous as Maddie. I was slim, not bulky at all. I took care of myself. But Maddie was all muscles and tanned skin. Gorgeous. I already felt self-conscious. "Let's start with talking," I said. "If that's okay."

He chuckled. "You're adorable. You know that?"

"I am?" I stretched out on the bed, trying to get comfortable.

"So, Professor Em, what are you wearing?"

"You saw me at the coffee shop." At his chuckle, I realized what an idiot I was. Oh, right. I quickly chucked off my clothes, trying to hold the phone at the same time so I didn't miss anything.

"You can put me on speakerphone."

Right. Could he hear my heart pounding? Speakerphone shouldn't be that scary. If he was here, we'd be making noise. It wasn't like anyone in the other apartments could hear us. I tried to push my thoughts of inadequacy away. I was the only thing that could mess this up for myself. I put the phone on speaker and finished undressing.

"Ready?"

I took a deep breath and blew it out. "Ready. Ask me again, Maddie."

"What are you wearing, Reid?"

"Absolutely nothing."

25

———————

MADDIE

Reid was adorable. The trust he put in me made my heart ache. The man was sexy as hell, and he didn't even know it. I hated that our first time sharing orgasms would be over the phone. But I wasn't willing to wait another month. And maybe this would be easier for him. Although, being Reid, he would still be insecure and unable to see my reactions to him. I had to let them know in other ways.

"You're so sexy all stretched out like that, Reid."

He half moaned, half chuckled. "You can't see me."

"I have a good imagination. But maybe you can correct that."

I heard a change in his breathing, a hitch, and I reassured him. "I'm not talking about switching to video. Describe yourself to me. Don't leave out any details."

"I'm not sure..."

"Are you laying down? Are you sitting up with your legs spread wide for me?"

"Oh fuck," he moaned. "How do you want me to be?"

"I want you any way and every way."

He took a deep breath. "I think I can come just from the sound of your voice."

I was already rock hard. I had to take this slow. I didn't touch myself. Not yet. "Descriptions, Reid. Now."

This time his chuckle sounded confident, like he knew what he was doing to me. Bastard.

"I'm laying down with a pillow behind my back. My legs are spread wide. My..." He hesitated. And I let the moment stretch on, letting him set the pace. "My cock is hard and leaking."

His inexperience really shouldn't have turned me on as much as it did. I was his first at everything. "I can't wait to see your body," I said. "Do you have hair on your chest?"

"Yes, but it's light across my chest and around my nipples, which are hard and tight right now. It trails down to my groin area, which I trim. I like things neat."

"You're driving me crazy, Reid."

"I'm about average size—"

"You haven't measured?"

"What? No. Have you?"

"Yes, but I'm not giving anything away. Let's say you won't be disappointed." I imagined Reid's face and body. "Do you want me to touch you?"

"Yes." His voice was wrecked. "Maddie..."

"Tell me." I couldn't see him, but just from his voice. I could tell he was blushing. Embarrassed. But turned on.

"My nipples. I want you to touch my nipples."

"With? My hand? My mouth?" I hesitated. "My cock?"

He let out a shuddering breath.

"Let's start with hands," I said. "Tell me what I'm doing."

"You're running your nail across my nipple..."

"Touch yourself, Reid. Imagine it's me."

"Yes." The word was panted out.

I couldn't help it. I took over. "I'm squeezing your hard nipples, rolling them, watching you react. You're so beautiful. I want you so much."

His breathing increased, and he made a whining sound.

I gave in and touched my cock. I wasn't going to last long. "Are you hard?"

"Yes."

"Spread your legs even wider, as far as you can. Let me in, Reid."

"Oh my God."

"Run your finger over the crown of your dick, spreading the precum." He wasn't speaking. All I could hear were gasps. "I'm wrapping my hand around you, pumping slowly. I love how gorgeous you are spread out for me. Waiting for me," I said. "I'm going faster—"

"No."

I stopped my words and my actions. I'd been following my own lead and stroking myself imagining it was Reid, his long fingers that I loved, touching me. But I'd been going too fast, and I should have known better. "Do you want to stop?"

"Oh, God no," he whispered fiercely. "Just slow down. I don't want it to be over too soon."

That made me smile. Reid was so stinking cute. "You realize we have all night?"

"I know, but I want you to tell me what you want."

I was still hard, but the edge was gone, but not far off. "I want you."

"More specific."

"I want you in my bed."

"Maddie."

I could picture him lying there, frustrated, and trying not to smile. That was the look he had when I was in his classroom. But that wasn't the reason I was being evasive. There were things I wanted. Specific things. That I'd never shared with anyone. I wanted to share them with Reid, but would it be better to do that in person? Maybe not. Maybe this was safer. Less intimidating. I couldn't say it all. So I gave him a part of it. "We hadn't talked about this."

"Just tell me."

"I want you inside of me."

"You do? You want me to top? I just assumed..."

I was losing some of my erection. I hated talking about this. I hated feeling like I was disappointing people. Disappointing Reid. I wasn't living up to his expectations.

"But I love the idea," he said, quickly.

"You do?"

"Yes. I like the thought of being the one in control, although I know that's not always the way it works."

"But you'd be okay with that?"

"Yes, Maddie," he said. "Absolutely yes."

"I wasn't sure."

"Don't hold out on me," he said. I could hear him moving around on the bed. "I want to hear everything. I want to hear what you want. You can tell me."

I nodded and realized how stupid that was, since he couldn't see me. "Yes."

"It makes sense, Maddie. Often people who have to be in control want a safe place where they can let go."

"Really, Reid? You're going to analyze me? In the middle of phone sex?" But I laughed because this was Reid. Always in teacher mode. And I did love teacher mode.

"But there's more. You're not telling me everything. I want you to trust me, Maddie."

"I do. I just...I've never told anyone."

"You mean I'd be your first?" He sounded excited and happy about that, and I couldn't resist.

"Yes."

"Then you have to tell me."

I hesitated, trying to think of how to word it, but Reid jumped back in.

"I mean, you don't have to tell me. Honestly, whenever you're ready is fine by me. I'd like you to tell me someday..."

"Reid, stop talking just for second. I'm just trying to figure out how I want to say it."

"Just say it."

"I've imagined it," I said finally. "Many times. We usually start in the classroom with you punishing me."

"How do I punish you?"

"You drag my pants down and bend me over your desk," I sucked in a breath, imagining it as I talked. "Then you slap my ass and I can feel the burn of your hand. It's humiliating but I'm so hard for you already. You slide your fingers into me hard over and over, telling me I need to be punished for not paying attention. Then you fuck me and tell me how good I am, taking my punishment."

The sounds on the other end of the phone were erotic as hell. His heavy breathing, whining, moaning, the slapping of his skin, and I was past where I was before, stroking myself but trying so hard not to come. Not yet. "And then you suddenly pull out of me and turn me around and..."

"And what? Tell me, please."

"You put your hands on my shoulders and shove me to my knees, grabbing my chin so I can't move. But you're not angry. Your eyes are sweet, loving as you look at me, and then..." Was I going to admit this to Reid? Yes, I was. "Then you come all over me, spraying my face. It's everywhere, in my hair, my eyes, my mouth...dripping down my chin. You're marking me. Claiming me."

Reid gasped and moaned as he came. Those sounds and the images of him standing over me holding his cock and coming all over my face had me coming harder than I could remember in a long time. Everything got quiet, and I wondered if he was going to hang up. Now that the high was gone, I was embarrassed. I reached for a tissue and cleaned myself up, waiting for Reid to say something. I didn't want to be the first one to talk. But maybe he was waiting for me?

We ended up saying each other's name at the same time, and I laughed, but it was more from relief. Relief that he hadn't hung up on me. But Reid wouldn't do that. I knew that with a certainty.

"Thank you."

"For the outstanding phone sex? Awesome orgasm?" I quipped, trying to lighten things up.

"For trusting me."

"Oh. Right. Yes." My heart warmed up.

"I trust you," he continued. "And you can always trust me. We're in this together. I don't want you to ever hesitate to tell me something,

Maddie. There might be things I don't like or I'm not ready for, but it doesn't mean I don't want to hear about them."

"You didn't like that?"

"That, I liked. I'm just saying. Odds are there will be something. Like I'm not sure I'd want you to pee on me."

"Good to know."

"That doesn't mean we can't talk about it."

"Me peeing on you?"

He laughed. "Anything. I'm all the way in this. I want you to know that."

"Me, too. Reid. All the way in."

I wished that I could hold him. Show him I meant what I said.

"This is the first time I actually...jacked off with another person. I'm not going to ask if you've done that."

I could imagine the blush he had from saying those words. "It won't be the last."

"God, I hope not," he said with a laugh. "But next time, I'd really like to try it with both of us in the same room."

"Soon. Very, very soon."

"You better study your ass off, Maddie. Ace every single class. Especially mine. If you don't, I'm going to hurt you."

"Promise?'

"Yes," he said, his voice somewhat stern. "But it will not be the fun kind."

THE MONTH LASTED at least a hundred and thirty days. I was so done with it. Not getting to be with Reid properly was torture. The brief moments we shared in class or, on occasion, the coffee shop wasn't enough. I needed him in my arms, right now. But we had to play by the rules. The school's rules, this time.

In class, Reid ignored me. Mostly. I'd asked him why during our many phone calls, and he said he was afraid of giving himself away. His heart eyes...and boner would probably do that. Hearing Reid talk about his boner initiated another round of phone sex. We'd moved up to video. And although Reid was nervous about showing me his body, I was able to coax him into stripping for me. God, it was hot as fuck. That man. And the fact that he didn't understand he was sexy made it even hotter.

During class, he called on Rae a lot more. She enjoyed the attention, at first. It didn't take long to get old.

"Tell your boyfriend to stop stalking me," she said after class one day.

"He's your professor," I countered. "He's allowed to call on you."

"Not when he's doing it so he can stare at you while everyone else is looking at me."

"Complain all you want, but I noticed that cute boy with the mess of blond curls, two rows down, was practically drooling over you."

"True," she said with a smile. "And if he doesn't man up soon, I'll have to take the initiative."

"Maybe you should take the initiative anyway. Isn't that what you'd tell me?"

"Shut up."

REID and I met at his office only once. We kept the door open. Professor Oliver walked by every five minutes. It creeped me out.

We survived on stolen touches during lab as Reid checked my work. It wasn't his style to grab my ass or anything like that. But somehow trailing his fingers on the inside of my wrist was just as, if not more, erotic. I fumbled through the explanation of my work, and he raised a brow.

"I'm not sure you understand the material, Mr. Evans. I'd like you to redo the experiment." Bastard.

I was different. Grabbing ass was my style. The opportunity didn't arise very often. But when it did, I took it. During one lab at Woodlands, we gathered tree samples. As I stood behind him, checking out the bark he was holding out, my hand may have slipped to his ass and squeezed. Reid let out an adorable squeak. More than once during our phone and video calls, we played out his fantasy of taking me right there in the classroom bent over his desk. I didn't tease him about it. He was embarrassed about having the fantasies in the first place. And it had taken a few times and some reassurance for him to relax enough to do it.

Staying away from each other was difficult, but it wasn't as difficult as I expected. I had to focus on my studies, so I needed the time apart. Having Reid around all the time would have made it impossible. I had to keep my grade point average up.

"Getting a B wouldn't kill you," Rae said to me one day at the coffee shop.

"Shut your mouth."

She rolled her eyes, sipping her dark roast.

"And I'm not giving Mt. Surly any excuse."

If Professor Oliver used tests with right or wrong answers, I was fine. If he gave an essay, it was up for grabs because he could interpret it however he wanted. And no way would that go in my favor.

The week of finals, I poured myself into my studies. My last final happened to be in Forest Ecology. I didn't hurry. I took my time to make sure I didn't make any mistakes. Bonus, the longer I was there, the more I got to see Reid. I was one of the last students to leave, and he raised his brow as I turned in my paper.

"Having difficulty, Mr. Evans?"

"A little," I said, my voice low, as I adjusted my cock.

He shut his eyes and took a deep breath. "You have to stop doing that."

"You have to stop asking me questions like that."

Only a few people remained in the room. We talked low enough that no one else could hear.

"Can I see you?" I asked.

"After I grade your final and turn the grades in."

"Really?" I couldn't help the smile on my face. "We don't have to wait till graduation?"

"Once the grades are recorded, I think we're okay. Besides," he said, lowering his voice even further. I had to lean in just to hear him. "I can't go another day without touching you."

I swallowed. I needed to get out of there before I hopped over his desk and into his lap. "Me, too."

"Thanks, Professor Emerson."

I jumped at the student behind me. Had he heard anything we'd said? I stepped aside so he could turn in his test. I think Sean was his name. Or was it James? I'd dated him sophomore year. Which consisted of us having one date and then sex. I hadn't called him after.

"No problem, Thomas. Have a good summer."

Thomas. Right. So close. He nodded to me on the way out. He didn't seem upset at all.

"Really?" Reid whispered. "Him, too?"

"I didn't say anything."

"You didn't have to. I can read you."

"The pupil has become the master."

I started to leave, but Reid grabbed my hand, dropping it almost instantly.

"Mr. Evans, do you have that book on trees I loaned you?"

I opened my mouth to remind him I didn't have his book, but he nodded to the last student in the room. I resisted the urge to roll my eyes.

"I think I lost it. Was it expensive? I may have to pay you back."

Reid tilted his head. Probably wondering where I was going with this.

I shot him a seductive glance, biting my lip. "I don't have any money. Any other way I can pay you?"

Reid choked, his face getting red. I heard the last student walking up to the desk.

"Are you okay, Professor Em?" she asked.

"Yes, fine. Just something went down the wrong way."

I had to turn away before I lost it.

She nodded, barely looking at me before rushing from the room.

"Choke on something?" I asked innocently.

"It was nothing." He cleared his throat.

"Do you want it to be something?"

"Maddie," he warned, but it was weak at best. He started this.

"Because I have something." I adjusted myself again, this time taking my time. My erection pressed tight against the zipper of my jeans. I wanted to pull it out and show Reid what he'd been doing to me.

He watched my hand, and his breathing became shallow. "We can't do this here."

"I know. I just wanted to make sure you thought of me all day."

"I didn't need you to practically masturbate in front of me for that to happen."

"So, no touching myself in front of you. Got it. Any other rules I need to be aware of?"

Reid stood and moved to the front of the desk, right next to me. I didn't need to look down to know his cock was hard. But I looked anyway. I wouldn't miss a chance to check out Reid's cock.

"I may be inexperienced," he said as if he were discussing the essay question on the effects of deforestation on climate change. "But I'm a quick learner. Don't think I can't punish you for insubordination."

"Are you going to spank me?"

This conversation was so inappropriate and dangerous. We'd played this fantasy out before but never in an actual classroom. And we only had a few more hours to wait, but the closer we got, the more urgent it seemed to be.

"But you do seem to need some help." Reid trailed his fingers lightly over my straining cock. I tried to hold in a moan.

"That's not helping."

"Sorry, I'm still learning." But the smirk on his face told me otherwise. He pressed his hand against me, harder than before.

"You're killing me, babe. I'm going to fuck you over this desk if you don't stop."

"That's supposed to deter me? You need to work on your negotiation skills." His hand moved to my face, cupping my cheek.

"I can't wait until tonight, Maddie. I need you."

I took his hand and kissed his palm. "You're strong, Reid. You can do it." I backed up before I lost the ability.

He nodded as I moved away. "See you tonight, Maddie."

"See you tonight."

REID WAS COOKING Creamy Pasta Pomodoro for me. As strange as it sounds, I'd never had a guy cook for me. It was probably because I didn't do relationships. Until now.

"What can I do?" I asked.

"I've got this." His hand shook as he added the tomato paste to the marinara sauce cooking on the stove. Was he nervous? He had to be. I was nervous as hell, and I'd had sex with lots of guys. But maybe that was why I was nervous. This wasn't any guy. This was Reid. What if I messed it up?

I stepped behind him and placed one hand over his as he stirred the sauce. I didn't want to mess him up. But I wanted him to hear me. I kissed his neck and leaned against him. "I'm nervous too," I admitted.

He set down the spoon and covered the pan, turning it to simmer. Then he faced me, cupping my cheeks in his hands. He leaned in and gave me a soft kiss. "You shouldn't be nervous. You know what you're doing. I don't have a clue." He kissed my nose and smiled. "Well, I do have a clue." He looked down my body, staring at my hardening cock, which liked the attention very much, thank you. "I actually have a big clue," he said with a smirk.

I stepped away from him. "No, no. You promised me dinner first."

"That I did. Tell me why you're so nervous."

I shrugged. "I'm supposed to know everything. I'm supposed to have all the answers, but this is your first time. What if I mess it up?"

"I don't think that's possible."

"I've messed things up. I'm good at messing things up."

He laughed. "You are. But not this."

"I've always been the student. The one learning. You're the teacher. I mean, putting sex aside how do you do this? Being responsible for students knowing what they need to know to be successful? That's a lot of pressure."

He kissed my forehead. "Everyone's responsible for their own learning. I give them information. If they learn it, they learn it. That's on them. Now if everybody isn't getting it, then okay, maybe I'm doing something wrong, but for the most part, I'm providing the knowledge. They are responsible for retaining and using it."

"What you're saying is I can teach you about sex, but it's up to you to take that information and apply it. If you fuck it up, it's not because I'm a bad teacher, but because you..."

"Need more practice. And I promise to be a good student and practice it over and over until I get it right. And then practice some more. You can never know too much."

"True. And I'll be showing you a few things, but I'm hoping you'll be showing me a lot of things, too. Especially one specific thing."

"My intelligence?"

"Close."

"My charm and wit?"

"Closer."

He leaned down and kissed me. "My huge cock?" he whispered against my ear.

"Did you measure it?"

"It's somewhere between above average and ginormous."

"Really?"

"Close...Well, close enough."

He kissed me again, and for a second, I didn't care about food. But Reid had gone to a lot of trouble.

I pushed him back. "Stop trying to tempt me with your gigantic cock," I said. "And focus on not burning our dinner."

THE TABLE SETTING WAS SIMPLE, yet romantic. A white tablecloth covered the table with a red runner and four white votive candles in the middle. Instead of roses, Reid had placed colorful wildflowers he'd gathered himself. The food tasted amazing. The creamy pasta pomodoro combined a creamy but light pasta sauce with a mix of noodles and sautéed vegetables. I loved watching Reid's face light up as he talked about it. I should have known he enjoyed cooking. The man almost never ate out. At least not until recently.

"I know you aren't a fan of vegetables, but I think you'll love this. It's cherry tomatoes, zucchini, mushrooms, and spinach. The extra ingredient is in the sauce. Cashews."

He watched me closely as I took my first bite. It had a tangy flavor that had me moaning in appreciation. Honestly, though, even if it had been awful, I would have pretended it tasted like chocolate cake just to see that smile on his face. And he would have believed it. I'm a good liar. Thankfully, I didn't need to fake it. I sat my fork down and took a drink of Pinot Noir.

"You're not going to just watch me."

"But I enjoy it."

"Eat your vegetables," I said, giving him a flirty look. "You'll need your strength."

He laughed, his wide smile showing off his beautiful teeth. I remembered thinking that Reid never smiled. And now he never stopped. Well, that wasn't true. I could piss him off like no other. And on those days, he growled. Unfortunately for him, I liked his growly face almost, but not quite, as much as his smile. Getting Reid riled up and out of his head was one of my favorite things to do.

But the look he had on his face right now was my least favorite. "What's this face about?"

He frowned. "Are you sure you like it? You're not just being nice?"

That was the problem with being good at deception. No one believed you when you were telling the truth. That, paired with his insecurities—I wanted to beat up everybody who ever made him feel inadequate. Had it just been people at school? Or had his family made him feel this way? He didn't talk much about them so I didn't bring it up. "If you take a bite, you'll see how amazing it is."

He rolled his eyes. Something I noticed he was doing more often.

Then he took a bite, and the insecurity on his face morphed into a grin. "This is damn good."

"I know right? How did that happen?"

"I can cook."

"It's all those years of refusing to get takeout." But I didn't say more on that. No sense in reminding him of why he never ordered takeout. I was also still nervous about tonight. The excitement had waned a bit, and I wanted to get that back. More importantly, I needed Reid to get that back. I decided to really enjoy my meal and show him how much I liked it. Spearing a cherry tomato, I slipped it in my mouth and rolled it on my tongue.

Reid sputtered and sat his wineglass down. "You should eat with your mouth closed."

I bit savagely into the tomato. It was sautéed, not fresh, so there wasn't a lot of juice left. But he still got the idea. I took another bite, wrapping my lips around the fork and moaning in appreciation.

"Are you trying to seduce me?"

I swallowed before answering him. His gaze dropped to my throat as he watched me and then back up to my mouth. "This food is amazing, Reid." I licked the remnants of sauce off my fork, watching him playfully. "Is it working?"

"Hell yes. In fact, let's just forget dinner. I'm tired of waiting." He used those puppy dog eyes that I normally couldn't resist. "Please, Maddie?"

I ran my foot up his leg. This may have been the first and only time I regretted his skintight pants. I couldn't slip my foot under to touch his skin.

He shut his eyes and said tightly, "I hope this torture means dinner is over."

"Nope."

His eyes flew open, and he pulled his leg away from mine. "Rude."

"You went to a lot of trouble, Reid."

"It was no trouble."

"I'm hungry."

"So am I," he said, his eyes heated, and I almost gave in. Almost.

"Eat your dinner."

He narrowed his eyes as if taking my words as a challenge. Fuck. Reid ate his dinner and enjoyed it thoroughly. By the time he swallowed his last bite, I was a mess. Hard. Aching. I wanted him so much. And we'd waited a long time for this. But that was the reason I didn't want to rush it. I wanted to draw out this sweet agony and watch Reid squirm.

Reid gathered our plates and put them in the sink for later. "Dessert?"

"Nope. I don't think so. Unless you're the dessert. Then hell yes."

"But it's ice cream."

I laughed. Reid loved ice cream. Enthusiastically. He had a boyish glow about him that he rarely showed anyone. I knew it was because he struggled all his life with people not taking him seriously and treating him like a child. But I loved that part of him. The joy and excitement when he did things like jumping into my arms off a brick ledge, twirling around in the butterfly house, hiding rocks, and exploring the riverbed. So while I wanted Reid naked and against me, like this second, I couldn't deny him ice cream. I nodded, and he grinned.

"Butter pecan or mint chocolate chip?"

"You choose."

"Butter pecan it is." He rushed to the kitchen and returned with a pint of ice cream. He put two scoops in a bowl and started to put the lid back on. "Two bowls or one?"

"Two," I said reluctantly. Finding out things about each other, our little quirks, was something I looked forward to doing. But not this. I was embarrassed about it. Just like my counting and having things straight and orderly, I didn't share food. Ever.

He handed me a bowl of ice cream and sat down, an excited look on his face. Then I could only stare because the man knew how to enjoy ice cream on a good day, but on a day when he was trying to torture me, he ramped that up by a thousand.

He moaned, and the look of pure bliss as he took a bite almost did me in. Opening his eyes wide and innocent, he asked, "Aren't you going to eat your ice cream?"

"I don't think I can."

His brow furrowed. "Why not?"

"Because ice cream is not what I want right now."

"You haven't even tried it." Was he really throwing my words back at me? "Here, try some of mine." He scooped ice cream onto his spoon and held it out to me.

I thought he'd understood when I'd asked for my own bowl. Now I had to break his little heart because I wasn't eating after him. I shook my head.

"Come on, Maddie." And there was that look of insecurity.

Didn't he realize this wasn't about him—it was about me? No. Because I hadn't told him. And I didn't want to. But I didn't see any way around it. I sighed. Loudly. "I don't eat after people. Like, ever."

His mouth dropped open, and he laughed. The fucker actually laughed. "Oh, wait. You're serious."

I glared at him, my face getting hot. All thoughts of seduction had vanished. I had my own issues with feeling insecure. It wasn't easy to get over almost twenty years of feeling inadequate. It would take time. I knew this would come up, but why did have to come up now?

"Maddie, talk to me."

I shook my head. "I just don't. People have germs."

He opened his mouth to say something and then shut it again, tilting his head. Then he shrugged. "Okay," he said, popping the spoon of ice cream in his mouth.

Was it really that easy? Somehow, I didn't think so. "But I like watching you eat ice cream." I wanted to bring the passion back in his eyes that I doused with my insecurity and weird habits.

He smiled, shyly. "Do you?" But I wasn't fooled. This wasn't his real shy smile. This was his turn-Maddie-on shy smile. Although there wasn't really much difference between the two. Then he ate another bite, moaning and licking his spoon.

"Are you almost done molesting the silverware?"

"Why? Would you like me to molest you instead?" And again, he said it not seductively but with that innocence that drove me crazy.

"Yes. And I'll beg, if that's what you want."

His smile widened. "Begging might be good. But later. I like the idea of molesting you, licking you like my ice cream." He took another bite. "Do you want to lick me?"

And although he said it playfully, there was this hint of insecurity. Like for some reason he thought I wouldn't want that. "Absolutely, Reid."

He bit his lip, his eyes sparkling. "Where?"

Okay, we weren't even done with ice cream, and we were moving on to dirty talk. Wasn't I supposed to be teaching him? "Your lips," I said. His eyebrows rose encouraging me. "Your neck? Your nipples." I could see the effects of my words on him. His breathing increased, and his hand shook slightly as he held his spoon. "Up the side of your body, even under your arms."

"Really?"

"I'm a sucker for underarm hair. What can I say?"

"Anywhere else?"

"Can I just say every inch of your body and leave it at that?"

He shook his head no.

"Okay, let's move on to the good parts. Your cock. Definitely, your cock. Every bit of it. Like a lollipop." Cheesy but worth the smile on his face.

Heat bloomed up his neck. "My hole?" he asked softly. I knew it wasn't easy for him to admit he wanted that.

I hadn't rimmed guys very often, but the idea of doing that to Reid and making him squirm underneath me was exciting. "Yes. Hell yes."

His face changed. The excitement was still there. The need was still there. The want in his eyes was still there. But the glare was new.

"What?" I asked, wondering what I'd done wrong.

"Really, Maddie? You'd lick my underarms? My hole, but you won't share a bite of my ice cream?"

My face flushed. It had been a trap all along. And he was right. It made no sense that I wanted to lick every inch of his body, that I'd had my tongue in his mouth, and yet I couldn't eat after him. Anxieties were almost never based in fact. But that didn't matter. I'd have to share a little bit of ice cream if I wanted to share any bit of him.

"Come here, you brilliant, devious man, and let me lick your ice cream."

He leaned in, holding his spoon out for me.

I ate the ice cream, ignoring my stupid, stupid brain and focusing instead on Reid and his beautiful eyes.

"There. That wasn't so bad, was it?" And then he kissed me as a reward.

I deepened the kiss and climbed into his lap. He was taller, but I was bigger. It worked. He could handle me. His hands went to my ass as I pushed my hard cock against his. "Are you ready? Or do you want more ice cream?"

"I'm done," he said. "But still hungry."

When we reached his room, I started to undress.

"Maddie, wait...." His face flushed red, and I could tell he was holding something back.

"I admitted I wanted to lick your butthole so you can share anything with me."

He laughed. "When you were my student, I had this fantasy..."

Oh, holy hell. "Tell me more."

"That day in my office you took off your sweater and your shirt rode up..."

"You know that was intentional, right?"

His eyes left my body and traveled to my face. "I figured. It was effective. And fueled many a fantasy. Strip for me..." he asked. "Slowly."

And so I did. I peeled each layer of clothing off, watching his eyes darken with hunger. Desire for me. I was the luckiest guy ever. After I was completely naked except for my underwear, I turned with my back to him and slid my briefs down slowly so very slowly. I barely got them past my ass when Reid was there, wrapping one arm around my waist as he pulled me flush against him. He rubbed his hard cock into my ass. I leaned my head back, giving his mouth access to my neck. He kissed me, and I threaded my fingers through his hair, pulling him even closer. "Reid," I moaned. "Want you."

"Striptease is over. Naked. Now."

He stripped his clothes off, and I removed what little I had left. Then he was suddenly shy again, and I remembered his insecurities about his body. He tried to hide, and I moved his hands. "You're gorgeous, Reid."

We made out. Kissing slowly...sweetly, but like a wildfire, it sparked quickly. We moved to the bed, rubbing against each other. I was barely conscious of what I was doing. My whole plan of seduction, of how I would show him things, flew out the window. All I could think about was getting closer to him, skin to skin. And then there was no thinking at all.

I pulled away, suddenly. "Reid."

"No, no, no." He grabbed for me.

"Stop, baby," I said. "I don't want it to be over so soon."

He shook his head. "We have all night."

"But this is your first time. I want it to be memorable."

He looked at me and laughed. "If you think I won't remember this for the rest of my life, you're wrong."

I knew he was serious, but I couldn't help poking at him. "That near-perfect memory, right?"

"Shut up and kiss me."

And so I did. "Tell me what you want, Reid."

"So much. I want everything. Well, maybe not everything."

I laughed. "That's right. No peeing."

"But for now, I just want to be close to you. Touch you. And watch your face as you come."

Fuck. I kissed him. "Where's your lube, babe?"

He had a panicked look on his face, and I kissed him again.

"Not for that," I whispered against his mouth.

"Right." He reached over into his nightstand and grabbed a bottle of lube.

I squeezed some in my hands and kissed him again as I stroked our cocks together.

"Oh, yes. That's so good."

I brushed soft sweet kisses over his flushed face. Moving from his cheeks, his eyelids, his nose to the corner of his mouth. As I stroked us, building the pressure and the need, I did everything I could to outlast him. We rubbed frantically against each other, and I could see the moment he was there. Reid called my name as he came, and I almost lost it. Almost, but I held back.

When his eyes were clear, I placed his hand on my straining erection. Covering his hand with mine, I built up a rhythm. "Watch me, Reid." He stared into my eyes as we stroked my cock together. It didn't take much. Having his hands on me...his eyes on my face.

He brushed his lips against mine. "My sweet Maddie," he whispered. "Come for me."

My orgasm surged through me, intense and wonderful, and I fell over the edge screaming his name.

Afterwards, he held me tight like he'd never let me go. I was sticky and gross, but in that moment, I didn't care.

"Thank you for making my first time so beautiful."

"Thank you, Reid."

"For not coming ten seconds after we started making out?"

"Well, thank you for that, but no. For making my first time memorable, too."

"Are you making fun of me?"

"No, my sweet nerd. This was my first time making love to someone. I've never had this connection before. Emotions made it so much better."

"Really?"

"Really." My eyes welled up, and I blinked back the tears.

"Why are you crying?"

I shook my head. "I'm just overwhelmed...I love you, Reid. So much."

He smiled that boyish, wide, all-in smile. "I love you, too, Maddox Evans."

We kissed soft sweet kisses that were almost painful in their intensity.

"I was wondering," he said, trailing his fingers down the inside of my wrist, "if you're not too tired...could you show me some other things?"

"Absolutely."

And I did. I showed Reid a few things, and he showed me much, much more.

THE UNIVERSITY EXPECTED instructors to be at graduation. Which was a relief. If it was optional and most professors didn't go, it might look odd for Reid to be there. Knowing he was expected made it easier. But it also meant Professor Oliver would attend. And I still had to deal with that asshat for two more years until I got my master's. My goal was still to move to Alaska and work at the state park. I didn't want to leave Reid, but we'd work that out when the time came.

Our first night had been amazing, and we spent every night after that together. I loved waking up in his arms. This was one of my firsts. I'd never spent the night with a guy before. I usually left or kicked them out. Reid had beamed when I told him that. So damn cute, I couldn't stand it. It had been one of my rules I was happy to finally break. Reid shattered every rule I had. My new rule was simple. Make Reid happy.

"When are your parents getting here today?" His hair stood up all over his head, and he had that sleepy-eyed look. And of course, we were both still naked.

"Let me put some clothes on and have some coffee before we start discussing my parents. Please."

He kissed my forehead, tucking my hair behind my ears. He was a very touchy person, something else I didn't expect from him. I loved that he felt comfortable showing affection. There was something about his touch that soothed me and excited me all at the same time. It was strange but wonderful.

"It's going to be fine."

"You say that, but you don't know that," I said. "Where's your empirical evidence? Sure, with my mom, it'll be fine. But with my dad? Not sure at all. Let's look at the facts, shall we? Fact—my dad has always been so practical it's painful. There was always more to strive for. Fact—he left me and my mom when I was five."

Reid shook his head.

"What?"

"I don't know your relationship with your dad," he said. "But if he's coming today, if he *shows up*, that means he's here for you. I'm not saying what he did was right, but sometimes things don't work out, and how long are you going to punish him for that?"

I sat up straight, pulling away from him. "You're right," I said. "You don't know my relationship with my dad. And I get that I should probably give him more of a chance than I have. But it's not like he's been bending over backwards to spend time with me."

Reid tilted his head, and I rolled my eyes. I really shouldn't have told him as much as I had.

"Okay, so he has tried to reach out, and I rejected him. But still, when I do see him, he just wants to take control of everything. Assess. Make a plan. Sometimes, I just need someone to listen to me. Sometimes, I just want him to relax and not have to control everything."

"Maddie—"

He didn't even have to say it. I could see it in his eyes. "Yes, I'm a little bit of a control freak."

"I wasn't going to say anything," he said, squeezing my leg through the sheet. "Sometimes, people just don't know how to express love until somebody shows them." The love and emotion in his eyes made me choke up.

"Okay. I'll give him a chance. If he shows up."

He smiled. "I'll be right there with you."

I tried not to panic at his words. "Um, about that..." Probably not the reaction he was expecting. "I want you there, Reid. I do. But do you think that's a good idea?"

He pulled away, no longer touching me at all. It felt like we were miles apart instead of inches.

"Reid, don't do that."

"It's fine. I just wanted to share this day with you and your family. I realize we can't tell them, yet."

I grabbed his arm and pulled him back down on the bed. "Okay."

"I don't want to make it uncomfortable for you."

"You're not," I said, trying to reassure him. I hated that sadness in his eyes.

"We agreed to take it slow, so I understand."

"That doesn't mean I don't want you to meet my family. I can introduce you as my favorite teacher. Because you are."

He grinned and let me thread our fingers together.

"And if they guess, so what? My mom won't think any less of me. My dad...okay, he might think less of me. Although he doesn't think much of me to begin with."

"Maddie."

I expected that reaction from him. "So we're doing this then?"

"Yes."

"Just think, after my parents leave, we'll have the whole summer together. I'll have to work because some of us don't get summers off."

"Will your parents expect you home for the summer?"

"No. I've usually had something going on. Summer classes, internships, things like that."

"And will you live..."

"No more questions, Reid. Let's just enjoy our day."

"Can I ask one more?"

He gave me those sweet innocent professor eyes, so how could I resist? "Fine. One more question. Make it good."

"Do we have time for..."

He hesitated, and I wasn't sure what he was asking. "Coffee? Breakfast? A ride on your scooter?"

He blushed. "You know..."

I finally got it. I pulled him closer and kissed him. "Babe, I always have time for *you know*."

∼

I GLANCED over at Rae as we sat waiting for commencement to start. She was several rows back, but she winked at me. We'd met with our families before the ceremony for a few minutes. After four years together at SMSU, we'd had plenty of interactions with each other's families. I loved her mom. Mrs. Watson was as fierce as her daughter. And my mom thought of Rae as part of the family. Would they accept Reid as easily? He hadn't met with us beforehand. We thought it would be better to meet naturally after the ceremony.

Reid was sitting with the other professors in a sectioned off area to the left of the graduates. Dean Albin, as department head, would be the one handing out the diplomas. Which worked out great since I liked Dean Albin. He seemed to care about Reid. Almost protective of him. And although Reid hadn't been good at reading people, his decision to be upfront with the dean in the beginning probably helped him in that regard.

I watched Reid laugh at something Gal said, and then he turned and looked at me, the smile still on his face. I gave a little wave, which he returned. Gal grabbed his hand and pulled it down. She probably thought we were being too obvious, but I was almost past the point of caring. I waved at her, and she shook her head at me.

I glanced at the audience. The graduation was outside since the weather was agreeable. My mom waved at me, and I waved back. My sister was able to come, which hadn't been a given. She was busy, but she told me the criminals could wait. Her brother came first. I hadn't spotted my dad yet. And I wasn't sure if I felt relieved or disappointed. Probably a combination of both.

The ceremony seemed to take forever. Each school had its own time slot. This ceremony was only for the School of Natural and Applied Science. It still took longer than I wanted. My legs shook as I reached the stage and shook Dean Albin's hand. As an Associate Professor, Professor Oliver was also on the stage. I walked past him without acknowledging him. I cheered when it was Rae's turn to walk. She looked radiant and happy. I hugged her extra tight when the ceremony ended with us all turning the tassels on our caps.

The professors came over to congratulate us first. They were seated closer to the graduates than the family members. I shook Reid's hand and tried to not look like I wanted to kiss him. Not sure I succeeded. Professor Ramon gave me a big hug.

"You be good to our boy. I know how to find you if you aren't." But she was smiling, so I figured I was okay.

"Yes, ma'am."

"Call me ma'am again and I'll cut you."

I laughed. "Got it, Professor Ramon."

"Gal is fine." She slapped my cheek. Then she hugged Rae. "Keep this one in line." She nodded toward me.

"Not my job anymore." She glanced over at Reid, who was grinning like a loon.

"Maddie?"

I turned, my heart pounding in my chest. "Dad?"

He stood with Mom, Harry, and Jen. "Congratulations. Well done."

"Thanks." I shifted awkwardly, not sure what to say.

"Hi, Mr. Evans. I'm Dr. Emerson, and this is Dr. Ramon. We were Maddie and Rae's professors. And we're immensely proud of them." Reid shook hands with my family and Rae's. Gal did the same. But watching him interact with my mom and my dad felt bittersweet. This was the moment my family was meeting my boyfriend, and they didn't even know it. I suddenly wanted to confess it all. But I held back. Now wasn't the appropriate time. And my dad honestly seemed proud of me. Would he feel differently if he thought I'd had an inappropriate relationship with my professor?

Rae left with her family, giving me a big hug and a promise that we'd see each other soon. My dad suggested we eat at a barbeque place, and everyone agreed. I invited Reid and Gal along. Gal told us both in a hushed voice that she'd go to lunch, but she wouldn't be our third wheel for long, so we needed to get our crap sorted.

It started out fine. I didn't sit next to Reid purposefully, so I wouldn't have the urge to touch him. I realized my mistake almost immediately when my sister kicked me under the table.

"What?"

"Are you shagging your professor?" she whispered.

"Gal is not my type."

"The other professor, dork."

I glanced at Reid. He was in a spirited discussion with my mom on gardening. I couldn't help the smile on my face.

"Oh, my God. You are."

"Have you been watching *Bridgerton* again?"

"You light up when you look at him. He can't keep his eyes off you. And you haven't rearranged any of the condiments. Maddie, are you in love?" Her eyes were wide as she stared at me with a huge smile on her face.

"Shh. If I say yes, will you stop talking about it?"

"I just never thought this day would come." She pursed her lips together, trying to hold back her smile, but she couldn't hide the gleam in her eye.

"Where's your lawyer face? Give nothing away. Reveal only what's necessary and nothing more. Blah, blah, blah."

"My baby brother is in love for the first time ever. Let me enjoy this."

"And the last," I said. "Reid is it for me."

She hugged me, unable to control herself.

"Jen. Stop. Everyone is staring."

"What?" she said loudly. "I can't hug my brother on the best day ever? His graduation day."

AFTER LUNCH, Gal and Reid said their goodbyes and went off to do professor-y stuff. We all went to my apartment. It was fine until Atticus came home... and grumped around the apartment. He'd been moody for the last week or so. I wasn't sure what that was about. At one point he sulked off to his room and slammed the door.

"We should probably go," Mom said. "I expect you to still come home over the summer."

"I will." I wasn't sure why she was saying this since I always spent part of my summer at home when I could get off work. Unless... I glanced over at my sister.

"She didn't tell me."

"Tell you what?" My dad looked from my mom, back to me.

"That Maddie and Reid are dating. I hope you both are happy together, but it won't be an excuse to ignore your family. I expect you to bring Reid with you."

"Wait...What? Isn't he your professor?"

I ignored my dad. For the moment. "How did you know?"

"You don't have much of a poker face, sweetie."

"Not true. I have a great poker face. I'm good at lying. I always get by with stuff." I tried not to look at my dad to see his reaction.

"Exactly. You *had* a poker face. But not today. Not with Reid. That, more than anything, told me what I needed to know."

"Wait." My dad held up his hands. "Did you sleep with your professor?"

"That's none of your business, George."

I was tired of the conversation being about me but not including me. "Reid and I are dating," I said, halting all the other conversations going on. "We were going to tell you guys...later. But I'm glad you know. Not that it's any of your business, Dad, but we waited until after grades were posted to...date. I earned my grades. Every one of them. I worked hard, so don't you dare imply..."

My dad hugged me, and I couldn't hold back my tears. "I'm glad you're happy, Maddie," he said. "And including me in your life."

And then everyone was hugging each other. Atticus walked out, looked at us all hugging and sobbing, shook his head, and retreated back to the safety of his room.

After they left, I didn't bother calling Reid. I just showed up at his door with a smile on my face and tears in my eyes. He pulled me in his arms and into his home and took care of me.

And he showed me that I didn't always have to be the one in control.

EPILOGUE
THREE MONTHS LATER

Reid

"I should shave my head." Maddie picked at his hair as he scowled at himself in the hall mirror.

"Good idea."

"And I hate this shirt. Should I go shirtless?"

"Sure."

He turned his glare on me. "Are you even listening to me?"

"I'm listening. I'm just not reacting." I checked my phone. "We have to go."

"I can't. My hair sucks, and I look like a troll." He ran his fingers through his hair, destroying the style it took him the last fifteen minutes to attain. We really had to leave now.

"You look amazing." I wasn't just saying that. The blue button-down brought out the azure color of his eyes. I slapped his hands away and fixed the wayward curls. His hair was getting long, but I liked it. Then I had to back away from that thought because of the reason I liked it. It gave me something to hold on to. So not the time for a boner. Not when it was the first faculty get-together of the new school year. And we were late.

Once I finally got him settled in his car, and we were on our way, I reached for his hand. "Talk to me."

He focused on the road. "Nothing to talk about. I'm running a few minutes behind. So what?"

"So, this isn't like you. Ten minutes early is late for you. What's going on?" I squeezed his hand.

He pulled it away. Was it a reaction to my question or so he could turn the blinker on? We were turning on to College Avenue. "This a big deal. And I'm not even sure I should be going." He gripped the steering wheel so tight I thought he might break it.

"You were invited."

"As a grad student. Not as your date."

Over the last three months, we'd gradually revealed our relationship. We hadn't officially announced it or anything, but we hadn't hidden it either. "Everyone knows we're together. Seeing us at the welcome event isn't going to change anything." He didn't respond. Maybe I needed to try the Maddie approach.

Push some buttons.

I shrugged, even though he was staring at the road and not me. "Maybe you're right." That earned me a confused glance. "We should both skip."

His mouth dropped open, and his gaze pierced through me. "Reid, you can't skip your first department party of the year. You're required to be there. It's imp-or—" His mouth shut with a click, and he smacked me on the arm. "You did that on purpose."

I chuckled. "You're such a good boy, Maddie. Always wanting to go by the rules."

"Not always."

That reminded me of every moment I'd had with him since I first saw him in my Forest Ecology class. He'd told me about his plan of seduction to keep from failing. He most certainly had not been a good boy, even though in the end, he'd done the right thing. That was closer to the real Maddie. His ways might have been questionable, but he always did things for the right reasons.

"Whatever. I'm obviously going since we're in the car, and I can see the university from here. I don't want to cause you any problems." He reached for my hand, and I threaded our fingers together.

"Don't antagonize Professor Oliver, and we should be fine."

"He should have lost his job."

"I'm actually okay with it." I squeezed his hand. "I don't want anybody else in our business. As long as we avoid him—"

He shot me a look. Right. He couldn't avoid the professor because of grad school. Maddie's area of concentration was agriculture. "I'll do my best to be nice to Mt. Surly this semester. You be nice to Atticus."

I turned the air conditioner up a notch. It was hot and humid, normal for August in Missouri. I didn't need to be a sweaty mess when we got there. I also didn't want to talk about his roommate. Atticus had taken a disliking to me. Dislike was probably too strong a word. It was more of an irritation. I wasn't sure if Maddie had figured it out, but I understood his annoyance perfectly. He was protective, and he didn't want to lose Maddie as his roommate. They'd started rooming together sophomore year and were very close. I had wondered if Atticus had a crush on Maddie, but I didn't dare bring it up to either of them.

I'd talked to Atticus about my plan of asking Maddie to move in with me. He'd hated the idea. Not that he told me. I'd just gotten better at reading the cues. I felt for him, but I wanted Maddie with me as much as possible. But asking Maddie to move in with me was risky. Up until now, he'd avoided commitment like Gal avoided black licorice and nice girls...and commitment.

I'd been ready the moment Maddie knocked on my door after graduation. His parents had left, and he was an emotional mess. I bundled him into my arms and my home, and I never wanted to let go again. Atticus had plenty to worry about. I couldn't say that to Maddie. He always got a little defensive when I talked about his roommate. And I had a plan for how I was going to ask Maddie. I wasn't going to let my fear stop me.

"I wish you two could get along."

There was a question in his voice, and I realized I hadn't

responded to his first comment. "I like Atticus. We're both very protective of you."

"Lucky me?" He was looking ahead, but I could detect a small smile on his face.

We arrived at Hudson Hall, and I practically dragged Maddie out of the car.

The get-together was in the basement in a large open area used for events. I recognized most of the people milling around, but there were a few new faces. New professors and even some new grad students who'd transferred in.

As we mingled with the other guests, I noticed Maddie had resumed his confident persona. The only outward sign he was nervous was that thing he did with his fingers. He would touch each one to something. His thumb. Or his leg. Or a desktop. It reminded me of his counting. Something he used to ground himself.

I'd always been awed by Maddie's ability to adapt to any situation. His charm and confidence attracted me but had also intimidated me. And although he wasn't like those other guys that tormented me, the more I got to know him, the more I understood that they *were* like Maddie. They were all as insecure as I was. Maybe not as insecure as I was since I took it to a whole new dimension. But they were feeling inadequate in some way and faking it.

Only a few people saw this side of Maddie. In fact, outside of his family, it was just Rae, Atticus, and me. I threaded my fingers through his, rubbing my thumb over his knuckles. He flashed me a brilliant smile I couldn't resist, and I leaned in and kissed him. Right there in front of everyone. Fuck them all. This was my Maddie. And I wanted everyone to know it.

"You two are just too damn cute. Stop it. You're giving everyone else a complex."

"Ha. As if that's possible," Maddie said with a wink. "You look gorgeous, Prof. Ramon."

She narrowed her eyes at him. "Maddie, we talked about this."

"Sorry, you look professional...?"

She put her hands on her hips, and Maddie laughed. I loved his laugh. He practically glowed. When had I become such a sap?

"No. You can always call me gorgeous. But call me Gal. We're colleagues now. You guys know Prof. Aubrey."

Delana stood behind her, but there were so many people I hadn't realized she was standing with her. Gal pulled her forward and put her arm through Delana's. So, it was like that.

Physically, they were complete opposites. Gal was dark—her hair, her eyes, and her wit. Delana Aubrey was sunshine—blonde hair, sparkling eyes, and light skin with a vivacious personality.

The differences weren't as noticeable until they were standing right next to each other, linked arm in arm. I wondered how and when that had happened. And why Gal was holding out on me. I raised an eyebrow at her to let her know we would be discussing this later.

"Always good to see you, Reid." Delana smiled at me and then touched Maddie's arm. "And sweetheart, you can call me gorgeous anytime. But call me Delana. No more Prof. Aubrey except in front of the students."

"I am a student," Maddie said. I could feel his hand waver slightly in mine. I squeezed again. I remembered how difficult the transition from student to colleague was.

"But you're one of us now. And you brought Reid out of his shell. You've earned this."

"He just needed a little knowledge." Maddie looked at me with a fond smile. "And a push."

"I needed a shove."

"Or a lure?" Maddie batted his eyes at me.

"A very attractive lure."

"I'm done." Gal put up her hand. "It was sweet at first, but now my teeth ache. Del, let's find a corner to make out in."

"Not happening. Not here, anyway."

"Can we accidentally trip Prof. Oliver?"

"As long as he doesn't fall on me."

"That's why I like you, Del, You're so practical."

"I'm sure that's why," Delana said with a laugh. "See you boys later." And they wandered off.

"That's new." Maddie watched them, shaking his head.

"I had no idea they were together, but I've been a little distracted."

"And you're fun to distract." Maddie bumped against me. "Do you think Gal's finally settling down?"

"Not sure. But it's nice to see her happy."

"Maybe she'll spend less time finding ways to torture us."

"I've hidden the cowbell so no more surprises when we're making out in my office." I pulled Maddie with me as I moved further into the room. We needed to get this over with. I spotted Prof. Albin and walked toward him. Right before we reached the dean, Maddie pulled his hand out of mine and slowed down so he was slightly behind me. I had no doubt he was trying to protect me. And I was having none of that.

"Dr. Emerson, are you ready for a brand-new year? I think we've got a good group of students coming in."

"Yes. I'm ready." I loved teaching. That was the best part about this job. "Of course, you know Maddie," I said, taking Maddie's arm and pulling him forward, "my boyfriend."

"How are you, Maddie?" His eyes twinkled, and again I thought back to the kindly old headmaster that he reminded me of.

"Hello, Professor—I mean, Dean Albin," Maddie stuttered. He really was nervous.

I put my hand on his back to reassure him.

"Are you excited about the new year? Graduate school is a lot of work. Papers to write with some reading involved."

Maddie laughed. It was well known that reading assignments given by professors at the master's level were unattainable. Unless you were a fast reader, like I was, it was impossible to read that much and retain it all. What Maddie didn't know was that to some professors, it was a game. They would try to outdo the other and justified it with building student character. I wasn't worried. Maddie would sail through it.

"Looking forward to it, sir."

Hard part over, Maddie seemed to relax. At one point we separated. Maddie had some students he wanted to talk to. I felt a slight twinge of jealousy. Just slight. I trusted Maddie absolutely. But I wasn't sure I trusted Ben. He worked as one of the receptionists for Hudson Hall. He was a sweet kid with a sunny personality. He saw the best in everyone. But his eyes lit up when Maddie approached him. They talked and laughed at something Maddie said. Ben was social in a way that I'd never be, no matter how many things Maddie taught me. But my boyfriend loved me, so I forced my feet to walk away so they could have their time.

I caught up with several professors to see what they had been doing over the summer and what new things they had planned for the year. They seemed surprised that I approached them but were happy to talk to me. We discussed our various research projects. My grants had all been approved so I was excited to get started on my research involving Missouri's red oak trees.

"I was right all along you know. You and your boy toy."

As soon as I heard his voice, my skin started to crawl. I turned to glare at him. "Our relationship is none of your business."

"It was then."

"It's not now. Stay away from him."

He chuckled. "That will be difficult considering he's one of our grad students."

"Is that a threat? Because if you step out of line, if you do anything—"

"Whoa," he said, putting his hands up. "Just an observation, Professor Emerson. As long as your boy does what he's supposed to do, he'll be fine. But he will have to do the work. He won't be able to gain any favors by sleeping with his professors."

I almost reacted, but I held back. I could see the excitement in his eyes. He wanted to rile me up. And I wasn't going to let that happen.

He tilted his head as he watched me. "Mr. Evans did us all a favor. Where did that bumbling professor go? This new Dr. Emerson can actually look me in the eyes."

I wanted to punch him. Would that be a bad thing to do on the

first faculty get-together? Punch another professor? And more importantly, would it be worth it? Maddie wouldn't be happy with me. That,
more than anything, made my decision easier. I unclenched my fists
and smiled. "It was nice talking to you Prof. Oliver."

As I turned to go, he said, "I think you're going to have an interesting year, Professor."

I glanced back at him. What did he mean? Was he talking about
Maddie? Or something else? He shook his head and chuckled to
himself.

I stood next to the food area like I was figuring out what I wanted.
Mostly I needed a moment to myself. I still wasn't a fan of crowds or
people. Even though most of these people were my friends and
colleagues. I felt overwhelmed. I wanted to go home and spend a
quiet evening with my boyfriend.

Some things would never change. Maddie was outgoing. He
thrived on attention. I needed my quiet time. It sometimes caused
rifts, and then Maddie would drag me out, or I would convince him to
stay in. We had a good balance. But at this moment, I was ready to go.
Strong arms wrapped around me. I could smell Maddie's cologne,
and it calmed me.

"Doing okay?"

"Better now."

"You think we've stayed the obligatory amount of time?" Maddie
asked, kissing the back of my neck and letting me know exactly
where his thoughts had gone.

"Absolutely." Every part of me was onboard. "Lead the way."

We almost made it to the door when we were stopped by Dean
Albin. "I'm glad I caught you before you left, Prof. Emerson. I have
someone I want you to meet."

I shifted my gaze from his smiling face to the person next to him.
A person I knew all too well. I pushed down the anger building in
me. I would not make a scene here in front of everyone. I looked
away, the familiar need to hide my feelings taking over. My legs
started to shake, and I fought back against the urge to scream in frustration. Maddie's hand in mine tightened, and I knew he noticed.

That, more than anything, gave me the strength to force my eyes up into the face of the man standing beside the dean. I wasn't that person anymore.

He was taller than Prof. Albin and had a presence about him that screamed *pay attention to me*. But it wasn't charming like Maddie's. It demanded attention. His eyes were on my face, but I didn't see any surprise in them. He knew I was here. Of course he did. How could he not?

He frowned, but he didn't seem angry, merely disappointed. Story of my life.

"Prof. Emerson. Maddie. I want you to meet our new adjunct professor, Dr. Morgan." His smile faded as he watched us, probably surprised by my reaction. I couldn't focus on that. I focused on Maddie's hand in mine and getting through this.

"Hello Reid," he said, holding out his hand. "It's good to see you."

I detected a note of warmth in his voice. Was he glad to see me? And did I hear exasperation and irritation as well? That I remembered. "Gabriel." I ignored his hand. He dropped it, nodding his head like he expected my reaction.

I could sense the curiosity, the protectiveness, rolling off Maddie. He wanted to know who this guy was and whether he'd hurt me. How would I answer those questions when they invariably came? Gabriel and I would probably give completely different answers.

Finally, Dean Albin spoke up. "Do you two know each other?"

Gabriel tilted his head, watching me and then Maddie before turning back to Prof. Albin. "I see Reid doesn't talk about me. We know each other quite well."

Maddie moved closer to me, his hand tightening in mine. Was he staking his claim? Which was ridiculous, but he didn't know that yet.

Gabriel chuckled, but it didn't match the look in his eyes. "I assume you are Maddie, Reid's boyfriend," he said, shaking his hand. "I'm Dr. Gabriel Morgan. Reid's brother."

Maddie

Reid gave one-word answers all the way to his apartment. That was going to change. I wanted to respect his boundaries, and I'd known there was a history with his brother, but he wasn't going to shut me out. As soon as we walked through the door, he started to head for his room. I grabbed his hand.

"Hey. Talk to me."

"There's nothing to talk about."

"Are you fucking kidding me? Your brother knows who I am. But I know nothing about him. Except that he's not a farmer, apparently." Okay, until that moment, I hadn't realized how angry I was.

His brow furrowed. "I never said he was a farmer."

"You did. When you told me about your intro classes and using a cowbell to wake them up. The bell you got from your brother's farm."

His face cleared, and he even smiled. A little. "I said he had a farm, Maddie. I didn't say he was a farmer."

This man was going to drive me crazy. "Who has a farm and isn't a farmer?"

Reid rubbed his head like he was getting a headache, and he probably was. All those people for that long of a time. Add to it the stress of seeing his brother. I'd be ecstatic to see my sister, so I didn't really understand what was going on. He always had a wariness when he talked about his brother.

"Fine. We'll talk about him. Briefly. But to do that, I'm going to need some ice cream."

We were settled on the couch, each of us with our own half pint of ice cream, and I motioned for him to start.

He sighed. "My brother's a professor at the University of Nebraska. Or was. He works with grain and GMOs. That's genetically —"

I waved my hand at him. "I know what it means, Reid. Get on with the story."

"You're cute when you're bossy…"

I glared at him and took another bite of my mint chocolate chip.

"Don't try to charm me. I thought we told each other everything or at least the big things. And yet you didn't tell me about your brother. But you told him about me."

His face fell, and I almost regretted my outburst. Almost. How could I help him if he didn't talk to me? He stabbed his ice cream instead of eating it.

"Let's start with the farm. It's not his. It belongs to the university. They do research...you know what I mean."

"Why do they need a cowbell?" Okay, that wasn't the most pressing question, but it's the one I was curious about.

He tilted his head with a smile. "It's a big university. They have animals on their farm. Gabriel gave me the bell when I was teaching at Maryville. I was having trouble getting students to pay attention..." All the amusement drained from his face. His jaw was tight like he wanted to hurt someone. I didn't want to push him too hard, but I needed more.

"Why don't you like your brother?"

His spoon had been halfway to his mouth when I asked the question. He stopped and stared at me. "What? What do you mean? I love my brother."

I wanted to throttle him, but maybe he didn't get what I was asking. Reid wasn't good at the social cues of other people, although he was getting better, so maybe he didn't understand the ones he was giving off. "Give me something, Reid," I said. "You need ice cream to talk about him. And your face looks like someone stole your ice cream and you want to hunt them down. All that adds up to something. I just don't know what."

He stuck his spoon in the container and placed it on the table. Then he stared at his picture of the Ozark Mountains on the wall. "Gabriel and I have different dads. And for much of my life, he lived with his father. When my mom got sick..." He paused, staring at his hands. "He moved back home to take care of us. And when my mom died, he was in charge." His voice had a hard edge to it by the time he'd finished.

"You guys didn't get along?"

"I was an angry teen. He'd never really been there except for visits over the summer. And suddenly he had control of my life, and it didn't matter what I thought. There's ten years between us, so he acts more like a parent than a brother. And he's fucking negative all the time." He turned to me, blinking back the tears in his eyes.

I put down my ice cream and pulled him into a hug. "That must have been hard."

He held on for a while before letting go. "I'm sorry I didn't tell you about him."

"But he knows about me?" I took another bite of ice cream. I still wasn't happy that he kept this from me.

"I told you, he's like a parent. Always wanting to know what's happening in my life. I thought telling him about you would shut him up. It made it worse. I stopped answering his texts and calls."

"And now he's here." Maybe this was Reid's chance to show Gabriel that he was all grown up. But I wasn't going to point that out. Not now. And I also felt he was leaving something out. "I have one more question," I said looking at him seriously.

He sighed. "What?"

"Want to make out?"

His eyes lit up, and he took my ice cream out of my hands and pulled me into his lap. "Absolutely."

By the next day, Reid didn't look angry anymore, but he still seemed jittery. Classes would start in a week, but I didn't think that was it. He'd been working on his syllabus for each class and had been excited anytime he talked about it. I couldn't pinpoint the issue. He just wouldn't sit still for long. We rode his Vespa to the river. This was another one of Reid's favorite places. Along with the butterfly house. I loved watching Reid teach kids about science. But going to the river and just existing in nature was something we both enjoyed. We gathered rocks and walked through the cool water that rippled over the larger rocks. It was a magical place and my place to take him when Reid was stressed. This time, it was his suggestion to go. We packed a bag with sandwiches and drinks and had a picnic in one of the small clearings.

We talked about various things as we ate, but Reid seemed distracted.

"Have you checked your Twitter account lately."

His eyes narrowed. "No. Why? And more importantly, do I really want to know?"

I laughed at the look on his face. "It's nothing major. We now have a couple name."

"Again, do I want to know?"

"I think it's cute. You were the one worried about how the students would react." I popped a grape in my mouth and took a drink of my water. "I think you should guess what it is."

"Or you could tell me."

"Fine. They call us Em&M. And the hashtag is Em&MHotties."

Reid scrunched up his face. "You mean like the rapper?"

I stared at him for a minute, trying to figure out if he was joking. "Like the candy."

"Of course. The candy."

I shook my head at him but then noticed the grin spreading across his face. "What?"

"I brought dessert," he said reaching in the basket.

Hopefully, he wasn't keeping ice cream in there. But in the next moment he brought out two bags of Peanut M&Ms and tossed one to me.

"You've been checking Twitter."

"Every day. Well, most days. And I love it when we're trending."

I wanted to ravish him right there, but I restrained myself. Not only because sex in the woods wasn't as fun as it sounded, but Reid still seemed nervous. His hand shook as he took another bite of his peanut butter and jelly sandwich.

"What's going on, babe?"

He dusted his hands off on his shorts and sighed. "I was going to wait until we were done eating, but I'm too nervous. I have something for you and a question." He pulled out a small box.

My heart pounded in my chest. Was he going there? We'd only been dating three months.

"No," he said, accurately reading my face. He put his hands up and laughed. "Not that. Not yet."

I didn't feel the panic I expected at even the thought. I'd been avoiding any type of commitment for so long even a fourth date had been too much. But now the thought of someday Reid and I getting married made me nervous but happy. We weren't ready for that and wouldn't be for a while, but I wasn't against the idea. When had that happened? "So, what is it?"

"You can say no," he said, "I mean it, Maddie."

"Of course I can say no. Humans have free will."

He rolled his eyes and handed me the box. I opened it up. It was a Zelda keychain with keys on it. I looked at him in confusion. "Is this a key to your apartment?"

"Yes."

I turned it over in my hand and squinted at him. "This is my key. The one you gave me a month ago."

"Yes, it is. But I know you like Zelda, so I got you the key chain. And the mail key is also on there."

"Okay…"

He reached for his tie, and realizing he didn't have one on, let his hands fall into his lap. "I'm messing this up."

I gathered his hands and held them in mine. "You're doing fine…I just might need a little more."

"I wanted to give you a key to our apartment."

"Our apartment?"

"If you say yes."

I grinned. "You're adorable, Reid." I held the key tight so he couldn't take it back. "You said there was a question?"

"I'm sure you know what is."

"Oh yes. But I'd like you to ask it."

"You enjoy being difficult." But he was grinning, and that made me happy. He was reading my cues, and he knew before he even asked what my answer would be. He'd come so far from the geeky professor who could barely look me in the eyes.

"Maddie?"

"Yes..."

"Will you move in with me?"

And then it clicked. "No wonder Atticus doesn't like you. He knows, doesn't he?"

"I mentioned it to him. I wanted to surprise you, but I also wanted to make sure you weren't locked into anything. I shouldn't have asked him." He shook his head.

"Reid, it's fine." I bit my lip, thinking about all the redecorating I could do, and how much it would drive him crazy.

There was no hesitation left on his face. "What's your answer?"

I leaned closer. "Read my lips."

And then my sexy but geeky professor pulled me into his arms and kissed me, earning an A-plus *plus* for getting that social cue exactly right.

~

The End

If you enjoyed My (Not So) Grumpy Professor, please consider leaving a review or rating. These help books get seen and find new readers.

ABOUT THE AUTHOR

D.K. Sutton has a background in social work and uses her learned knowledge and experience to develop flawed characters you can't help but love. As an introvert, she has always been a little awkward (and a lot geeky). Turns out, those are handy traits for an author. Her Broken Series is M/M fiction. It's full of love and angst, and it challenges the rhetoric around being gay and religious. Her Trials of Love Series and Sloan Brother Series are both M/M romance. She doesn't believe in hate and clings to the idea that there's good in most people. She has a passion for writing LGBTQ+ stories because the world needs more love and inclusion. For a list of all her books, please turn the page.

For more books and updates sign up for her newsletter here or check out her website at dksuttonwrites.com. You can also visit her reader group at facebook.com/groups/cafedk/

ALSO BY D. K. SUTTON

(Not So) University Series

My (Not So) Slutty Professor

My (Not So) Grumpy Professor

My (Not So) Straight Professor

Broken Series:

Broken Sidewalks

Trials of Love Series

Trial & Error

The Virgin Pirate

Chasing Santa-A Trials of Love Christmas Novella

Sweet Regrets and Other Holiday Stories

Sloan Brothers Series:

Talk to Me

Equal Opportunity Player-A Sloan Brothers Short

Standalones

Accidental Detour

AS ADDISON LLOYD

<u>Y/A LGBT ROMANCE</u>

Dublin High & Westbridge Academy

Reading Order

Merry Little Lies Aaron & Cian

Invincible Me Rob & Caleb

<u>Waiting for Her</u> Carli & Maia

<u>When September Comes</u> Boonie & Dylan

<u>Starr Struck</u> Jade & Mark

Facebook.com/addisonlloydwrites

Pinterest.com/addisonlloyd605

Addison Lloyd on Amazon

Made in the USA
Monee, IL
16 May 2025

17553567R00142